To Sarah!
Enjoy!

BE MORE LUCY

Suzanne Lissaman

For K.H.

One day I might write about you ;-)

ISBN-13: 978-1-7393575-1-1

Also by Suzanne Lissaman

BE MORE OCTOPUS

PROLOGUE
August 2018

Lucy turned over on Em's sofa bed. There must be some position where there wasn't a spring or a crossbar sticking into her back. She moved a little to the left. Slightly better. It hadn't felt this uncomfortable when she'd slept on it last night, but she'd had so much to drink yesterday she'd gone out like a light as soon as her head hit the pillow.

She looked at her phone. 11.35 pm. It was a bit early for being in bed alone on a Saturday night.

Lucy considered knocking on Em's bedroom door to ask if she'd got a spare blanket to put on top of the mattress. It might make it feel less lumpy. But Em was probably asleep already. As soon as they got back from the hospital half an hour ago, she said she had a headache, and she hurried off to bed. Lucy suspected it was an excuse to avoid talking about what had happened with Jack earlier.

It was so frustrating watching those two screw things up. Jack was the perfect man for Em. He was charming, had a good job as a history professor, he was well-educated, he always smelt lovely, he had no obvious bad habits, he was an excellent cook, and he was good-looking. Too clean cut for Lucy but totally Em's type. And Em was ideal for him - funny, caring, equally good-looking and, with nearly 30 years of dealing with that barking mad, controlling mother of hers, probably the only woman who understood the hell Jack was going through trying to divorce his narcissistic wife, Isabella.

Lucy wasn't sure what had gone wrong this time. Jack and Em had been flirting with one another in the restaurant, and the banter continued in A&E while they were all waiting for Lucy to have a fishbone removed from her throat. But when Lucy had rejoined them after the doctor had done her stuff, there was an atmosphere between them that you could cut with a knife. The drive back to Dashford had been tense, to say the least. Jack's best mate, Mark, hadn't got a clue what had gone wrong either, judging by the whispered conversation Lucy had with him in the back of the car.

Gorgeous Mark. Deep brown eyes with a roguish twinkle. A nice line in risque jokes. Lush, curly, medium brown hair - just the type of locks she'd enjoy running her fingers through. He had a healthy tan, too, thanks to living in Spain, she guessed. She'd like to find out where those tan lines ended.

Mark was the complete opposite of Lucy's boyfriend, Lars. *Don't think about Lars! He's an ex-boyfriend now, or he will be when you send him the "You're dumped" text.* Yesterday's Instagram post of Lars enjoying himself with a scantily clad woman during his friend's stag party drifted back into her mind. He was probably still fondling women in Mallorca this evening. Well, Lars could do what the hell he liked now. There was no way Lucy was letting him back into her bed. To think she had believed he was serious about their relationship after he invited her to meet his parents in Canada.

Lucy needed to find a new man to entertain her, and Mark would fit the bill nicely. Some people might think it was indecently hasty, but why wait around for him to be snapped up by someone else?

She was pretty sure Mark wanted to find out where her, albeit much paler, tan ended, too. He'd been very attentive over dinner and seemed genuinely concerned when she'd started choking in the restaurant. He'd volunteered to come with her to see the doctor in A&E, and he'd even held her hand while she had that big metal instrument shoved down her throat. He said how good she'd been. Perhaps he was impressed by her lack of gag reflex. Lucy felt a warm glow, thinking about the implications of that.

Then there had been that spark of attraction when their fingers touched. It was a long, long time since she'd felt that sensation. Not since Dylan. *Don't think about Dylan, either!* What was wrong with her inner voice, conjuring up unreliable exes one after the other? Think about the future, not the old disasters!

And now Mark was on the other side of the courtyard in the big Georgian manor house that had been his childhood home. He might still be awake.

Lucy got off the sofa bed and looked out of Em's living room window. The house was in darkness, except for one first-floor window. That could be Mark's room. Or it could be his mother, Nancy's. She could try texting him.

She found Mark's number on her phone and tapped out a message:

```
Any news on why Jack and Em were
ignoring one another?
```

Three dots appeared almost immediately. Great - he wasn't asleep.

```
Em read one of Jacks texts while he was
in the shower earlier. He thinks she's
as bad as his ex.
```

Lucy knew about the text. Em hadn't been spying on Jack - reading it had been an accident. She ought to try to make things right.

```
Pls tell Jack that Em didn't do it
deliberately
```

Another quick reply:

```
He's not here - he went back to his
cottage with a headache!
```

Jack and Em really were perfect for each other. They even sulked in the same way. Well, she'd done her duty as Em's best friend. Time to find out whether Mark was in the mood for some company.

```
Are you alone?
```

Mark:

```
Yes. Mother dearest is out partying with
her hang-gliding cronies.
```

Typical Nancy! She was always on the go. If Mark were anything like her when he was 74, he'd still be fun to be around. But she ought to confirm how fun he was now before planning the rest of her life with him. Another text from Mark.

```
How's your throat? X
```

A kiss this time. Lucy replied

```
Still a bit sore. Thanks for asking
```

She added a kiss as well. He immediately started typing again.

```
Fancy coming over here for some ice
cream? x
```

Intriguing. She texted back:

```
And what am I going to do with that?
```

The three dots appeared and disappeared several times. Either his response was long, or he was editing it a lot.

```
I thought you could eat some to soothe
your throat. But I'm open to
```

`suggestions.`

No kiss this time, but a wink emoji instead.

Promising. Very promising. Lucy sprayed herself with perfume, pulled on her jeans and a jumper, laced up her trainers and quietly let herself out of Em's flat.

Part One

July 2019

1

Em walked through the arch into the ceremony room. The scent of roses was overwhelming. The early afternoon sunshine flooded through the tall windows, reflecting off the shiny marble floor and white walls. This room would look bright even on the darkest of days, which was exactly why Em had chosen the venue two years ago. What a pity Connor was standing at the end of the aisle now.

He'd noticed her. He looked very suave in his light grey suit and dusky pink tie that matched the flowers perfectly. Once upon a time, she'd found that cheeky grin appealing. Now, it reminded her of all the heartache he'd caused her last year, first by cheating on her weeks before their wedding day and then by trying to scupper her relationship with Jack.

Where was Jack? She scanned the room. He was four rows from the front on the bride's side. He turned and waved. He looked smart in his best suit, but she would have preferred to see him in his usual jeans and a linen shirt or, better still, nothing at all. *Don't think about that now.* He squeezed her hand as she sat down beside him.

'Did you find Lucy?' he asked.

'No sign of her. It's really odd.' Lucy was a stickler for being on time. Em was worried something serious had happened.

'I'm sure she'll arrive any minute now,' Jack said. 'How are you feeling about being here?'

'I'll be fine in a minute. It's a little unsettling, that's all.'

Perhaps they should have stayed away. But Ella had been insistent. 'I want you at my wedding. You're one of my closest friends. Don't let Connor's presence put you off. '

Em leaned on Jack's arm. He kissed her on the forehead.

Her skin prickled as if someone were staring at her. She turned around. It was Connor, scowling this time.

Jack must have noticed Connor looking their way as well. He put his arm proprietorially around Em's shoulders. Sam, the groom, whispered something in Connor's ear. Connor started patting his pockets. Em guessed Sam must have asked about the rings.

A kerfuffle at the back of the room distracted her. She looked around, expecting to see the bridal party, but it was Lucy making a late entrance on her own. At least she'd made it. She slipped into an empty seat on the aisle end of the back row.

'No Adam?' Jack whispered to Em. Lucy's latest boyfriend had lasted longer than the others. They were coming up to their six-month anniversary. He was meant to be here today.

'He was supposed to pick her up from her flat this morning.'

Em looked around again. Lucy was smoothing down her dress. She looked flustered and slightly sweaty. Not her normal cool, calm self at all. She was too far away to talk to without shouting down the aisle.

'You could text her to see if she's alright,' Jack suggested.

'I haven't got a phone signal. And that snooty woman at reception refused to give me the Wi-Fi code. It's for residents only, apparently.'

Jack pulled out his phone. 'I haven't got a signal either.'

Em tried mouthing 'Are you ok?' at Lucy.

Lucy responded with some weird face-pulling and hand signals that implied she wanted to strangle someone, Adam presumably.

A cough interrupted their conversation.

The registrar was standing at the front, staring at her. 'We're ready for the bride now,' she said pointedly.

***

The wedding guests were spilling out onto the hotel terrace. Jack went in search of the gents while Em made a beeline for Lucy, who was talking to their old school friend, Charlotte.

'Hey, Em.' Charlotte gave her a hug. 'What a lovely wedding ceremony.'

'Yes, it was beautiful. Even Connor didn't screw up!' Em turned to Lucy. 'What happened to you?''

Lucy rolled her eyes and sighed. 'Bloody Adam. He was supposed to be stopping at mine last night, then he texted me to say he was working late and he'd come around first thing. But he didn't turn up, so I phoned him several times. All I got was his voicemail. I thought something awful had happened. Then he finally called me back, saying he had an emergency at work.'

'I thought he was an accountant,' Em said. 'What sort of accountancy emergency justifies missing a wedding?'

'Perhaps a spreadsheet wouldn't add up?' Charlotte suggested.

Lucy grimaced. 'I'm sure it's just an excuse to get out of coming today. And there's one thing that's bugging me. When he phoned, I swear I could hear a baby crying in the background.'

'In the office?' Em asked.

'When I asked about it, he said he was in a coffee shop. Why would he be in a coffee shop when he's in the middle of a crisis at work? And it didn't sound like a busy cafe either.'

'He could have needed a caffeine hit,' Em suggested. 'It must be challenging keeping awake looking at all those numbers.'

Lucy swirled her champagne thoughtfully. 'I think he might have someone else.'

Charlotte looked uncomfortable. 'Whereabouts does he live?' she asked.

'He's got a flat in the Rotunda. Why?'

'Oh. It probably wasn't him then.' Charlotte looked even more unsettled now.

'Who wasn't him?' Lucy asked.

'I was at a family christening in Moseley last Sunday, and there was this guy in the congregation who was the dead spit of Adam. I thought he must have an identical twin.'

'Adam's an only child,' Lucy said. 'And he's an atheist. Anyway, he spends every Sunday morning at the tennis club. That's why he doesn't stay on a Saturday night. He likes to go home to get plenty of sleep. He's very competitive.'

'Every Saturday night on your own?' asked Charlotte. 'I don't think I'd like that.'

'We get to spend most nights together during the week and Sunday nights, too, so I don't mind catching up on my sleep on Saturdays.' Lucy looked on edge.

'Well, it can't have been him,' Charlotte said, 'because this guy was with a woman and a couple of kids.'

A waiter approached them with a plate of canapes, stopping Charlotte from elaborating further. 'I'm just going to get another drink,' she said.

As Charlotte walked towards the bar, Lucy started drumming her fingers on her champagne flute.

'It can't be Adam,' Em said. 'You'd have found all that out

when you started dating him.'

'What do you mean?'

'Your detailed online research would have revealed a wife and family.' Em remembered the extensive dossier Lucy had produced on Jack when Em had first met him.

Lucy didn't say anything.

'You did Google him, didn't you? I thought you always did that when you went out with someone new.'

'Of course I did, but I couldn't find anything on him. When I challenged him about it, he said his job meant he wasn't allowed on social media.'

'An undercover accountant. Interesting.'

'It sounds stupid, but I'd no reason to think he was lying. Not everyone plasters their lives over Instagram and Facebook.'

'But surely someone with such an important job would have a LinkedIn account at least?' Em hadn't forgotten the first time she and Jack had met Adam. He'd delighted in crowing about how essential his role was. 'Not a phoney job like being an academic or an artist,' he'd said. An interesting list of professions to mention. Surely Lucy had told him Jack was a professor and Em was a portrait painter as well as a concierge. Obviously, endearing himself to Lucy's friends wasn't a priority for Adam.

'He told me he didn't need to be on there. He's well known in his industry, so he gets recruiters head-hunting him all the time without needing to show off online.'

'I can believe he said that.' Em thought Adam was an arrogant knob, but as Lucy seemed to like him, she'd kept her opinions to herself.

'I know he can be an arsehole, but he's always been very good to me.' Lucy didn't sound as confident as she usually did.

'So why are you looking worried?'

'Because having a wife and family would explain some of his absences.' Lucy looked thoughtful. 'What if he tells her he's working away, so he waves goodbye to her on Sunday evening, and then he comes back from a hard week's work to fall into her loving arms on Saturday morning?'

'Or Friday evening this week?'

Lucy knocked back the rest of her champagne. 'Bastard.'

Better steer Lucy away from thinking too much about Adam's potential lies. Anger wasn't a good look for a wedding guest. It would ruin the group photo. 'That's just us speculating. He might have a double?' Em suggested. 'Or maybe he was working late last night?'

'Or he's secretly working for MI6, and he's been called away to sort out a coup in Uzbekistan? Which do you think is more likely?'

2

Jack pulled the seat away from the table for Em. She still hadn't got used to his excellent manners. Connor would have left her to sort herself out. 'Are you ok here?' he whispered in her ear when she sat down. He must have noticed her eyeing up the top table.

'Yes, I'll be fine. We're as far away from Connor as we can be without being in the corridor,' Em said, as he sat down next to her.

She'd checked where Connor would be sitting when she'd looked at the table plan earlier. He was at the end of the top table in the opposite corner of the dining room. Ella had kept her word about seating them as far apart as possible. If Em leaned on Jack's shoulder during the speeches, the large floral table centre would obscure Connor's annoying face completely. But she'd still be able to hear his voice. A walk around the grounds after the meal might be a better option.

Lucy was sitting on the other side of Jack. She was still looking pensive.

'Excuse me a second,' Jack said, pulling out his phone and typing something. He passed his phone to Em. She read the note.

```
Why the atmosphere? Lucy looks furious.
```

Em tapped out her response.

```
It's Adam. I'll explain later.
```

'Are you two taking notes?' Charlotte asked.

'On what?' Em asked, trying to look innocent.

Charlotte raised her eyebrows. 'I just thought you would want to remember which parts of the wedding you enjoyed and which you didn't. That information could come in handy for any celebrations you might be planning.' she said with a cheeky grin.

Em glanced at Jack.

He looked unsettled. 'Shall we run a book on how long the speeches will be?' he said, changing the subject.

***

The waiting staff were clearing the dessert dishes and topping up champagne glasses, ready for the speeches. Time for Em to disappear for a while. 'I'm going to get some fresh air,' she announced, getting up from the table.

'Do you want me to come with you?' Jack offered.

'No, I need some time alone, thanks.' The introvert in her wanted to get away from everyone, even her beloved Jack. She needed to unwind.

'If you're sure.' He looked disappointed.

'How long do you reckon the speeches will take?'

Jack consulted his handwritten notes on the back of the menu. 'Current bets range between twenty minutes and a massive two hours,if you add it all up.

'Two hours?' Charlotte looked horrified.

'You're the one who suggested Sam was going to ramble on for 90 minutes.' Jack laughed.

'19, Jack. I said 19 minutes!' Charlotte protested.

'I'll be back in about half an hour,' Em laughed, slipping

through one of the open French doors and onto the terrace.

She headed down the steps and along a path to the end of the garden, where a wrought iron gate opened onto a large meadow. She'd spotted it earlier when they were on the terrace. It looked like the ideal place to get away from the hustle and bustle of the day.

The meadow was empty apart from the groom's brother, Tom, kicking a ball around in the short grass at the edge with his two young sons.

'You avoiding the speeches too?' Tom shouted.

'Yes,' she laughed.

'You can join our footie game if you like,' he offered.

The oldest boy scowled. 'Daaaad!'

Tom looked appalled. 'Don't be so rude. Em can join in if she wants.'

'It's ok. I don't think my footwear's up to it,' Em said, aware that now she was standing still, her stilettos were gradually sinking into the ground, tilting her precariously backwards. She stumbled out of them before she lost her balance completely, trying to style it out so Tom didn't think she was drunk.

Em extracted her shoes from the soil, waved bye-bye to Tom and the boys, then set off along a well-trodden path uphill through the long grass with only her thin cotton shoe liners on her feet.

The meadow was bathed in the golden glow of the early evening sun. It brought back happy memories of that late summer evening last year when she and Jack had finally made love for the first time in the meadow by Dashford Grange. She glowed at the thought. Perhaps she should have let him join her now. He might have carried her up here if nothing else. Then she'd have avoided the stabs of pain when she trod on the occasional stone. How did those barefoot models in perfume ads run effortlessly through the grass?

They must have an army of minions clearing the path ahead of them.

Em took a few more steps over the brow of the hill and found a comfortable spot to lie down out of sight of the hotel.

She looked up at the clouds slowly moving across the pale blue evening sky. A swallow swooped and dived in the warm summer air. Em pulled out her phone and videoed it, pondering how to capture its movements in a painting.

Her thoughts wandered back to Jack. Was it really only a year since she'd first met him? He'd reminded her in the car as they drove to Birmingham yesterday evening. It felt like a proper partnership now he'd moved into her flat at Dashford Grange.

The warmth of the sun and the buzz of the insects were making Em feel drowsy. She checked the time. Connor would still be talking. She'd stay here for a few more minutes. Em closed her eyes.

3

'Lost her again?'

Jack turned to see Connor walking towards him across the terrace, clutching a half-empty pint of lager in one hand and a cigar in the other. He had that annoying smirk on his face. The same expression he'd had when Jack had found him in Em's flat last summer. Jack couldn't get that image of Connor out of his mind. Standing in Em's hallway naked except for a towel and doing his best to make Jack believe he'd just screwed Em.

Jack squared up to him. 'She went for a walk. She didn't want to listen to your speech. I can't imagine why.'

'Didn't want reminding that she'd lost a good man, I should think.' Connor said, taking a drag of the cigar.

Cocky bastard. Jack resisted the urge to call him something far worse. *Keep your cool. Em may not be with you now this minute, but she isn't with Connor either.* Not that he'd really believed she would be anywhere near Connor, but Jack had noticed that Connor was on his own today, and Em had been gone nearly an hour now. Jack was imagining all sorts of scenarios to explain her disappearance. The hotel wasn't that big. How had she managed to vanish into thin air?

'Jack!' Charlotte was walking towards them both. 'Ella wants to do the bouquet throw now before her gran has to leave. I'm sure you don't want Em to miss it. Is she still in the meadow?'

The meadow. Why hadn't he thought to look there? It was the obvious place for her to go. Em loved walking in the countryside, especially when she wanted to relax. And it would be the perfect place for that on this gorgeous summer evening.

'I'll fetch her,' he said, ignoring Connor and heading to the bottom of the hotel garden.

Jack walked through the gate in the hedge and scanned the long grass in front of him. No sign of Em. He headed up the slope. Still no sign.

'Em. Em!' He called as he walked.

He heard a rustling nearby and spotted a flash of blue fabric.

'Hello, you. I've been worried.' He bounded over to her.

'Sorry, I must've nodded off.' Em sat up, looking half asleep. 'Do we have to go back indoors?'

It was so tempting to stay out here, just the two of them, but he suspected Charlotte would come looking for them if they didn't return soon.

'Yes, my darling, sadly we do,' he said, holding out his hand to help Em to her feet.

4

'Stand there.' Lucy steered Em to the middle of the dance floor. 'That's the optimum place for catching the bouquet, I reckon.'

'Why don't you stand here then?' Em asked.

'It doesn't look like Adam's marriage material, does it? Or rather he is, but not to me.' Lucy seemed quite matter-of-fact about the potential Adam situation. Em was glad she seemed to be taking it in her stride now. It was amazing how she rarely wallowed in self-pity. She always had the attitude that they weren't worth crying over.

'Yeah, it's definitely your turn to get the bouquet this time.' Charlotte said to Em.

Em rolled her eyes. 'It's a load of superstitious nonsense. You caught it at Mia's wedding last year, and you've been pipped to the altar by two people now.

'Thanks for rubbing it in,' Charlotte laughed.

The rest of the unmarried female guests were gathering around them.

'You might need elbows to fight off Ella's cousin Rachel,' Charlotte whispered in Em's ear. 'She looks determined.'

Rachel did seem keen. She looked like a goalkeeper poised to deal with a penalty kick. Rachel's younger sister, Rosie, was standing on the other side of her, looking equally focused.

'Watch it, ladies! We've got competition,' Lucy said as Ella's gran manoeuvred her wheelchair in front of Em.

She looked over her shoulder and grinned at them. 'Caught three, married three,' she said, rubbing her hands together.'

'Have you got anyone in mind today?' Lucy asked.

'Cyril. He is the perfect bridge partner, still has his wits about him, and he has decent teeth and an index-linked civil service pension. What more could a single girl wish for?'

'Is he here?' Em asked.

Ella's gran nodded towards a small, frail bald man who looked to be in his nineties. He was slumped on one of the sofas at the back of the room, snoring loudly with his mouth open. 'He's saving his energy for later.'

Em didn't ask for more details about why Cyril would need to save his energy. Judging by the twinkle in Ella's gran's eyes, it probably wasn't for a hand of cards.

The DJ turned on the microphone. 'Is everyone ready?'

Ella was standing on the stage holding a small hand-tied bunch of freesias.

'That's not your bouquet,' Ella's gran objected.

'It's a special throwing bouquet, Gran. I'd take someone's eye out if I threw the real one.'

Ella's gran appeared to think momentarily, then rolled her wheelchair forward a couple of metres.

'She knows what she's doing,' Lucy whispered to Em. 'That small bouquet isn't going to travel that far. I reckon you should move forward too.'

'I'm fine here, thanks. Far be it from me to stand in the way of love's young dream,' she said, nodding at Ella's gran.

'Ella, turn your back on the guests.' The DJ instructed. 'Right, everyone, we're going to do a countdown. 3 … 2 … 1 …'

Ella threw the bouquet over her shoulder.

Ella's gran had seriously miscalculated. The bouquet flew over her head straight towards Em. Em instinctively raised her hands to catch it just as Rosie hoisted Rachel in the air like a forward in a rugby lineout. Rachel lurched in front of Em, snatching the flowers in mid-air.

There was a loud gasp from the wedding guests as Rosie overbalanced and fell towards the dance floor, taking her sister and two other women down with her.

Undeterred, Rachel emerged victorious from the pile of polyester and stilettos, brandishing the bouquet, a small trickle of blood making its way from her left nostril. Rachel's boyfriend looked terrified and scuttled off towards the garden.

'I think we need VAR,' the DJ announced to the stunned onlookers.

5

Em relaxed in Jack's arms as they slowly moved around the dance floor, swaying to the soothing sounds of Adele. The taxi would be here soon. Then they could head back to her dad's for the night. By this time tomorrow, they'd be back home in North Devon, far away from Connor.

'Have you enjoyed today?' Jack murmured in Em's ear.

'More than I thought I would.' She nestled closer into him.

'I thought you were robbed earlier.'

'What do you mean?'

'The bouquet throw. It was heading straight for you. I'm sure Rachel's technique is against the rules.'

Em chuckled. 'I'm not bothered. It's all superstition.'

'Do you think we should be next?'

What had he just said? Em tensed. 'Next for what?'

'To get married. I want to marry you.'

Why was he saying that now? In Em's head, this was a conversation they should be having in a couple of years' time, not today. 'Let's go outside. We can't talk properly here,' she said.

She led Jack out onto the empty terrace. The cold night air

made her shiver as it hit her bare shoulders. He put his arms around her and pulled her in close. 'Emily Gillespie, will you marry me?'

Em gulped. A panicky feeling started in her stomach, and she felt her chest muscles tense. Just concentrate on breathing.

'Are you ok?'

She nodded. 'Jack, I love you, and I don't want to be with anyone else. But after Connor cheated on me and the nightmare you had with Isabella, I thought we'd agreed we would keep our relationship informal for now?'

'I know we said that. But that was months ago. I'm sure we're right for each other. I'd like to show the world how serious we are. I saw the way Connor looked at you today.' His expression clouded over.

'I'm not going back to Connor. Not ever. Why would you think I would? We agreed we were going to buy a house together. Isn't that a big enough commitment to one another?'

'No,' Jack looked exasperated. 'It's not the same.'

'But what if getting married makes you feel trapped?'

'I'm not Connor. I won't go looking for love elsewhere. You're the only woman I want. I'm absolutely sure. I wouldn't be asking you if I wasn't.'

He wasn't budging. She turned away. 'I really do love you, but please don't pressure me.'

He let her go and stood back, looking disappointed. 'I won't beg you, but if you change your mind, let me know.'

Jack went back inside, leaving Em standing alone on the terrace. She leaned her forehead against the cold stone of the pillar next to her. *Oh god, why now just when everything was going so well?*

***

A few minutes later, Lucy appeared at Em's side. 'What's wrong?'

'What makes you ask?' Em didn't want to discuss it,

particularly given Lucy's situation with Adam.

'You're standing here alone in the dark looking like you've just accidentally flushed a winning lottery ticket down the bog, and Jack's sitting by himself at the bar, nursing a double scotch on the rocks. I may not be the most observant friend sometimes, but I think something isn't quite right.'

Em would have to tell her. 'Jack's asked me to marry him.'

'But that's fabulous. Why are you looking like he's left you?'

Em was shocked. 'I thought you were dead against marriage?'

'I was. I hate the whole idea of being given away like some prize cow. And taking someone else's name as if they own you. But you don't have to do either of those now. My biological clock's ticking. And so is yours.'

'What's that got to do with anything? You don't have to be married to have children,' Em said.

'No, but it makes life simpler if you are. And you've just confirmed you are feeling broody.' Lucy looked almost triumphant. 'I thought that when you were showing me those pics of Jack's niece and nephews the other day. We're both 30 now. Our eggs are ageing and not like fine wines. We can't leave it too long. If someone like Jack asked me, I would say yes now. I might even propose to him.'

Em looked daggers at her.

'Someone like Jack, not Jack. He doesn't make my heart skip a beat like he does yours. There are only two men who've ever done that.'

'Two?' Em asked. She knew about one - dishy Dylan from Lucy's uni days. But who was the other?

'Em? You zoned out then. Are you ok?'

'Sorry, I was just running through all your exes. I think my brain overloaded.'

'Charming! It doesn't matter. It's all in the past.' Lucy

looked like she'd regretted saying anything.

'You promised me after I left Connor that if I ever said I was getting married again, you'd talk me out of it.'

'If you ever said you were marrying Connor or some other shit again, yes. But Jack's different. He's straightforward.' Lucy sighed. 'Unlike any of the men I attract.'

Which was true. Lucy's boyfriends had all turned out to be liars, whereas Jack was honest, loving and caring. 'So why am I scared getting engaged will ruin everything?'

'Because you think it ruined everything with Connor, but I bet he'd still have cheated on you even if you hadn't agreed to tie the knot.' Lucy hugged her. 'Do you love Jack?'

'Yes.'

'Do you think he'd cheat on you?'

'No.'

'Can you see yourselves growing old together?'

'Yes.'

'Does he want to marry you for your money?'

'He's going to be seriously disappointed if he does,' Em laughed. Jack had a good job, and a very healthy balance on his savings account thanks to his divorce settlement. Meanwhile, Em had her holiday let concierge job and some extra income from her art business. But she still earned a fraction of what Jack did.

'I guess I need to get used to the idea. I always thought we'd get married, eventually. I just never thought he'd ask this soon. It's taken me by surprise, that's all.'

'Even if it's still a no, you need to reassure him that you two are still ok. He looks like he's been kicked in the balls by a herd of angry elephants.'

6

Em woke up to a buzzing sound. She picked up her phone from the bedside table. Lucy. She didn't usually call at 9 am on a Sunday. Em got out of bed and walked out onto the landing so as not to wake Jack. She could hear her dad and his partner, Cynthia, chatting in the kitchen downstairs.

'Oh good, you're up.' Lucy's voice was very bright and breezy for someone who'd been knocking back tequila shots a few hours previously.

'I am now.' Em said, rubbing the sleep from her eyes. 'What's wrong?'

'Can I borrow you for an hour?'

'When?'

'Now?'

'Now? I'm not sure how much use I'll be to you. I hardly had any sleep last night.' Em had been mulling over Jack's proposal before she'd finally nodded off at about 4 am.

'Neither did I, but we'll be fine. I need to see if Adam really is at the tennis club this morning.'

'Why do you need me for that?'

'It's Jack's car that I need. Adam won't recognise it.'

Em yawned. 'But you're not insured to drive it.'

'No, but you are.'

So much for a lie-in. Lucy was difficult to refuse when she'd got an idea in her head. 'Shall I come and pick you up then?'

'No need. I'm outside.'

Em looked out of the landing window. Lucy waved from the pavement. 'I got an Uber to drop me here.'

'It's a good job I said yes,' Em laughed. 'Do you want to come in for a drink while I get dressed? I'm sure Dad and Cynthia would like to see you.'

'Much as I love your dad, not this time. We need to get going. Time is of the essence, as they say.'

Em went back into the bedroom, where Jack was gently snoring. She tore a page from the notebook in her handbag and left him a note.

***

Five minutes later, Em was reversing Jack's car off the drive. 'I need to be back here by one o'clock. Cynthia's cooking Sunday lunch.'

'That's fine. We aren't going very far.' Lucy tapped the destination into the car's satnav. It was only three minutes away.

'Are you sure you've got the right address? I thought the tennis club was in the other direction?' Em said, as she started following the satnav's instructions.

'We're not going to the tennis club. We're going to Adam's house.'

Em raised her eyebrows.

'I couldn't sleep when I got home, so I decided to do a bit more research on Adam. I know the church Charlotte's family goes to, so I looked through their Instagram feed, and there he was in a photo with some kids.'

'And it was definitely him?'

'The caption read "Thanks to Adam Washington for helping with Sunday school this week".'

'I thought his surname was Jones?'

'That's what he told me. But, unless he's got a double who's also called Adam, it's Washington. He's listed on the church website as the contact for the youth group, and it gave an address for sending in application forms. That's where we're going now.'

'But that could be where the person who does the youth group admin lives?'

'I wondered that too, so I did a Land Registry search on who owns the house and, lo and behold, there was his name along with a Mrs Eve Washington.'

'Adam and Eve?'

'I know! They were obviously made for one another.' Lucy rolled her eyes.

Em turned into a wide, tree-lined suburban avenue. The satnav announced they'd arrived.

'Pull in there.' Lucy indicated a space by the side of the kerb. 'Perfect. We'll have a great view of his house from here. It's that one over there with the dark red door. I checked on street view.'

Em looked across the road to a classic bay-windowed 1930s semi with a large, neatly cut front lawn and herbaceous borders bursting with late summer colour. Whoever lived there had green fingers or could afford to employ someone who did.

'So he does have another life with a wife?'

'And at least one child as well. There was a photo of him at the Church Christmas Fair carrying a toddler who looked remarkably like him.'

'With a bald head and a heavy 5 o'clock shadow?'

Lucy rolled her eyes. 'You're not taking this seriously.'

'Sorry! It all feels a bit extreme. I know you hear about people living double lives, but how's Adam managing it?' Em continued. 'I thought you spent at least one night at his flat most weeks?'

'I do. He doesn't own that either, but I wasn't expecting him to. He told me he's renting it until he can find his perfect house. I'm starting to think it's a friend's, and he borrows it while they're working away or something. He's always insistent that I shouldn't leave anything there. I thought he was afraid of any hint of commitment.'

'Or he really does live at the flat, and he's separated from his wife but likes to co-parent at the weekends?' Em was doing her best to find a simple explanation that meant Lucy hadn't hooked up with yet another lying waste of space.

'So why did he tell me he's never been married, and he doesn't have any kids? Or "none that he knows about" as he said with that annoying blokeish tone. I should've run a mile as soon as he uttered those words.'

'It's not looking promising.'

'No, it's not.' Lucy looked at her watch. 'I reckon it will be another ten minutes or so before Adam leaves for tennis, if that's where he's going.'

'What shall we do?' Em suggested.

'You can tell me how you got on with Jack after Charlotte and I left last night. I'm assuming you're still together as we're sitting in his car.'

'Yes, we're still together. He said to forget he'd ever asked when I went to him at the bar. Then we carried on dancing as if nothing had happened. But I can't forget. The more I think about it, the more I think getting married now is a good idea.'

'But your gut reaction was no?'

'I know. I think it was a control thing. I've enjoyed being in control of my own destiny since I left Connor. I was the one who decided that Jack and I should get together again, then it was me who suggested he moved into my flat, so subconsciously, I think I wanted to be the one who decided when we got engaged.'

'What are you going to do?'

'There's a bottle of champagne in the fridge at home, left over from his book launch. When we get back tonight, I'll surprise him with a glass of that and suggest we make a toast to becoming Mr & Mrs Carver.'

Lucy brightened up. 'That should work.'

'He might change his mind!'

'I bet he won't.'

***

Ten minutes later, they were still waiting around. Nothing had moved in the house or the street.

'My bum's gone to sleep.' Lucy shifted uncomfortably in the passenger seat.

'Heads up! I spy with my little eye something beginning with A.' Em nodded towards the house.

A man was opening the curtains in the first-floor bay window.

'Is that Adam?' Lucy asked. 'It's difficult to tell with the reflections in the glass.'

The man moved to the other side of the window. He was easier to see now. He was wearing a white shirt, but it wasn't buttoned up.

'It is Adam.' Lucy slid down onto the floor.

Em looked at her, puzzled.

'He might spot me,' Lucy explained from the passenger side footwell.

'We're in Jack's car. You said he wouldn't recognise that.'

'I know, but if we can see him, he can see us. I should've thought about wearing a disguise. Hopefully, he won't recognise you.'

'I very much doubt there's any chance of that. He's only met me twice, and he mostly ignored me on both occasions.' Em tried not to sound too bitter.

Lucy changed the subject. 'I should've asked you to bring your camera!'

'I'm not a paparazzo. I'd need a huge lens for that. Anyway, it's not as if you need evidence. I assume you're just going to challenge him if anything isn't right?'

'If? He's given me a false name, and he's currently getting dressed in a house he owns with another woman who shares his real surname. I think we can safely say that something is not right.' Lucy was angry again now.

'Look - the front door's opening,' Em said.

A woman, who appeared to be around Adam's age, walked outside.

Lucy pushed herself up slightly so she could see out of the driver's window. 'That must be Eve.'

A toddler followed the woman outside and held her hand. Both of them looked back towards the open door.

'Who's that with her?' Em asked.

'A child.'

'Nothing gets past you, does it?'

'I meant Adam's child. He looks like the little boy I saw in the photo.'

A pram emerged from the door. A second later, they could see that Adam was pushing it.

'He's got more than one child,' Em said.

'That explains the baby crying in the background when he phoned me yesterday.' Lucy looked seriously pissed off.

'Eve could be his sister-in-law? That would explain why she's got the same surname.' Em knew she was clutching at straws, but for Lucy's sake, she felt she ought to try hard to find an excuse for Adam being there. 'They're all dressed up for some special occasion or church?'

'They are definitely not dressed for tennis. Shit! They're coming this way. Put your coat over me.' Lucy ducked back down into the footwell.

'Because that doesn't look suspicious at all.'

'Don't argue. Pretend to be looking for something in the glove box so he doesn't see your face.'

Em obliged.

She could hear Adam and Eve chatting amicably as they crossed the road and walked past the car. They were talking about where they were going to take the children after they'd been to church.

As their voices faded away, Em risked a look in the rearview mirror. She watched as Eve put her arm through Adam's and whispered something in his ear. He leaned down and kissed her, and not in a family peck on the cheek kind of way either. They headed off along the street, looking like the perfect couple.

'What's going on?' Lucy's muffled whisper came from under Em's coat.

There was no way to dress this up. 'He's just snogged her.'

'Bastard!'

'I'm so sorry.'

'The lying, cheating shit!'

'Do you think you could come out now? It feels weird being sworn at by my own coat.'

Lucy pulled the coat away from her face and found her phone. She launched WhatsApp.

'What are you doing?' Em asked.

'Letting Adam have one last chance to give me an innocent explanation for all this.' Lucy showed Em the message she'd just typed.

```
Hi darling. Hope your emergency is over.
Come over to mine and I'll cook you
lunch.
```

She added a kiss emoji and pressed the send button.

Adam and his family were still in sight. The little boy picked up something from the grass verge and showed it to Eve. Adam took the opportunity to check his phone. He started typing.

Em was flabbergasted. 'Surely he's not going to reply to you while he's standing next to his wife.'

Ping. Lucy got a new message. She showed it to Em:

> `Sorry stuck at the office - still got an issue. Nearly sorted. See you this evening as usual. Love you Xxx`

'What an arsehole! What are you going to do?' Em asked.

'I'm not sure. But I've got a few hours to think about it.'

7

Eating at Em's dad's was a lottery now that Cynthia had taken up permanent residence. Em's mother had been a difficult woman to deal with, but at least she could cook. Cynthia's talents lay elsewhere, but she always gamely had a go at producing a meal with varying degrees of success. Today's offering was better than the rock-solid lasagne she'd served the last time Em and Jack visited, but it still presented a challenge.

Em looked at the grease slick floating on top of the gravy boat. How was she going to pour the gravy without transferring the fat onto the over-cooked roast chicken? Perhaps she didn't need to. The bread sauce looked palatable. She could use it to moisten the dry chicken enough to make it edible.

The roast potatoes were a different matter. Em attempted to cut one in half, but her knife slid off without making a mark. Bread sauce wasn't going to soften these beauties. There were NASA rockets with weaker outer casings. She was going to have to deal with the grease after all. Em poured a pool of gravy onto the side of the plate so she could separate the fat there.

'You're not eating much, Em. Surely you're not on a diet?' Cynthia asked.

Em smiled. 'I'm still full from all the food we ate at the wedding yesterday.'

'How was it?' her dad asked.

'Beautiful. Ella and Sam pushed the boat out. No expense spared.'

'So when are you walking Em down the aisle, Jack?' Cynthia asked.

Em gulped.

Jack glanced at her. 'We've decided we're not getting married. We're fine as we are,' he said, not sounding convinced.

'That's a shame,' Cynthia continued. 'I was hoping for another excuse to get a new frock. Though I will be getting one soon.' She looked at Em's dad expectantly. He was deep in thought, having similar concerns about tackling the greasy gravy, Em guessed. She noticed Cynthia kick him under the table.

'Oh, yes.' Her dad rejoined the conversation. 'We've got some news. I asked Cynthia to marry me, and she said yes.' He beamed at Cynthia and held her hand.

'That's fantastic news, Dad. Congratulations to both of you.' Em was surprised but pleased. Cynthia made her dad happy. Em felt less guilty about living 200 miles away, knowing he wasn't alone.

'That is fabulous news,' Jack said. 'It's exciting when someone's willing to commit to spending the rest of their life with you.' He started pushing the potatoes around his plate, avoiding Em's gaze.

'Our news is hot off the press,' Cynthia said, oblivious to Jack's discomfort. 'We haven't told anyone else. And we haven't set a date yet, either. Your dad's taking me to the

Jewellery Quarter this week to choose an engagement ring. A sapphire with diamonds like Princess Diana's, I thought. What do you think, Roger?'

'Whatever makes you happy, my love,' he said.

'We're not going to have a big do,' Cynthia continued. 'I'll be asking my two little great nieces to be flower girls. No grown-up bridesmaids.' Cynthia put her hand on Em's. 'I hope that's not a disappointment.'

'No, that's absolutely fine.' Much as she liked Cynthia, Em had no desire to walk behind her up the aisle. She glanced over at Jack. He had put his cutlery down and was looking absent-mindedly out of the window.

'Roast parsnips, Jack?' Cynthia asked, waving a dish of what looked like wedge-shaped charcoal sticks at him.

***

Jack had barely said a word since they'd driven away from her dad's house half an hour ago. It wasn't a companionable silence - the atmosphere in the car was tense. Em couldn't stand it any longer.

'What's wrong, Jack?'

They were approaching a motorway services. He silently took the exit, drove into the car park, found a parking spot and switched off the engine. He turned to look Em in the face.

'I think we should have a break,' he said.

'Yes. I could do with a drink.' Em undid her seat belt. Whatever was bothering him, it would be easier to discuss it face to face over a hot drink.

'No. I mean a break in our relationship. Live apart. Go out with other people. See if we genuinely do love one another.'

Em froze. Where the hell had that come from? 'How have you gone from wanting to marry me yesterday to wanting to split up today?'

'You seriously don't know?' He laughed, but he looked like

he was about to cry too. 'You've spent most of this afternoon enthusing with Cynthia and your father about their wedding plans as if marriage was the best idea ever. But you don't want to get married to me. It hurts, Em. It really hurts.'

She was going to have to bring her proposal forward before this all ended disastrously. Em went to put her arm around him, but he moved away. 'Jack, I ...'

He cut across her words. 'No. I understand you've had a bad time emotionally. But so have I. I need someone who's willing to commit to me. And you don't want to do that. I know it sounds crazy when it took me years to get out of my marriage to Isabella, but I trust you. And yet you want to be able to walk away if you ever need to. I can't live like that.' He looked out of the window.

'I'm not going to leave you. I don't want anyone else. I love you. I want us to grow old together, have children together, and not necessarily in that order. I've been thinking it through since you asked. Jack, I do want to marry you.'

He looked exasperated. 'And now I feel I've emotionally blackmailed you into it.'

'No, you haven't. I was going to talk to you about it when we got back home tonight.'

'Are you sure you're not just saying that?' He turned to look at Em again.

'No. Yes. I mean, I am sure. You caught me by surprise yesterday. I've had time to think it through properly since then. Ask Lucy if you don't believe me.' Em took his hand in hers. 'Jack Carver. Will you marry me?'

He looked as if he didn't know what to say. She realised he was holding his breath.

'Well, will you?' Surely he wasn't going to change his mind now.

He remembered to start breathing again and let out an enormous sigh. 'You've taken me by surprise.' He kissed the hand that was holding his face. 'Yes, I will.'

'Not quite the marriage proposal I thought we'd have.'

'No. I'm glad you didn't plan it to be like this,' Jack laughed. 'Gloucester Services would have been so much better.'

8

Lucy looked at the large clock on the kitchen wall. 7 pm. Any minute now. The doorbell rang right on cue. Adam was always punctual on Sunday evenings, she'd give him that.

Lucy strode to the door and checked the video feed. Yes, there was Adam in his usual jacket and jeans. She pressed the entry button and watched him disappear from the screen as she opened the front door to her apartment. His footsteps grew louder as he ascended the stairs several steps at a time. He was keen this evening.

'Hi, darling. I'm so glad to see you,' he said as he walked through the door.

Always darling, never Lucy. When she'd thought back over all their previous encounters looking for clues to his double life, she'd realised that Adam never used her name. No risk of accidentally calling her the wrong one that way, she guessed.

He bent down to kiss her, but she backed away.

'Still upset over the wedding? I've bought you a gift to say sorry. We can try it out later,' he said with a smirk.

He handed her a plain white gift bag. Lucy opened it while

he hung his jacket on her coat rack.

A whip. He'd been hinting he wanted to experiment in the bedroom. Lucy admired his confidence, handing a potential weapon to an angry woman. 'Excellent. I get to punish you for standing me up,' she said, cracking the whip on the floor.

'Whatever turns you on.' He gave her a wink.

Forty-eight hours ago, she might have found that appealing, but she was looking at him in a whole new light now.

'Can I use your bathroom?' he asked, heading there before she had time to respond.

'Sure. You know where it is,' she said as he shut the door.

Perfect. She quickly went through his jacket, looking for his wallet. It should be easy to find as it usually contained a large wad of notes. Adam always paid cash, flamboyantly counting out the notes and leaving a generous tip. Now she knew why: no unexplainable transactions on his credit card bill.

Found it. She pulled out a credit card. "A Washington" was embossed on the bottom. No surprise there, but at least she'd got physical evidence now. He couldn't try to get out of it by claiming he had a double. She slipped the credit card into the back pocket of her jeans and returned the wallet to the inside pocket of his jacket.

When Adam walked back into the living room, Lucy was casually sitting on the sofa, pretending to read emails on her phone. He looked across at the kitchen area. 'I can't smell anything cooking. What are we eating this evening?'

'I thought you could make up for yesterday by taking me out for dinner.' Lucy got up and put her arms around his neck. She wanted to watch him closely when she told him where they were going. 'Em recommended a lovely little Italian on Moseley High Street. I've booked us a table for 8 o'clock.'

The restaurant was only a five-minute walk from his

house. He'd probably been there with Eve. She saw a brief flicker of panic in his eyes before he was in control again. He was good at this. Lucy wondered whether he'd had practice at cheating on his wife with other women.

'Darling, I'm so tired after working all weekend. Can we send out for takeout instead?'

'I understand.' Lucy tried to look sympathetic as she backed away from him. 'It must've been very stressful having a work crisis that lasted two whole days. I'm sure your wife missed you as well, especially with two small children to look after on her own. Perhaps you should use our booking to take her out instead?'

'What are you talking about?' Adam was still outwardly calm. Impressive. He should be a spy. Perhaps her sarky remark about him dealing with a coup in Uzbekistan hadn't been that wide of the mark.

'Mrs Washington?' Lucy said.

'Are you on something?'

Was he seriously trying to brave this one out?

'You mean you're not Adam Washington, joint owner of 17 Ferndale Avenue, with Mrs Eve Washington? I'm sure an estate agent would describe it as "a well-maintained 3-bedroomed pre-war semi-detached in a much sought-after road in the catchment area for the best primary school in Birmingham". That will come in useful when your children are a bit older.'

Adam laughed. 'Darling, don't be so silly. I'm Adam Jones. You know that. There are loads of Adams in Birmingham. I've no idea why you think I'm Adam Washington.'

Arrogant bastard. Lucy pulled the credit card out of her pocket and threw it between them onto the coffee table. 'I better phone the police then, as you seem to have stolen at least one of Adam Washington's credit cards.'

'How dare you go through my wallet! I should be the one

calling the police.'

Mock outrage. Lucy could cope with that.

'I think you'll find that morally, that's a lesser crime than cheating on your wife. But as an atheist, I guess you set your own moral standards. I'm not sure what the vicar at St Margaret's would think about that, though.'

He stared at her. Surely he'd worked out his number was up as far as Lucy was concerned.

'You've been spying on me!'

'I wouldn't call it spying. More casually observing the lesser spotted cheater in his native environment. A bit like David Attenborough but with fewer cameras.'

'Is it over then?'

'Of course it's over. I'm not screwing a liar who has a wife and a family. I have standards. I suggest you go and see one of your other women. The Tuesday one might be sitting at home twiddling her thumbs.' Adam never saw Lucy on Tuesdays. "Tennis club session night" he used to say whenever she suggested it. It was a pure guess that he spent Tuesday nights in someone else's bed.

'I might just do that. She's hotter than you anyway,' he said as he grabbed his credit card and jacket and left.

***

'Just checking you're ok?'

It was 9 pm on Sunday, and Em had called Lucy, who was sitting on her sofa pondering what to do next about her love life.

'I'm fine,' Lucy replied without thinking. Was she? Disappointed but not surprised would be a better description. After all, Adam was the latest in a long line of liars and cheaters.

'Adam didn't deny it then?'

'He tried, but he realised I knew far too much for him to

give me some flannel, I guess. And there's at least one other woman.'

'Seriously! What a shit. Are you going to tell his wife?'

'I considered it. But why spoil things for her purely for the satisfaction of getting revenge on Adam? She probably knows already but chooses to ignore it. And if she doesn't know, it's not my job to tell her.' Plus, Lucy didn't want any backlash. If Eve were blissfully ignorant of Adam's philandering ways, she would probably assume Lucy was some bunny-boiling maniac. Lucy hadn't missed the extremely loving look Eve had given Adam when he came out of his house this morning.

Lucy changed the subject. 'How are you and Jack?'

'We're fine. He's off to London tomorrow to discuss his latest television programme.'

'I didn't mean in general. Did you ask him to marry you?'

'Are you sure you want to know?'

'Of course I do. Just because I seem to find more than my fair share of arseholes doesn't mean I begrudge you any happiness.'

Em filled her in on the proposal.

'Wow. That's different.' It was a complete contrast to Sam and Ella's proposal. Sam had got down on one knee at the top of the Eiffel Tower. 'I can honestly say that you're the first couple I've heard of who agreed to get married during an argument in a motorway services car park.'

'You know we don't like to do anything the normal way,' Em said with a laugh. At least she looked genuinely happy.

'Congratulations!'

'I'm just relieved we're back on an even keel again. Don't say anything to anyone yet. I need to tell Dad, and Jack needs to tell his parents before we go public.'

'And Nancy? She doesn't miss a trick. There's no way she won't notice that you and Jack have got engaged.'

'We might have to tell her first.'

'So when's the big day?'

'Give us a chance. We've not worked out when or where yet. But I hope you'll be my maid of honour again.'

'Of course I will.'

Always the bridesmaid, never the bride. *Come on, Lucy Thomas, if you ever want a family, you're going to have to up your game.*

9

'You're in early. It's not even 8 o'clock yet.' Lucy's PA, Kizzy, hung her jacket on the office coatstand.

'I couldn't sleep, so I thought I may as well crack on with my To Do list,' Lucy said.

'Isn't Sunday night an Adam night? You're always in late after those.' Kizzy gave her a knowing look.

'I've told him where to go.' Lucy updated Kizzy on the weekend's events.

'What a first-class shit! So you're back on the dating apps then?'

'No. I seem to be having a run of bad luck with men online and off.' Adam had been an online match, she'd met Lars in the sandwich shop queue, and then there was Mark. She sighed. She missed Mark. 'I'm starting to think I'm meant to be single.'

'Don't be ridiculous. You're intelligent, you run your own business, you own a fancy apartment in the middle of Birmingham, and best of all, you're not a minger. They should be queuing around the block for your attentions.'

'Thank you for that glowing description. But I didn't have

to fight my way through a line of eligible bachelors to get in here today. Did you?

'Only that homeless guy who's usually by the shop over the road. He's moved into our doorway.'

'He always does that when it rains - we're more sheltered. I'm sure he's very deserving, but I'd prefer someone without an addiction.'

'Well, if you're going to be fussy,' Kizzy laughed. 'Cheer up. It will work out eventually. Not all men are lying bastards. Thea's just moved in with her man.'

Thea was Kizzy's sister. Kizzy often shared updates on her love life, whether Lucy wanted to hear them or not. 'He's gorgeous. Got a weird thing about alpacas, but you can't have everything.'

'Alpacas?' Kizzy came out with some odd tales about her friends and relatives, but she'd never mentioned South American mammals before.

'Thea thinks it's because they remind him of his late nana.'

'Why? Did she run around fields and spit at people?' Lucy's only experience of alpacas was on a school trip to a farm. Having thirty noisy, fidgety infant school kids pointing at them had spooked the whole herd. It hadn't ended well.

Kizzy looked at her as if it were obvious. 'It's that fluffy hairdo they all have. It looks like his nana's perm. And then there's the teeth.'

'So what does he do?'

'He's an electrician,'

'I meant, what does he do with alpacas?'

'Oh. He's got a big collection of fluffy toy ones, he's saving up for a trip to Peru, and he sponsors one in an alpaca rescue. He takes Thea on a special trip to Kent every year just to visit it.' Kizzy leaned in closer to whisper, even though no one else was in the office. 'I swear it looked different in the picture he took this year. I reckon the rescue swapped it out for another one and didn't tell him.'

'How could you tell?' Lucy whispered back.

'Different hair do - straighter, darker.' She pulled a face. 'Very suspicious.'

Lucy couldn't quite believe she was having this conversation. 'Perhaps it fancied a new look?'

'No, it was definitely a different one. The old one had to die sometime, so why put off telling him? But don't worry. I doubt you'll meet another alpaca fancier in Birmingham. He's not mentioned meeting up with any anyway.'

Kizzy busied herself with making tea while Lucy tried to get the image of a grown man with a collection of cuddly alpacas out of her mind.

'Have you thought about signing up for an evening class?' Kizzy continued.

'On alpacas?'

'No! To widen your social circle. How about pottery?'

'Do you think I might get a bit of wheel action with a Patrick Swayze lookalike?'

Kizzy grinned. 'Ghost was my mum's favourite film. I always knew when she'd split with her current boyfriend because she'd spend every night for at least a week watching it on repeat, sipping from a bottle of Lambrusco. She wore the VHS tape out. We were the first house on our street to get a DVD player.'

She plonked a mug of tea on Lucy's desk. 'Or there's life drawing?'

'Definitely not! I can't draw, and Em's dad is a life model. I'd die if he walked in naked.'

'How about learning a foreign language?'

'The class would be full of retirees. Everyone else learns on apps these days.'

'An older man might be more appreciative of you?'

'I don't want someone loudly snoring beside me in bed

every night. Adam's heavy breathing was irritating enough.'

'Snoring is what you get in the long run, so you may as well get used to it now.'

'I don't see you practising what you preach on that score. Your boyfriend is barely legal.'

'He's 21. He's only six years younger than me. I'm not in the market for a long-term relationship just yet. I prefer a man who's closer to his sexual peak.'

Lucy smiled. That was exactly how she'd been until recently. But since she'd turned thirty, she just wanted to settle down. That's why she'd chosen Adam. She thought a sensible-looking man with qualifications and a career was the safe option. So much for that.

'How about our postman, Paul?' Kizzy was still trying to find Lucy her next date.

'He's nowhere near his sexual peak. He must be at least 20 years older than me. How do you know his name?'

'I've got this amazing technique for getting information out of him: I talk to him.'

Lucy rolled her eyes.

Kizzy continued. 'He's widowed, so he's not someone else's cast-off. He's very fit, a bit of a silver fox, and he's always happy. Postmen usually are. I think it's all that fresh air. Human beings weren't meant to be stuck in offices. We should be out in nature.' Kizzy waved her arms in the direction of the window, with its view of several large office blocks and not a lot else.

Lucy took in Kizzy's long acrylic nails, perfectly contoured makeup, false eyelashes and four-inch stiletto heels. She couldn't imagine her surviving for five minutes in the great outdoors. 'All human beings?'

'Well, some of us have evolved to manage better in an indoor environment. But I do love the outdoors, as long as it's at least 25 degrees and I've got access to a sun lounger and a swimming pool with a swim-up bar. Anyway, Paul is attracted to you. He said you reminded him of his late wife. Hopefully, before the accident.' Kizzy sat down at her desk. 'You should give him a try. Do you want me to ask him? He usually turns up around 11.30.'

As lovely as she was sure Paul was, he hadn't made enough of an impression on Lucy to feature on her list of fuckable men.

'No, thanks. I'm giving up dating. It's the single life for me from now on.'

10

Jack usually looked forward to getting home, but today's trip to London to meet with his production company hadn't gone to plan and Em wasn't going to like the outcome.

She opened their front door before he could get his key in the lock.

'Hello, you,' he said nervously.

She beamed at him with that fantastic smile of hers. Perhaps he could charm her into bed. She might be more receptive to his news afterwards.

'You're back early. I'd have had dinner ready if I'd known,' she said while he put down his laptop bag and hung up his jacket.

'My fault. I should've texted you.' He kissed her.

'Are you sure it wasn't deliberate?'

He tried not to look guilty. He had remembered that there were a couple of good steaks in the fridge, and he didn't want Em to try cooking them. Steaks weren't her forte.

'I was distracted.' Which was true. 'Do you want me to start cooking, or do you want to do something else first?' He gave her his best 'I want to fuck you now' look.

She looked at him quizzically. 'Is something wrong?'

Em was too good at reading his mood. 'Not exactly,' he said.

'Oh god. They haven't sacked you, have they?'

'It's not that bad. I'll tell you later.'

'I'm imagining all sorts. Put me out of my misery. What happened?'

Jack sighed. He better get it over and done with. He led her into the living room. They sat down together on the sofa.

'I'm still going to be presenting. But they've had a focus group, and they think we'll get more viewers if a female presenter is working with me, particularly as the new series is about women pirates.'

'That's reasonable, I suppose. But are there any female academics who specialise in your area?'

'None that I know of.' *Stop drumming your fingers on the arm of the sofa. She'll know you're nervous.*

'But they have they got someone in mind?'

'Yes.' Em was going to work it out any second now.

'It's Clara, isn't it?'

Jack's former friend Clara was a newsreader and TV presenter. They'd had been much more than friends for a while, but that had been way before Jack and Em had got together. And he'd kept Clara at a distance ever since she'd been rude about Em last year. Em didn't know the whole story about that, though.

Jack sighed. 'Ian said we needed someone with gravitas.'

Em hesitated for a second. 'I don't mean this nastily, but why has she agreed to work on your programme? It's not as if it's shown on the mainstream channels she's used to.'

'I thought the same, but Clara's struggled to get a presenter role since that unfortunate interview with the animal trainer.'

'The one where she punched the poor man's chimpanzee in the face when it reached out to her? I'm surprised the

RSPCA didn't bring charges.'

'In her defence, she said its hand was heading straight for her crotch.'

'It didn't look that way. Anyway, when did you have that conversation? I thought you'd been avoiding her for months?' Em did not look happy.

'She was in the meeting.' He looked away. 'And we had lunch afterwards.'

'Lunch?' Surely, Em didn't think something was going on. *Stop behaving so shiftily otherwise that's precisely what she'll think.*

He looked her in the eye. 'Just lunch. Nothing else, I promise. I thought I better offer an olive branch if we were going to be working together.'

Em relaxed slightly. 'I guess Clara thought "I need a job, why not approach good old Jack Carver, who's got a soft spot for me?"'

'No.'

'Yes.'

'Ok. Possibly. But she didn't approach me. She contacted Ian.'

'Knowing he'd ask you and you'd say yes.'

'I didn't have a choice.' Which wasn't entirely true. He could've said no and walked away, but this project was his baby, and he didn't want to let it go, even if it did mean working with Clara.

'I'm not interested in her. Not that way. She knows that.'

'But you were once. Could she be hoping you could be again?'

'I can't help being irresistible.' He grinned.

Em glared at him.

You misjudged that one, Carver.

'I guess you could work in different places,' Em suggested. 'Clara could do the Italian episode, and you could be in Spain talking about another pirate.'

'We could, but Ian wants us both on screen together most of the time.' He decided not to mention that Ian thought Jack and Clara had excellent chemistry. *You should've put up more of a fight.* If Em had just announced she was planning to work with that lecherous bastard of a personal trainer, Ben, he'd have exactly the same expression on his face as Em had now.

'When is it going to happen?' she asked.

'During October and November. They're sorting out the locations, accommodation and flights this week.'

'I trust you, Jack.'

That was a relief.

'But I don't trust Clara.' Em looked upset. He hated to see her like that. He needed to float the idea he'd come up with on the train home. He put his arm around her.

'There is one thing we could do,' Jack said. 'You could come with us as my assistant.'

'How many days?'

At least she was considering the idea. 'Six. Possibly seven. I'll know when they finalise the shooting schedule in a couple of weeks.'

Em still looked thoughtful. 'We're still busy with guests in October. I'll have to check with Nancy.'

'But in principle?'

'Yes.' Thank god her big beaming smile was back.

11

Lucy walked across the gym to the cardio equipment. She'd been furious with herself for not putting two and two together about Adam sooner, but at least she'd been able to channel that anger into smashing her personal best on the weight machines tonight.

She was knackered after her long day in the office, but she wasn't going to quit now. She'd not missed any of her gym sessions this year, and all she needed to do to complete this one was ten minutes on the cross trainer, followed by a quick set of stretches. At least that was one personal goal she was on track to meet. Pity about the other one she'd written in the front of her 2019 journal: find a reliable partner.

Surely that wasn't too much to ask? Seeing Jack and Em at New Year had made her realise it was time to stop messing around. Despite the shaky start, they were so relaxed and in love with one another now. Lucy needed some of that in her life. After nine years of changing boyfriends several times a year, she wanted someone she could trust to come home to.

You thought you had that with Dylan, and then he'd abandoned you right when you needed him most.

She mustn't think about Dylan in public. It always made her cry. Lucy climbed onto the cross trainer and flicked through the channels on its display. Soaps, football, quizzes - nothing appealing. Then she found a documentary featuring a couples' therapist. She might get some relationship tips from that. She put on her headphones and watched the screen as she moved her limbs backwards and forwards.

A couple were sitting on a sofa, looking miserable. The psychologist nodded thoughtfully as the woman described her disappointment with her partner's infidelities with her best friend, their nanny and a random Deliveroo driver. Why wasn't he telling that poor woman to leave the bastard? Lucy had a strict 'one strike, and you're out' policy. She knew some women were more tolerant, but this was ridiculous.

What would the therapist say if Lucy were sitting on that couch? He might suggest picking unsuitable men was a self-preservation mechanism after her experience with Dylan. Lucy was pretty sure that's what her subconscious had been doing all this time. But it was ten years since the Dylan problem, and she'd experienced that spark again with Mark last year. Ok, he'd proved to be yet another cheat, but at least it meant there was hope she could find another man who made her feel special. Perhaps she'd been a bit hasty when she told Kizzy she was giving up dating. She'd have one last attempt at achieving that remaining 2019 goal.

12

'I need a favour,' Nancy said as soon as Em walked into the kitchen at Dashford Grange the following morning. 'Had you got any plans for this afternoon?'

Em usually did admin for the holiday lets on Wednesday mornings, but the afternoon was her own.

'I was thinking of sketching down by the harbour, but the weather forecast says it's going to rain. What do you want me to do?'

'We need to revamp the holiday cottages.'

'This afternoon?' Nancy was always in a rush to implement new ideas, but Em wasn't sure what she was expecting her to do about such a potentially large project today.

'No, no, no. Nothing so strenuous. I want you to come shopping with me.' Nancy put the iPad she'd been using in front of Em. 'What do you think of that?'

Em looked at the screen. It was displaying the website for Dashford View, the new holiday accommodation down the road. All very modern, with minimalist furnishings. Em scrolled through the site. Attractive, competitively priced, and they had a better view over the bay.

Nancy sighed. 'Serious competition. We need to up our game. Our setup looks very dated by comparison.'

'A lot of our clients like the cosy, country look.'

'But not the ones with money. I've been looking at the stats for next year's bookings, and they're down compared to this time last year. I have a suspicion that Dashford View might be to blame. Tea?'

Em nodded. 'Yes, please.' Nancy always preferred to discuss major decisions over a cup of Earl Grey.

'We can't do anything about the view,' Nancy continued. 'Not unless we blow up the stables, but I think Historic England might have something to say about that. However, we can improve the decor.'

'What are you thinking of doing?'

'I'd already budgeted for upgrading the kitchens and bathrooms over the next three years,' Nancy continued. 'But we need to do something much sooner to make them look more appealing to the younger market. I've phoned Clive, the decorator, and got him lined up for redecorating over the autumn. So now we have to do the fun part: deciding on colours, fabrics and accessories. My only disappointment is having to give up my plans for going husky sledding to fund it all.'

'Husky sledding? You haven't mentioned that before.' It sounded pretty tame for a Nancy activity holiday.

'Haven't I? Oh, it's fabulous. You spend a week going deep into the wilds of Finland with just a pack of dogs and a sled. And a tent, of course, living very simply. It's physically demanding, but I'm still in peak condition after Kilimanjaro, so that wouldn't have been a problem. I was all set to book it this week as well.'

Not that tame, then. Nancy was never going to be content with relaxing on a cruise ship.

'Can't you persuade one of your sons to invest?'

'I very much doubt it. Nigel will want a fully costed, detailed business plan for him to dither over for six months and then say no. I've been down that frustrating path before. And Mark would probably have been game if he still had a decent job as a solicitor, but now he's messing around hiring out jet skis on the Costa del Sol, I doubt he's got any spare cash to help. No, the huskies will have to wait until next year, sadly.'

Nancy placed a steaming mug of tea in front of Em. 'So, will you come with me to Exeter to choose furnishings?'

An afternoon's shopping sounded fun. Em would enjoy wandering the aisles of John Lewis. She might even get some ideas for her and Jack's new home when they managed to find one. 'Yes, I'm up for that.'

'Excellent. I've done some preliminary work.' Nancy switched the iPad screen to a mood board of photos from interior design websites. A sea of shades of grey with the occasional pop of colour, all with sleek furniture. A big change from the pastels and flowery fabrics the holiday cottages had now. 'Are you ok to leave about 12 o'clock?'

***

'Ready for the off?' Nancy asked as soon as Em had finished the sandwich she had made her.

'I better tell Jack where we're going,' Em said.

'No need. I told him earlier. He was busy editing. He didn't look too pleased that I'd disturbed him. We ought to leave him in peace.'

'Ok.' Em was puzzled. It wasn't like Jack to be anti-social, even when he was writing.

They walked out into the courtyard together.

'Shall we take the Fiesta? There's more room in the boot than your sports car, in case we find lots of things we like.'

Em held the passenger door open for Nancy before she could object.

'I don't think I've driven you since I first picked you up from the station all those months ago.' Nancy said as they pulled out of the gate onto the lane.

'No, it never seems to work out that way, does it?' Em tried to sound innocent. After her initial hair-raising journey to Dashford Grange, she'd vowed never to let Nancy drive her again. She needed to change the subject quickly.

'I meant to ask you earlier. Would you mind if I had some time off in October and November? Jack's going away filming his TV programme, and he's asked me to come with him.'

'How lovely. But will he be able to spend any time with you? I don't think I'd enjoy sitting down and watching everyone else work. And October is still busy.'

'I know, but I'm worried about Clara.'

'Clara? What's it got to do with Clara?' Nancy was giving Em her full attention now.

Em explained the situation.

'You go. I'll manage.' Nancy was adamant.

'Are you sure?'

'Absolutely. I saw how she looked at him at your award ceremony last year. That woman reminds me a lot of Isabella.'

'I thought it was just me being uncharitable.'

'No, always trust your instincts. I wish I'd done that with Xander years ago. Jack is so kind. He seems to attract manipulative women - present company excepted, of course.'

That was an intriguing statement about Xander. Em had never met Nancy's late husband. He'd died 15 years ago in interesting circumstances. Em didn't feel comfortable asking for more details. They carried on in silence for a few miles.

'You've not told me much about Ella and Sam's wedding,' Nancy eventually said.

Em had tried to keep off the subject in case she let slip

about her and Jack's engagement. They'd decided they weren't going to tell anyone until they'd sorted the ring. *Just stick to the wedding facts.*

'We had a good time. Ella looked gorgeous, but I knew she would. She's always had a great sense of style. Sam scrubbed up well too.'

'And Connor?' Nancy had met Connor once and hadn't been impressed.

'He was just being Connor. Life and soul of the party, dodgy jokes, revelling in being the best man.'

'And are you and Jack ok?'

Nancy was fishing now. Em needed to distract her with something else.

'Yes, we're fine. Lucy had a hard time, though.' She filled Nancy in on the Adam situation.

'Shame. Pity she split up with Mark. Did you ever get to the bottom of that? Mark told me he couldn't get over here for an event because he lost his passport, and she's ghosted him ever since. Seems an extreme reaction.'

'All she told me was that he cheated on her.'

'I can believe he lost his passport, but he's never been the sort to two-time his girlfriends. He saw how his father's behaviour affected me.' Nancy went quiet for a moment. 'But then I am his mother - I suppose I see the best in him.'

13

'You're back early,' Jack shouted from the kitchen as Em walked into their flat.

'Yes, we found everything we needed, and the traffic was quite light considering it's holiday season.'

'Don't come into the living room yet.'

Em took off her trainers and put them on the shoe rack. 'Why?'

'It's a surprise.'

'Ok.' Em said apprehensively. What was he up to? She'd had enough surprises for one week.

'Don't go into the bedroom either.'

'Am I allowed to use the bathroom? I'm desperate. I'll need you to give me a bucket if not.'

'I love the air of mystery you like to exude.'

'Jack!' Em was really uncomfortable now.

'Yes, the bathroom's fine.'

Two minutes later, Em was back in the hallway. 'Are you going to be long, Jack, because I'm starving? Nancy usually treats us both to afternoon tea when we go shopping, but she made some excuse about being on a special diet today. Do you know anything about that?'

'No.' He sounded distracted. She heard saucepans being dumped in the sink and then footsteps coming towards the living room door.

Jack flung the door open. 'Welcome to Restaurant Jacques,' he said in a terrible French accent. When he stood back, she could see the curtains were closed, the main lights were off, and strings of fairy lights lit the room instead. He'd moved the table out of the corner of the kitchen and into the main living room, covered it with a white table cloth and laid it properly for a three-course meal. He'd even added a silver candelabra with red candles, which were flickering nicely, adding to the cosy ambience. Was Jack trying to make up for the Clara revelation yesterday?

'This is amazing. What's all this in aid of?'

'This is what my marriage proposal should've looked like,' he said, 'if I hadn't got carried away at the weekend.'

He pulled out a chair for Em to take a seat at the table.

'I thought I may as well do it anyway. I've made your favourite sweetcorn soup for starters, with that olive bread you like from the bakery in the village.'

'But they don't make that on Wednesdays.'

'They do if you ask nicely,' he said.

'Was Nancy in on this?' Em asked as Jack busied himself in the kitchen

'I might have suggested that I'd like you out of the way for the afternoon. But she doesn't know why. I just said I wanted to surprise you with a meal. Have you said anything to her about the weekend?'

'I told her all about the wedding and Lucy's situation with Adam. But I didn't mention that we got engaged. I thought we said we were going to tell her together once we'd sorted out a ring.'

Jack appeared with a bottle of Chablis. 'Would madame

like to try the wine?'

'Merci monsieur,' Em replied. She may as well get into the spirit of the occasion.

He poured her a glass, which she sipped delicately.

'It's perfect. My compliments to the sommelier.'

'The soup will be ready in ten minutes. Mind if I join you?' he asked, grabbing the other glass from the table.

'Be my guest,' she laughed. 'Where did you get all this stuff?'

'I borrowed the candelabra from Nancy. I ordered the rest online and had it delivered to Phil at the gallery. I didn't want you to open the parcels by mistake. Phil and Simon have had it stashed at theirs for a fortnight.'

A fortnight? So he'd been planning this for a while. Well, if Jack was getting all romantic, she ought to change into something more beguiling than the jeans and baggy t-shirt she'd been wearing all day. Time to break out her posh lingerie again. 'I'm sure I don't meet the dress code for Restaurant Jacques. Do you mind if I get changed?'

'That would mean going into the bedroom.' Jack looked less than keen on the idea.

'Yes, it would. What have you done in there?'

'I suppose I could let you have a look.'

Em headed back into the hallway and opened the bedroom door. More fairy lights. Rose petals were strewn over the bed, there was a diffuser heating her favourite Jo Malone scent on the dressing table, and a bottle of champagne chilling in an ice bucket on the bedside stand, with two champagne flutes next to it.

'You have gone to town, you old romantic you. I didn't know we even had a champagne bucket.'

'We didn't, but we have now. I couldn't find Nancy's.'

Em kissed him.

'Do you want any help getting changed?' he whispered

into her ear as he slid his hands under her t-shirt, a twinkle in his eye.

'That might be nice. I think you should get changed as well,' she said, undoing his belt.

'I better turn the soup off first. I'm hoping this will take longer than ten minutes.'

***

'Are you ready for your dinner now?' Jack asked as he lay next to Em in bed.

'I seem to have worked up even more of an appetite after the amuse-bouche,' she said, rolling towards him and kissing him.

'Before we head back to the living room. I've got something to show you.' He leaned over and pulled a small box from the bedside table drawer. Em's heart sank. It looked like a ring box. She was hoping they'd choose the ring together as she had a specific one in mind.

'I think I'm meant to go down on one knee at this point,' he said.

'No need for that. Stay here.' She pulled him close to her so he wouldn't be able to see her expression if she didn't like it. He flicked the lid of the box open, revealing a platinum ring with a lozenge-shaped sapphire set in a very unusual way. It was the exact one she wanted. Phil's husband Simon made contemporary jewellery, and she had been lusting after it for weeks, working out how many paintings she needed to sell to justify buying it when she really ought to be saving any extra cash for the house fund. 'How did you know to pick that one? I was so disappointed when Phil said it had been sold a couple of weeks ago.'

'I noticed you were admiring this one when we went in there the other week. Phil said he thought you wanted it. If it doesn't fit, Simon says he can adjust it. And if you'd rather have a more conventional one as your engagement ring, they're happy to take it back.'

'No, it's beautiful. I don't want anything else.'

Jack took the ring out of the box, gently took her left hand and slid it onto her ring finger.

'It fits perfectly. Thank you so much.'

'Emily Gillespie, will you still marry me?'

'Yes, Jack Carver. I still will,' she said, kissing him again.

***

'I'm absolutely starving now.' Em snuggled up to Jack.

'It's your fault. You keep distracting me.'

'Get back in the kitchen, husband-to-be.'

'Where I belong?'

'I wouldn't say that. But you are particularly talented in there.'

'Only in the kitchen?' He asked, kissing her again. He got out of bed, put on his dressing gown and blew her another kiss as he walked out the door.

Em picked up her phone and took a quick photo of her new ring, then sent it to Lucy, with the caption 'Lucky me!'

Lucy called her straight away. 'Is that the one you were lusting after?'

'Yep - Jack spotted me looking at it in the gallery when we were dropping off some pictures a few weeks ago.'

'Nice that he pays attention. It's beautiful. No regrets then?'

'Absolutely none. How are you? I feel guilty rubbing it in after what happened with Adam.'

'I'm ok. He had the cheek to text me today, asking for his whip back. I'm tempted to drop it off at his house.'

'You're not going to, are you?' Em was horrified.

'No, I've got more important things to do. I'm off to the beauticians. I've got a date tomorrow.'

'Already?'

'Yep. There's no point hanging about. Life is far too short. I'm giving online dating one last try.'

***

Jack and Em were back at the dining table tucking into the main course now - venison steaks, perfectly cooked by Jack, with a red wine jus and several vegetable accompaniments.

'How did you have time to make all this?'

'Messrs Marks and Spencer might have helped with the veg.' Jack poured her another glass of wine. 'So when are we going to get married?'

' It would be lovely to have some of our wedding photos in your meadow.'

'Yes, it would. Though we'll have to remain fully dressed this time.'

Em blushed.

'Early summer then. I don't want to have to wait for you until next August.' Jack said.

'How about late May? I could have a bouquet of peonies then.'

'Perfect. That gives us eight months to get organised.' He gathered up their now empty plates. 'Ready for dessert?'

'Definitely.' Em followed him into the kitchen, pulled him close to her and gave him a kiss.

'I meant chocolate mousse,' he laughed.

'Can that wait?' she asked, starting to unbutton his shirt.

14

'What's that on your finger?' Nancy asked.

Em had been in the kitchen of the main house for less than 30 seconds. 'You're very observant,' she said, kicking herself for not taking her engagement ring off before she left the flat that morning.

'Has somebody finally popped the question?' Nancy asked.

'It's supposed to be a secret. We were going to tell you together this evening.'

'Is it believable that I wouldn't notice a ring like that? Nigel might assume I am too old and frail to notice a double-decker bus heading straight for me, but Jack knows I'm still fit and healthy.' Nancy always seemed annoyed at how her eldest son assumed she was one step away from needing a care home. 'I've been on high alert for any signs of an engagement since we got back from Exeter yesterday.'

'Was it that obvious? Jack often does the cooking.'

'But he doesn't borrow a silver candelabra every time he decides to whip up a stir fry. There aren't many reasons a man goes to town cooking a special meal for his girlfriend.'

Nancy looked pleased that her suspicions had proved to be correct. 'Congratulations, my wonderful girl!'

She gave Em a big hug.

'Do you think you could pretend you don't know?' Em asked.

'Goodness me, no. I'm hopeless at acting. You'll have to tell Jack I guessed.'

Nancy made herself breakfast while Em settled down at the desk by the Aga to sort out the bookkeeping.

'When's the big day?' Nancy asked.

'We haven't set a date yet. Probably May next year.'

'You're welcome to have a marquee in the garden here. It will be my wedding present to you both if that's what you'd like. I'll cover the catering as well.'

'Oh Nancy, that's too much.'

'Nonsense. It would be a pleasure. And I might get to see Mark. Apart from that flying visit at Christmas, he seems to be permanently stuck in Spain again since he fell out with Lucy. I don't think his latest girlfriend likes me.'

'Hannah? Don't take it personally. I don't think she likes anyone much - except Mark, of course. And Jack.'

Hannah was an estate agent in Spain specialising in selling properties to Brits. She was always immaculately turned out, even when they were only going for a stroll on the beach. Em got the impression that Hannah disapproved of Em's more laid-back approach to clothes.

'Everyone likes Jack. I assume Mark is going to be Jack's best man?'

'I guess so. We haven't discussed that yet.' Of course, Jack would want Mark as his best man. But that could make things awkward with Lucy. Having them both involved in the wedding could be challenging.

'You don't look too happy? Brides are supposed to enjoy all the planning,' Nancy said.

'Are we? I find it all quite stressful.' And not just because of Mark and Lucy. 'I hated it when I was getting married to Connor. But then he wanted all these over-the-top things that I didn't want to waste money on. What was Jack's wedding to Isabella like? I've never felt able to ask.'

'Very lavish.' Nancy pulled up a chair in front of the desk, cradling a steaming hot cup of tea. 'When the bride's father is an Earl, a certain amount of pomp and ceremony is expected to show off his wealth to his friends and family, and Isabella was more than happy to comply.'

Em had only seen one photo from Jack's wedding to Isabella. He'd been dressed in a morning suit, and Lucy had found the picture on a society website, so Em should've realised it wasn't a quiet affair.

Nancy must've noticed the look of horror on Em's face. 'I'm not sure Jack had much say in it at all. I very much doubt he'll want the same for your wedding. He and Isabella got married in the church on the estate. All very formal.'

'But Jack's not religious?'

'Neither is Isabella, but when you have your own family church, you're expected to use it. There must have been four hundred guests, including a few minor royals. The church was full to the rafters. Then they had the Earl's 19th-century horse-drawn carriage take them up the drive to a huge marquee in the garden. Champagne reception with a small orchestra.'

'Not a string quartet?' Perhaps Nancy was exaggerating.

'Oh goodness me, no. There were at least 30 musicians plus a conductor and an opera singer. Then we had a five-course meal. More flowers than the Chelsea Flower Show. One of the great aunts had to go home because her hay fever tablets weren't strong enough to counteract the effects of all that pollen.'

Em's vision of a small ceremony followed by a hot buffet

would be a real comedown for Jack. She wished she'd never asked.

'Huge ornate cake with six different flavoured layers surrounded by a sea of cupcakes covered in icing that looked like flowers,' Nancy continued. 'Another buffet in the evening. An ice bar. Ridiculous thing. Dancing until midnight with a band and a DJ afterwards, I think, but I'd gone back to the hotel by then.'

'Ours will be a much smaller affair. I'm not sure we know 400 people to invite.'

'Very sensible. There were people there who had never met Jack and Isabella before. Ludicrous. Not what a wedding should be about at all. I always thought it was more of an opportunity for her father to show off to his business contacts rather than a declaration of lifelong devotion. It seems I was right on that one.'

Em decided to change the subject slightly. 'What was your wedding to Xander like?'

Nancy laughed. 'A complete contrast to Jack's. We got married at Marylebone Register Office, much to my mother's disgust. But if it was good enough for Paul and Linda McCartney, it was good enough for me and Xander. My parents refused to attend, and Xander's father was something big in the British embassy in Washington at the time and didn't make any effort to come home. So the only people there were a few close friends, including Jack's mother, Olivia, of course, and my brother and his girlfriend. We took them for tea at The Ritz afterwards.' Nancy smiled, then picked up her mug and put it in the dishwasher.

'I loved every single minute of it. Ask Jack whether he enjoyed his wedding,' she said as she left the kitchen.

15

Considering it was late on a Thursday afternoon, Lucy's favourite cafe was still really busy. She checked the time on her phone. Her date was ten minutes late. He'd seemed keen when they were texting online, and he was the one who'd suggested they meet in person. He might just be stuck at the office. She'd give him a bit longer.

'Excuse me.' A man walked up to Lucy's table. Brown eyes to die for, looked about her age. Beard - not ideal, but at least it was neatly trimmed, not one of those shaggy hipster numbers that probably held the remains of the owner's last two meals. Smartly dressed as if he'd just left an office. Much better looking than his profile pic. He really should update that. He must've taken it after a heavy night's drinking. But perhaps she'd keep that advice to herself if he turned out to be as good as he looked.

'Hello,' said Lucy, giving him her best smile.

'I'm expecting someone, but I can't find a table with two seats. Would it be ok if I borrowed this chair?'

Perhaps he didn't recognise her, though Lucy thought her profile pic was reasonably accurate. 'Is your name Andrei?'

'No,' he said, looking puzzled.

Not her date. Bloody typical. No wonder he looked better than his photo. That would've been a first.

Lucy sighed. 'I'm waiting for someone too, but he's late, so you may as well take it.'

'Thanks,' smart guy responded. He sat down at a table across from hers, got out a notebook and pen and started doodling.

Lucy picked up her phone and went through her notifications. No more matches today. There were a couple of business emails that needed attention. She replied to those and checked the time again. Her date was twenty minutes late now.

She finished her latte. No point in getting another one. If "Andrei, 34, Solicitor" couldn't be bothered to tell her he was running late on their first date, she was crossing him off her list of potential life partners.

As Lucy got up to go, she felt someone looking at her. She turned and saw it was smart guy.

'Did he stand you up?' he asked.

'Yes, looks like it.' Lucy noticed the chair he'd borrowed was still empty. 'Yours not turned up either?'

'No,' he said. 'Can I get you another coffee?'

She wasn't sure if he was waiting for a date or not. He might have been planning to meet a colleague. No ring on his left hand, though. Not that that meant anything. Adam hadn't worn a wedding ring either. At least, not when he was with Lucy. *Stop thinking about that bastard.* 'That depends.' she said.

'On what?' Smart guy asked.

'On whether you're straight, single and looking for a relationship, not just a quick shag?'

'You don't waste time getting to the point,' he laughed.

'I don't believe in messing around, unlike half the men

online, it would seem.'

'Women are just as bad.'

'What made you swipe right on yours?'

'She had a nice smile. Just my type. Slim, brunette.'

'Not her interests, amazing qualifications and her high-powered career?'

'I've given up selecting on that basis. They exaggerate it all anyway.'

He was right. Lucy had pretty much given up on selecting on anything other than looks as well. 'They invent everything,' she said. 'What's the worst lie you've been told?'

He appeared to be mulling over her question. 'I went out with someone who claimed she ran her own chain of hairdressers across the West Midlands. It turned out she'd got one mobile salon in a battered old caravan, which I suppose could move anywhere in the West Midlands if you're being pedantic. How about you?'

'The guy who claimed to be a 35-year-old gym instructor, which was probably true in the 1980s. He turned up here looking ready to claim his old age pension and walking with a severe limp.'

'So you'd prefer someone with a full set of working limbs, then?'

'Not necessarily. I once dated an ex-soldier who'd lost his lower left leg in Afghanistan. But he was honest about that at the start. We had a very enjoyable time until he decided to go back to his ex-girlfriend in Germany.'

'What had she got that you hadn't?'

'His spare leg.'

He was chuckling now. 'Are you making this up?'

'Sadly, I'm not.'

'So how about that coffee, then? I can tell you all about the rest of my failed dates. But I warn you, I don't think they're as entertaining as yours.'

'Ok, then. A regular skinny latte, please.'

'You look like someone who prefers a large one.'

Was that an attempt at double entendre? Judging by his cheeky grin, it was. Lucy shook her head. If he turned out to be a bore, a large latte might take too long to drink. 'I'm fine with a regular - quality, not quantity.'

He moved the spare chair back to Lucy's table. 'I'm Josh, by the way.'

'Nice to meet you, Josh. I'm Lucy.'

'Don't run away, Lucy.' He made an obvious look at her legs under the table.

'I'm not in a rush,' she said, admiring Josh's rather cute backside as he headed towards the counter.

16

Jack had promised to treat Em to dinner at the Fisherman's Arms in the village. Now would be a good time to follow up on her conversation with Nancy that morning. He was often more talkative about awkward topics when they were walking side by side.

'Did you enjoy your wedding?' Em asked.

'No. I've tried to wipe it from my memory.'

'Nancy told me all about it.'

'Good, that saves me from reliving it.' He didn't sound like he wanted to discuss it further.

Em decided to focus on the future. 'What type of wedding do you want this time?'

'A fun one. Not one where I'm paraded about like a prize pony to meet people I have nothing in common with and never want to see again. How about you?'

'A small ceremony and then a relaxed party afterwards, with just the people we care about there?'

'Sounds perfect. Do I get an invitation?' He smiled.

'If you play your cards right,' she grinned. 'What do we do about Mark and Lucy? I assume you want Mark as your best man?'

Jack nodded. 'Yes, I've already asked him.'

He walked through the gate into the wood and held it open for Em. 'It shouldn't be a problem. If we're keeping it simple, there's not much for them to do. Certainly, nothing they need to liaise with one another about. We'll have to plan it that way.'

'I'm sure they'll behave on the day.'

'Is Lucy still angry with him?'

'She's fuming, which is odd because normally, when she falls out with a man, she likes to give off an "I don't give a fuck" air. Has Mark ever worked out what he did?'

'He still has no idea why she ghosted him. He said if she wanted to be like that, he was well rid of her.'

They walked a little further in silence.

'I'm guessing Lucy is organising a hen do for you?' Jack eventually said.

'We haven't discussed it yet, but I'm sure she'll want to.'

'Are you going to have a weekend away like last time?' Jack asked. He sounded a bit on edge about the idea.

'I'm not sure.' Everyone had enjoyed what turned into the non-hen do in Newquay last year, but having another trip away seemed a bit cheeky. 'It's a big time commitment for everyone.'

'I thought they were keen to do it all again?'

'That's what they said last year, but we've just had one for Ella. I'm going to suggest we go out for a meal on a Saturday night in Birmingham as an alternative.'

'I think Nancy and my mother are hoping to get an invite. They enjoy a good party.' He went quiet for a minute. 'If you do go away, can you promise me one thing?'

'What?'

'No naked chef this time.'

He was still smarting about Ben, obviously. But Jack

should've been more decisive and not left her thinking he wasn't interested. She changed the subject. 'Are you going to have a stag do?'

'Mark has suggested we could all to visit him for a long weekend in Spain.'

'As long as it's not like the stag do Lars went to.'

'I promise I will not be fondling scantily clad women.'

They had reached the end of the wood now. The path led out into a quiet cul-de-sac of 1960s bungalows. They continued down the road to the harbour.

Bunting left over from the previous weekend's Morris dancing festival fluttered in the breeze. Em noticed the colourful patterns the reflections were making in the water. They would make an interesting picture of the harbourfront. Phil at the gallery reckoned that she needed to paint more bright and cheery summer scenes, and this view would fit the bill. She stopped to take a photo.

The view didn't look as good on the phone. She headed a few yards down the quay to try a different angle, Jack tagging along behind her.

'I love you.' Jack slipped his arms around her waist and pulled her close to him. She turned around so he could kiss her properly.

'What prompted that?' she asked.

'Does it matter?'

'I enjoyed it, so it would be handy to know what gets you in the mood for snogging me.'

'It might have been seeing your hair shining in the evening light, the wonder in your eyes as you watched the sunlight sparkling on the sea, or the fact that I'm hungry and I don't want to stand around for ages while you take lots of photos.'

'I wish I hadn't asked now,' Em laughed.

'Get a room.' Mary, the local beach cafe owner, was walking towards them, smiling. 'I haven't had a chance to say congratulations on your engagement. I wish you a long and happy life together.' How had she heard about them getting engaged already?

'Thank you,' Jack said.

'It must be very cosy with the two of you in your little flat, Em.'

'We're going to start looking for somewhere bigger in the autumn.' Em said.

'Extra bedrooms for guests or little ones?' Mary raised her eyebrows quizzically.

Jack gave Em the "Do not tell her anything else" look.

Mary leaned in conspiratorially. 'I've heard Eddie Earle's family are going to be putting his house up for sale, now he's moved into the old folks' home. It needs a lot doing to it, but it's in a beautiful spot. It's a big plot as well. You'd have room to extend and still have a big enough garden for children to run around in.' She pointed up to the row of Victorian houses towards the top of the cliff. 'It's the big one on the end. I can put you in touch with his daughter if you want to get in before everyone else. You know how difficult it is to buy property here. '

Jack looked thoughtful, but Em was keen not to get stuck in a conversation about their plans. Mary was a terrible gossip. The whole village would know anything they told her within 24 hours. 'Thanks so much, but we've got to dash. We've got a table booked at the pub, and we're late already.'

'No problem. Just say if you want me to introduce you.' Mary waved as she headed towards the main street.

Jack looked thoughtful as they continued walking to the pub. 'Mary's right about it being hard to buy property in Dashford.'

'I know. Anything the slightest bit habitable disappears off the sales listings within a few days.'

'So shall we follow up on that house she mentioned? The

location's ideal.' He looked up at the cliff.

It was perfectly placed. The views would be spectacular. Em would have no shortage of inspiration for her paintings living there. 'We've got to do something. There are only so many times I can trip over that pile of books you've left by our bedroom door before I get pissed off.'

Jack grinned. 'I'll pop in to see Mary in the morning.'

17

It was Em's turn to be eager to get an update on Lucy's love life for a change. After all, as Lucy put it, Em was all sorted now. As soon as Jack went out for an evening run, Em grabbed a cup of tea, made herself comfortable on the sofa and FaceTimed Lucy. 'How did your date go yesterday?'

'Apart from the fact he didn't turn up?'

Em was confused. Lucy had a great big grin on her face. She didn't look like someone who'd been stood up. 'Why are you looking so happy?'

'Because someone else was there, waiting for his online date, and she didn't turn up either. We had a coffee together.'

'What's he like?'

'Attractive. Laughed at my jokes. Asked about me. Didn't bore me about his extensive train collection.'

'He has a train collection?'

'Hopefully not. I'm just comparing him to my previous failures. There doesn't seem to be anything wrong with him.'

It sounded like Lucy had had struck lucky for a change. It was the happiest Em had seen her in a long time. 'What's he called?'

'Josh. He's working at the uni for a few months. He usually lives in Cheshire.'

'What does he do?'

'He's a car designer.'

'Is he, though?'

'Oh, yes. I'm not being caught out again. I spent the evening researching him when I should have been working on a client's marketing campaign.'

'Was that wise?'

'Probably not, but given the choice of analysing bathroom fitting suppliers or looking up a handsome man, I chose the man. Toilet seats can wait.'

'Toilet seats? I thought you specialised in luxury items?'

Lucy laughed. 'Heated toilet seats are a luxury. Anyway, I've decided to delegate that particular job to Kizzy. She's been pestering me to give her her own account.'

'Does Josh give you that heart-skipping feeling that Mark did?'

'Unfortunately not. But there's potential. He gave me a delicate peck on my hand when we parted company. Very gentlemanly.'

'Is Josh a time traveller from the 18th century?'

'If he is, he's slotted perfectly into 21st-century life. He races cars at the weekends and plays rhythm guitar in a band. He's a couple of years younger than me.'

'You didn't feel the urge to snog his face off, then?'

Lucy grinned. 'I restrained myself, but I might give it a go tomorrow.'

'Second date already?'

'Yes, we're going for dinner at that posh new Italian on George Street.'

'Handy for your flat afterwards.'

'Very handy. I've even invested in new bedding - 1000 thread count Egyptian cotton.'

'He's worth expensive bedding, then?'

'I don't know yet. But I am.' Lucy never lacked confidence.

'You usually get new lingerie. That's what you recommended for Jack.'

'I know, but I think Josh is the sort who might not keep a woman waiting in her lingerie for long.'

***

Jack walked into the living room just as Em ended her FaceTime call with Lucy. He was shivering.

'You're back early. I thought you were going to do a 5K?'

'I was, but it started hailing, and it hurt, so I headed back.'

'Poor darling.' She hugged him. 'You feel cold.'

'I'm going to have a bath to warm me up.' He kissed her. 'Care to join me?'

'I might do.'

'You don't need to bother with lingerie.' He started kissing her neck, running his hands underneath her top, searching for her bra clasp.

'You heard what Lucy said then?'

'Yes, I did.'

'Ooh!' His cold fingers made Em flinch.

'Sorry.' He scooped her up and carried her into the bathroom.

'Jack, do you think we'll have room for a big freestanding bath in our new house? Like the one Nancy has in her London flat?'

'We haven't even seen the house yet. And right now, my mind is not thinking about interior design.' He gently put her down on the edge of the bath, put the plug in and turned the taps on.

'It would be lovely, though,' Em said as she helped him undress.

'I was hoping we hadn't reached the stage in our

relationship where bathroom fittings were more interesting than sex.'

She grinned at him cheekily. 'But a big rolltop bath would give us a lot more room for that.'

He grinned back. 'I see I'm going to have to work much harder to take your mind off Homes & Gardens magazine.'

Jack picked her up and dumped her, giggling in the water.

***

Half an hour later, Em and Jack were snuggled up in bed together.

'Are we going to get on with planning our wedding?' Jack asked. 'If we decide to buy Eddie Earles' house, we won't have time to think about it for months.'

He had a point. 'Where shall we start?' Em asked.

'The guest list?'

Em reached for her phone and created a new note. 'Fire away.'

'You and me.'

Em started typing. 'Lucy. Possibly Josh.'

'Who's Josh?'

'Lucy's latest love interest. They're having their second date tomorrow, but I've got a good feeling about him.'

'Really? I bet she'll have got through several men by the time we walk down the aisle.'

'Don't be so mean.'

'But it's true. She may as well install a revolving door on her apartment.'

'That is really judgy. She doesn't have much luck with men, that's all. She had a long-term boyfriend years ago. Dylan. We thought he and Lucy would be partners for life. They seemed so good together.'

'What happened to him?'

'We never got to the bottom of it. They broke up when I

was living in London. One day, they were all loved up and pretty much living together, the next, she didn't want to mention his name. She didn't go out with anyone else for at least a year afterwards.'

'She's making up for lost time now.'

Em glared at him.

'I'm sorry,' he said, 'but Mark was seriously cut up about her ghosting him. She could at least have given him an explanation.'

'Well, we're not going to resolve that now. I'll put Lucy plus one.'

'Mark and Hannah.'

'Do you think they'll still be together next May?' Em felt mean, hoping they wouldn't, but she didn't get on with Mark's latest girlfriend.

'She's lasted longer than most.'

'I'll put Mark plus one. Ella … Sam … Nancy. Who else?'

'Parents?' Jack suggested.

'My dad, Cynthia, your mum. What about your dad?'

Jack went quiet. He'd been cagey about how his father had reacted to the news of Jack and Em's engagement when he'd phoned him earlier. His mother had been delighted, but Jack's father lived in France, and they rarely saw one another. Em still hadn't met him in person. Whenever Em suggested they visit, Jack said he hadn't got time for a trip.

'I suppose we'll have to invite him and Catherine.'

'You don't sound too keen. I thought we were only going to ask people we actually wanted there. '

'I'm not keen, but I wouldn't feel happy excluding them.' Jack looked deep in thought.

'Are you going to tell me what he said?'

Jack sighed. 'He said I was on the rebound. I should enjoy my newfound freedom after the divorce and sow a few wild oats. Not get hitched to someone else so quickly.'

No wonder Jack had kept quiet.

'And do you think he's right?' Em asked.

'Of course not! I wouldn't be lying here next to you discussing our wedding if I did.'

'Was he happy about you marrying Isabella?'

'Yes, he was fine with the idea of her as a daughter-in-law.'

'So it's just a Brummie artist who's not good enough for Peter Carver's son?'

'No, it's not that. He hasn't even met you yet.'

'But your ex was Lady Isabella, and I'm just plain old Em.'

Jack pulled her in close. 'Don't do yourself down. You're worth a million Isabellas - never forget that. It says more about what he thinks of marriage than anything else.'

'But he's been married twice?'

'No. Only once. My sister and I refer to Catherine as our stepmother, but technically, she isn't. My mother is the only person to get him to walk up the aisle so far. He's shown little interest in me since I was born, so why should I care what he thinks?'

'But I sense you do care.'

Jack sighed. 'I try not to. At least he's taught me how not to behave towards a son. I won't treat our children like that if we're lucky enough to have any.'

He looked sad. Em put her phone down and wrapped her arms around him. 'Shall we finish this later?'

'Perhaps we should stick to discussing your rolltop bath idea.' He grinned at her.

'I thought you'd never ask,' she said, reaching over to grab her interior design magazine from the bedside table.

18

Mary had put Jack in touch with Eddie Earle's daughter, Kerry. And now Em and Jack were carefully picking their way through the overgrown garden to the front door of his house.

'Good omen,' said Jack, nodding towards the door.

'What do you mean? Oh!' Em spotted the brass door knocker in the shape of an octopus.

'I think you should knock as it's your lucky symbol,' Jack said.

'Is it, though? I usually think of octopuses when I'm having a stressful time.'

'Perhaps it will ward off awkward people.'

A woman opened the door. 'Hi, I'm Kerry. Welcome to Octopus Cottage.'

'Even the name fits,' said Jack.

Kerry looked puzzled.

'The door knocker?' Jack said.

'Oh, I always forget about that. Mum found it in a car boot sale years ago. The house has been called Octopus Cottage since it was built in the 1880s, even though it's a bit too big for a cottage. I think there was a previous house here that was called that.'

A whiff of mothballs hit them as Kerry stood back to let them inside.

'You're not seeing it at its best.' Kerry led them into the dining room. 'Dad's been in the care home for six months, but I've been so busy, I've not had time to clean thoroughly, and my brothers live away, so they're no help. I wasn't expecting to be showing potential buyers around just yet.'

'I'm sorry about your father. It must be difficult,' Jack said.

'It'll be odd seeing another family living in this house. Me and my brothers grew up here. But it's just been Dad rattling around for the last ten years since Mum died. It's time it was full again. Have you got any children?'

'Not yet,' said Jack.

'Feel free to wander around. Ask if you need to know anything. I'll be in here,' Kerry said.

The kitchen was large but needed updating. No surprise there. 'Good sized dining room and separate living room with original features,' Em said as they walked into the other rooms.

'You're starting to sound like an estate agent. You'll be telling me it's in the catchment area for an outstanding school next,' Jack laughed.

'Actually, it is. I checked.'

There was a layer of dust over everything, but it looked like it had been well-maintained structurally. Despite the 1990s decor, Em felt it had a good vibe. She was already starting to visualise living here with Jack.

'Shall we go upstairs?' Jack said.

They walked into the front bedroom. 'Wow! That view's even more stunning than I thought,' Jack said.

'And the room's huge,' Em said.

'You're thinking about your bath, aren't you?'

'Possibly,' she grinned.

They went back a couple more decades when they walked into the bathroom. 'Why did anyone ever think this was a good idea?' Em said, looking at the avocado suite.

'Give it another twenty years, and they'll probably be all the rage again.'

'Not with me.'

'It's not just the bathroom that needs ripping out. There's a lot of work to get it up to scratch,' Jack said. He didn't sound as positive about the place as she was feeling.

'But it means we should get it for a good price and we can make it exactly how we want it. We can carry on living at the flat while we do it up. And we could manage by leaving some of it as it is for a while once it's been cleaned.'

'Where would you paint?' Jack asked as they walked back downstairs.

Kerry must've overheard them. 'Come out into the back garden. I think you're going to love this.'

She pointed to a big summer house at the end of the garden, with windows along one side.

'It's north facing. Perfect for artists,' she said as she unlocked the door. 'My mother was a ceramicist. She loved working in here.'

Kerry was right. Em did love it. 'It's my dream studio.'

It was full of boxes and old furniture, but Em could picture it tidied up and set up with her painting materials. There was room for an easel, a big table, and a drying rack for the paintings she was working on. Plenty of room for shelving and space to store finished pieces. She could even squeeze in a sofa and table at one end for meeting portrait clients. Kerry left them to it.

'I can imagine you working in here.' Jack smiled.

'Where would you write?'

'I'm bagging that end bedroom.' He nodded at the window

in the side of the house, looking out over the sea.

'So we both love it then?'

'Sounds like it.'

'Can we afford it?'

'I think we can. I did some rough calculations this morning. Kerry's keen to get it all sold. Let's hope her brothers are too. Shall we put in an offer?'

Part Two

Autumn 2019

19

Monday was Em's day off. She decided to take advantage of the lovely weather to sketch the sea from the garden at Dashford Grange. The view looked almost Mediterranean in the early autumn sunshine.

Jack walked over from the courtyard and sat beside her on the grass. 'Life's about to get hectic.'

He was grinning, so it must be good news. 'Is it the house?'

'I've just had an email from the solicitor to confirm that we've finally exchanged contracts. We complete the purchase next Tuesday.'

'At last.' Em put down her pencil and threw herself into his arms.

He fell backwards, laughing. 'It'll be weeks before it's habitable.'

'I know, but it's ours now. Well, nearly.' She snuggled into him.

'It's going to be a lot of hard work.'

'Are you determined to put a damper on my excitement?'

'I just want to manage expectations, that's all.'

'We've been discussing it all summer. I haven't suddenly

forgotten that long list of changes we made. It'll be fun turning it into our forever home.'

'I'll remind you of that when we're knee-deep in paint. '

'If we're knee-deep in paint, we've got other worries.'

'We could buy the decorating stuff this weekend.'

Em pulled a face. 'There's a slight problem with that. I've invited Lucy here to discuss hen party plans and go wedding dress shopping while Josh is watching a bike race in France.'

'Oh.' Jack didn't sound very enthusiastic.

'We can get the DIY things one evening this week.'

'It's not that. Mark's coming over from Spain on Friday. He's got business to sort out in Bristol, then he's coming here afterwards. He only told me yesterday. I forgot to mention it. Sorry.'

'Oh.' It was Em's turn to sound worried. How were they going to handle Mark and Lucy being in the same location at the same time?

Jack was obviously thinking the same. 'It's not a disaster. Mark's only here until Saturday lunchtime, so we just need to keep them apart for Friday night and Saturday morning.'

'Except Nancy's offered to put Lucy up in the main house. She was adamant that it would be too cosy for all three of us to be in our flat. And I know our sofa bed's not the comfiest, so I didn't argue. She said nothing about Mark being there as well.'

'Nancy knows full well he's coming here on his own. She must be up to her old tricks again,' Jack grinned. 'I imagine she's keen to get son number two married off to someone who lives here rather than abroad.'

With Nigel living in New York with his family and rarely putting in an appearance at Dashford, Mark was Nancy's last hope for having grandchildren she could see regularly. Em couldn't blame her for trying. Getting Mark and Lucy coupled up again would also suit Em. Life would be a lot more fun if Jack's best friend had a partner she could get on with. But he hadn't been faithful to Lucy, so that was a non-starter.

Em kissed Jack on the forehead. 'Nancy did alright on the matchmaking front with us, but I don't think she'll succeed with Mark and Lucy.'

'No, Mark won't go back to Lucy, despite what Nancy thinks. He reckons she's - what was the phrase he used? - batshit mental.'

20

'If we're discussing hen and stag dos this weekend, we ought to settle on the date for our wedding,' Jack said as they finished dinner later.

Em sighed. 'We can't do that without finding a venue, and that's been impossible.' Every venue they'd approached so far had no availability for next May. It had been so disheartening Em had given up looking a few weeks ago.

'You still want to get married, don't you?' Jack looked concerned.

'Of course I do.'

'And we've agreed we're not doing it in a church.'

'Yes. So we either need to widen the area we're looking in or push the date back.'

Jack got down from the table, sat on the sofa and grabbed his laptop. He searched the map for licensed wedding venues. Em sat next to him, looking over his shoulder. She recognised most of the names on the list as ones they'd already eliminated.

'I don't remember us looking at this one,' Jack said, pointing to a dedicated wedding venue called King Arthur's

Crag. He clicked on the website link. "New for 2020" was displayed in a big banner across the top.

'I thought King Arthur lived in Cornwall?'

'I suppose they allowed him over the border occasionally.'

'It's not going to work. Look, we have to have the meal there as well. We're stuffed.' Em sank back against the back of the sofa and looked at the ceiling.

'I don't want to wait another year.' Jack looked fed up as he scanned the map again. 'Remind me why we crossed the Bay View Hotel off the list? It's in Dashford, so it's the closest one.'

'Nancy put me off. She got food poisoning there in 1989.'

'But we won't be eating there.'

'It wasn't just that. She thought the manager was rude. "Had the attitude of a walrus with a raging tusk ache" was the phrase she used.'

'Surely it can't be the same manager after 30 years? We don't have to book if we don't like them when we look around.' Jack clicked on the website.

Em read the details over Jack's shoulder. 'Wedding ceremony room overlooking the bay.'

'I felt the clue was in the name.'

'It could have been overlooking the bins at the back.'

'I like the sound of that,' Jack said as he scrolled down the page.

'What? The bins?'

'No, the view over the bay. Let's give them a call.'

***

'We can't sue them under the trades description act. It does indeed have a view of the bay,' Jack said as he and Em got out of the car in the hotel car park the following evening.

'You can see our new home from here.' Em pointed across the bay. 'It would be a nice touch to have it in the background of the photos.'

Jack nodded. He looked around at the building and the gardens. 'It looks like a lovely hotel. I'm not sure why I've never been here before.'

They walked inside together. A middle-aged woman in a smart navy suit appeared from the office behind the Reception desk.

'I'm Lesley, the events coordinator. Pleased to meet you both.' She smiled and gently shook their hands. 'My notes say you're looking for a civil wedding ceremony venue, but I assume you want your reception here as well?'

'No, we've got the use of a marquee at home for that,' Em smiled back encouragingly, hoping the Bay View Hotel didn't have the same policy as King Arthur's Crag.

'Oh.' Lesley looked disappointed. 'You must have a large garden then.'

'Yes, we live at Dashford Grange,' Em said.

'Oh. I thought Nancy Farnham lived there?'

'She does. I'm the concierge for her holiday cottages, and Jack is her godson.'

'Oh.'

There were a lot of ohs. Lesley didn't seem at all excited by the prospect of hosting their wedding.

'Is Mrs Farnham on your guest list?' Lesley asked tentatively.

'Yes, of course,' said Jack. 'We're very close.'

'Ahh.' At least Lesley had moved on to a different letter sound.

'Is that a problem?' Em asked.

Lesley looked uncomfortable. 'It might be. You won't be able to have her as a guest at your wedding.'

Since when did hotels dictate who could be on your guest list? 'Why not?' Em asked.

Lesley looked nervous. 'She's barred from entering the

hotel.'

'Barred?' Em was shocked. 'Nancy is an upstanding member of the local community. How can she be barred?'

'There was an unfortunate incident in 1989,' Lesley continued.

'What incident?' Jack asked. 'I'd heard you poisoned her. But why does that warrant a 30-year ban?'

'I don't believe we did poison her. And it's a lifetime ban, actually.'

'Were you here in 1989?' Jack sounded uncharacteristically sharp.

'No, but it's one of the first things I learnt when I started working here. The owner is adamant Mrs Farnham is not allowed on the premises. We even have a photo of her pinned up in the office so we can easily identify her if she attempts to even set foot on the driveway. I can't tell you anything else about it because of data privacy laws. You'll have to ask Mrs Farnham. Would you still like to look round?'

Lesley was an optimist - Em would give her that. 'Nancy's a big part of our lives. Her attendance at our wedding is non-negotiable. We'll have to look elsewhere. Thank you for your time.' Em headed back outside with Jack following.

'What was all that about?' she asked Jack when they were both back in the car

'I have absolutely no idea. I was only six in 1989. I don't recall any major incident.' Jack started the car engine. 'But it explains why Nancy put you off looking here.'

'I don't feel comfortable asking her about it. She'd have said if it was anything she wanted to share.' Em sighed.

'My mother might know, but it doesn't sound like they're going to budge, so I guess it doesn't matter. What are we going to do now? That's every venue in or near Dashford eliminated.'

They drove in silence down the hill into the village, Em

racking her brains for other solutions. 'We could have a celebrant, then we can have our wedding ceremony anywhere we like. That's what one of Ella's work colleagues did. They had a traditional Celtic wedding, including jumping the broomstick.'

Jack didn't look impressed. 'Sounds more like a fake Victorian version of a Celtic ceremony to me. I'd be the laughing stock of the history department.'

'Actually, it is a genuine Welsh tradition, Mr Cynical. But we don't have to include anything you don't like. We could even write our own vows.'

'I promise to love and cherish you and follow you around picking up your clothes wherever you've discarded them till death do us part, probably due to me breaking my neck tripping over them?' he suggested with a grin.

'I was thinking something less passive-aggressive. And your books are a bigger trip hazard than my clothes, so you're on dodgy ground there, professor.'

'Joking apart, we'd have to have a register office ceremony first, so we'd already be legally married. It wouldn't feel the same.'

'No, I guess not,' Em said sadly.

21

It was Friday night, and Em and Jack were in the courtyard at Dashford Grange getting into Jack's car.

Em's phone pinged as Jack started the engine. A text from Lucy.

> `At the bar in the Fisherman's. Please save me from this prick!`

Em frowned. Jack looked over at her. 'Everything ok?'

'Looks like Lucy's in the pub already.' She texted back.

> `What prick?`

Lucy replied almost immediately.

> `Mark. Who do you think?`

Em turned to Jack. 'Why's Mark at the Fisherman's Arms?'

'Because that's where I'm meeting him.'

'But I thought you two were meeting at the Kingfisher.'

'No, you're meeting Lucy at the Kingfisher.'

'No, Lucy and I are going to the Fisherman's Arms.'

'You definitely said the Kingfisher. You've not done this deliberately, have you?'

'No! I swear I said the Fisherman's. I thought you weren't listening properly when we discussed it last night.'

Jack sighed. 'Too late now. So much for keeping them apart. We better get down there ASAP.'

A few minutes later, they pulled into the car park by the harbour.

'Ready?' Jack asked as they headed towards the pub. 'Whatever is through those doors, we have a better chance of survival if we work together,' he said, doing his best Russell Crowe impression.

Why were men obsessed with Gladiator? 'Come on Maximus Decimus Meridius. We'll be fine. Lucy was planning to leave her scythed chariot at home this weekend. I gather it's a bit tricky to drive it down the M5.' Em slipped her hand into Jack's as they walked across the road to the pub.

'Hi!' Em waved at Lucy, who was sitting at one end of a long table. Mark had his back to her at the other end. Both of them were concentrating on their phones and ignoring one another.

'Drink?' Jack made a hand signal for a glass of something.

'No, thanks,' Lucy and Mark said in unison.

'Jinx?' Mark looked expectantly at Lucy.

She just scowled and muttered 'child' under her breath.

Mark sighed and looked at Em and Jack. 'I will have that drink after all.' He headed to the bar with Jack.

'What's he done now? I thought you said you were going to be civil to him if we bumped into him and Jack tonight?' Em asked as she sat beside Lucy.

'It's more what he hasn't done. We've been sitting here for at least ten minutes, and he's made no attempt to say sorry for the way he behaved last year. Anyway, I thought you said it would just be the two of us tonight?'

'There was a bit of a cock up with the venues. And I don't

think Mark knows what he's meant to be apologising for.'

'For cheating on me, of course.'

'But he claims he didn't.'

Lucy huffed.

'Can we at least have a truce for this evening? Mark's going back to Spain tomorrow morning. Jack doesn't get to see him that often.'

Lucy sighed. 'I'll try.'

***

'Do you hate everything I suggest on principle?' Mark challenged Lucy, as the waitress cleared away their plates.

'No. You just come up with ridiculous ideas that are a waste of breath.'

'I don't think it's a ridiculous idea at all.' Jack looked exasperated that hostilities had broken out again after half an hour of relative calm while they were eating. 'Or it wouldn't be if you two were speaking to one another.'

Mark had suggested having a combined stag and hen weekend. 'Other couples do it. If we do separate ones, the stag do will just be me, Jack, Phil, Phil's husband and two of Jack's old uni friends, one of whom is a woman. We're not going to be having a classic weekend of drunken debauchery with the local womenfolk.'

'That must be a disappointment for you,' Lucy said.

Mark looked like he was biting his tongue.

'Aren't you inviting your dad?' Lucy asked Jack.

'I don't want him there. He made it perfectly obvious he was annoyed enough about making the trip from the Dordogne for our wedding.' Jack got up and went to the bar.

'Excuse me,' Em said as she got up and followed him.

'Are you ok?' said Em.

'I'm just tired. I like the idea of a combined celebration, but it won't work with Lucy sniping at Mark all the time. Can't you get her to talk to him about it? Clear the air?'

'I'll try, but it might be easier back home.'

'Let's settle up and go then.'

Jack drove them all back to Dashford Grange, Mark in the front passenger seat and Lucy in the back with Em, behaving as if Mark didn't exist.

'I'm exhausted,' Lucy said to Em as she got out of the car. 'I've had a long day with one thing and another.' She glared at Mark, who had his back to her. 'I'd like an early night,'

'I'll come with you.' Em looked at Jack. 'I'll see you in a bit.'

'Can you tell Mum I'll be over later?' Mark said, following Jack to the flat.

Em let Lucy into the main house. Nancy was in the kitchen.

'Lucy darling. It's so lovely to see you again.' Nancy hugged Lucy tightly. 'Has that hopeless son of mine made peace with you yet?'

'No. He won't apologise.'

'Hmm. Perhaps I should have a word with him.'

'It's too late for that. I'm sorry, Nancy, but I've had such a stressful day. Would you mind if I went straight to bed?'

'Not at all. You can tell me all your news over breakfast. I'll show you to your room.'

Em left them to it and went back across the courtyard to the flat. She heard Jack and Mark talking as she walked through the door.

'I tried to get things on a civil footing, but she's still determined to be angry with me.' Mark said. 'I can't believe at one point, I thought she might be the one.'

That was news to Em. 'She's waiting for you to say sorry for two-timing her,' Em said as she walked into the living room.

'But I didn't. That's what's so frustrating.'

'Why don't you have a proper talk to her? Find out why

she thinks that.'

He sighed. 'I tried that in the pub before you arrived, but you saw what she was like with me. She wouldn't even let me say two words to her.'

Em had noticed. It was really odd. Normally, Lucy moved on quickly when a relationship failed, but tonight, she seemed to be determined to stay angry with him.

Mark sighed. 'I'll give it one last go, for your sakes.'

22

Lucy was lying in bed, looking at the ornate mouldings on the ceiling. She was tired, but being in close proximity to Mark all evening had wound her up. She couldn't relax, and she felt bad about upsetting Jack. Was she genuinely annoyed with Mark? Or with herself because he still made her heart skip a beat when he looked at her. Perhaps being angry with him was her way of making sure he stayed away from her because, as soon as he'd walked into the pub earlier, she knew she was still attracted to him. What a mess.

There was a knock on the door.

'Can we talk?' Mark.

Come on, Lucy Thomas. You've got to find a way of being civil to him. The skipping heartbeat thing will wear off, eventually. Lucy sat up and pulled the duvet up around her neck. 'Ok'

The door opened slightly, and a coat hanger with a white t-shirt hanging off it slid through it, followed by Mark's face. 'Truce?'

Trying to make her laugh. She'd always found that appealing, but she mustn't lose sight of the fact that he'd lied to her. Lucy pointed to the chair by the window.

Mark walked in and sat down.

'I'm listening,' she said.

'I don't know why you ghosted me, but it's been almost a year, and we've both moved on. Can we find a way of being in the same room without you sniping at me, for Em and Jack's sakes?'

Bloody cheek. Still no sign of an apology. 'So it's all on me, is it? You're still claiming that you're the innocent party?'

'I explained why I missed your awards ceremony. I didn't lose my passport deliberately. I'm not sure why that warranted you ghosting me, but we've got to move on from that now.'

'I accepted your apology for that, but you lied to me about why you hadn't got around to inviting me to Spain.'

He looked confused. 'I told you I was busy. It's really hard not to be dragged into doing business activities when I'm there, even when I've got cover. I didn't want you to fly all that way and then be on your own for most of the weekend. I thought I was being considerate.'

Very plausible. That's why she'd believed it when he spun her that line last year. 'You think I'm an idiot, don't you? Well, I am. I am idiotic enough to buy a plane ticket to Malaga and turn up on your doorstep the morning after the awards as a surprise, thinking you'd be fed up and lonely without me. But you weren't fed up and lonely, were you?' She looked away. She was in serious danger of bursting into tears. *Deep breaths. You've got this.*

'I don't understand. I had no idea you'd flown to Spain.'

'Because I didn't hang around once I found out what was going on. When there was no answer at your house, I was worried in case you'd sorted out a temporary passport, and you were on your way to England. So I knocked on your neighbour's door to ask if she knew where you were. She said she'd bumped into you earlier, and she thought you'd be working all day because you'd said the guy who was meant to be looking after the jet skis had phoned in sick, so you were having to cover. Then she said your girlfriend - GIRLFRIEND - usually came home about 11 am if I wanted to talk to her. Note that she said usually. So it wasn't a one-off, having a woman living with you.'

Mark looked like he was about to say something, but Lucy had waited months to have this conversation. She was going to get her full story out first, whether he liked it or not. 'I waited. And, lo and behold, five minutes later, a tall olive-skinned beauty walks up to your door, jangling her keys. I thought, "Don't jump to conclusions, Lucy". So I said hello and that I was looking for you. She said you wouldn't be home till the evening.'

Mark looked stunned. Lucy carried on. 'I could see what you saw in her, what with her amazing looks and that sexy Spanish accent. But just in case I was still mistaken, I asked her outright. Are you and Mark together? And she said yes! You had been all summer. ALL SUMMER. So you were with her when we first met. You told me a blatant lie, Mark Farnham. You said you were single.'

Mark looked downcast. 'It was an Italian accent,' he said quietly. 'That was Gabriella. She is not and never has been my girlfriend.'

Lucy was angry again now. 'So you're not a liar, but your neighbour is, and so is this Gabriella woman. Is that what you're saying? Don't insult me by carrying on with this complete fabrication. There's no point. We're never getting back together. Show me some respect by telling me the truth.'

'Gabriella's my sister.'

'Sister? She looks nothing like you. We're here in your childhood home with no evidence of you having a bloody sister. Nancy even said to me once that Em was like the daughter she never had.'

'Keep your voice down. Mum's not her mother. Gabriella is my half-sister. Mum doesn't know she exists. I didn't know she existed until last year.'

'Well, that's bloody convenient. You pass off your girlfriend as a sister, but I can't confirm that with anyone. So why did she say you were together if she's your sister?'

'Because she saw me every day, I guess. She was sharing my house. She's not a native English speaker. I suppose she didn't understand what being together inferred', he said.

'OK, let's carry on with your interesting story. If she is your sister, why didn't you ever mention her?'

'She never came up in conversation. She was lodging with me while she was improving her Spanish. I didn't see a lot of her. I guess I was used to not talking about her to anyone who knows Mum in case it got back to her. I would have told you eventually, I'm sure.'

Lucy shook her head. 'Mark, please just be a man and own up. I'd think better of you if you did.'

'But Luce, it's the truth. I swear.'

'On your fictional sister's life, no doubt. Please get out.'

Lucy got off the bed, marched over to the door, and opened it. 'Get. Out.'

He did as he was told. She slammed the door behind him and flopped down on the bed. Did Mark honestly think she would fall for that load of crap?!

***

Em's phone buzzed on her bedside table.

'Leave it. It can wait till morning.' Jack murmured in Em's ear, pulling her closer to him in bed.

'I won't be able to sleep if I don't answer it. What if Dad's ill? Or Nancy needs help?'

'Nancy never needs help.'

'One day she might, and what if today's the day?' Em

picked up her phone. A text from Lucy.

'That's odd.' She showed Jack the message.

`Pls ask J if M has a half-sister.`

'Does he?'

Jack looked uncomfortable. 'I'm not supposed to say.'

'So that's a "Yes" then?'

'Mark asked me not to tell anyone. His father worked in Rome for six months back in the late nineties. And we all know what Xander was like. He needed a woman to keep him company. Gabriella was the result.'

'Nancy's never mentioned it.'

'She doesn't know. The only other Farnham in on the secret is Nigel. He's been helping Gabriella out with her university fees.

'She's definitely Xander's daughter?'

'Yes. She contacted Nigel out of the blue last year. She must've got his details off Xander's will. He insisted on a DNA test to make sure it was her before he handed over any cash.'

'Have you met her?'

'No.'

'Why would Lucy be asking about her?'

'I have no idea.' Jack sighed.

'What shall I say?'

'Don't reply yet. I'll message Mark.'

Jack picked up his phone.

`Why is Lucy asking about Gabriella? What should I say?`

Em looked over his shoulder

'It's delivered, but he's not read it yet,' Jack said.

'I can't leave Lucy hanging.'

Jack flopped back on the pillow. 'Tell her I'm asleep like any normal human being would be at 12.10 am.'

Em glared at him.

'Ok. Leave that last bit off.'

'I'll say I'll ask you in the morning,' she said, tapping out the reply.

23

Jack heard a knock on the front door of the flat. He turned over and looked at the clock. 7.55 am. It was probably a guest wanting to ask about something before they checked out. Em's side of the bed was empty. She'd deal with them. He pulled the duvet closer around himself and closed his eyes again.

'I knew you'd be up early. Can you drive me to the station?' Lucy's voice.

'Aren't you staying until tomorrow? I thought we were going into Exeter to look at wedding dresses together today?' Em sounded disappointed.

'I'm so sorry. I really need to get home. I don't want to be anywhere near Mark. I promise I'll come back another weekend when he's not here.'

Jack sighed. He better be sociable and say goodbye to Lucy.

Em was putting on her trainers as he emerged from the bedroom, bleary-eyed.

'Did Em ask you?' Lucy looked directly at him.

'And good morning to you too,' Jack smiled. 'Ask me what?'

'About Mark's imaginary sister.'

Jack had forgotten about the conversation last night. 'Just a minute,' he said, going back into the bedroom to pick up his phone. There was a reply from Mark.

```
She thinks I'm a liar.
```

The reply was only ten minutes old. Jack typed his response.

```
Do you want me to confirm you have a
sister?
```

Mark replied straightaway.

```
Yes pls
```

Jack walked back into the hall again. He looked at Lucy. 'Mark does have a sister called Gabriella.'

Lucy looked stunned. 'Shit.'

'Do you want some tea? It's a bit early for anything stronger.' Em asked, ushering Lucy to the sofa in the living room.

'I'm going to have to apologise.'

Jack was curious why all this mattered. 'What's his sister got to do with anything?'

'I thought he was having an affair with her.'

Em looked baffled. Lucy summarised what had happened in Spain last year.

'Why didn't you let him explain at the time?' Em asked.

'I thought he was the second man to cheat on me in two months. I wasn't going to hang around to be humiliated again. I blocked him and got a taxi straight back to the airport.'

Em put her arms around Lucy. 'What a mess.'

'It's an understandable conclusion to jump to,' Jack said. 'Why don't you go back over to the house and apologise? I'm sure he's just relieved to know finally why it all went wrong.'

The quicker Lucy went to find Mark, the quicker Jack

could get back to bed and possibly persuade Em to join him.

'It's embarrassing,' Lucy said. 'Anyway, it doesn't make any difference now. We've both moved on.'

'He might not be in a relationship for much longer. They never seem to last for more than six months. I reckon they get clingy, so he breaks up with them.'

Was Em seriously suggesting that? Nancy's matchmaking tendencies were rubbing off on her. Jack needed to nip this in the bud.

'I hate to rain on your parade, but Hannah seems to have more staying power than the others,' Jack said.

'Yes, but …'

Jack guessed what Em was about to say, but that wouldn't be helpful. He glared at her. She took the hint and shut up.

But Lucy knew Em too well. 'Come on, spit it out.'

Em avoided catching Jack's eye again. 'Mark was upset last night. He said at one point he used to think you were the one.'

Exactly what Jack thought Em had been about to say. Encouraging Lucy to think there was a chance she and Mark could get back together would not help the situation.

Lucy went quiet for a moment. 'I thought the same about him.'

This was so not going to end well.

'Shall we invite Mark over for breakfast?' Em asked Jack.

Jack sighed. There was no chance of going back to bed now. But, on the positive side, if Lucy did apologise to Mark, they could have that joint stag and hen do after all. 'Fine,' he said.

'What are you expecting me to do?' Lucy didn't sound keen on the idea of Mark joining them, either.

'You can make peace with him. See where it goes.' Em got up. 'Jack's just going to get dressed.' She shepherded him into the bedroom and shut the door.

'You've given Lucy false hopes. I don't think Hannah's going anywhere soon,' he said.

'But Hannah's not here now, is she? She couldn't be bothered to make the trip over from Spain.'

'I told you - she's working. I know you don't like her, but Mark does.'

'I take it Mark's awake as you were texting him.' Em said. 'Are you going to invite him over here, or shall I?'

'It's going to be a bit cosy here with all four of us eating around our tiny table. Why don't we go over to the main house and have our breakfast there?'

'Lucy can't apologise about Gabriella with Nancy potentially in earshot,' Em whispered. 'We'll make an excuse to leave the two of them alone.'

Jack sighed. 'Ok then. In the interests of world peace.'

He texted Mark.

    Breakfast at ours?

***

Five minutes later, Jack was welcoming Mark into the flat.

'That was perfect timing. Mum was grilling me about what Lucy and I were arguing about last night.' His expression clouded over when he saw Lucy. 'Ready to have another go at me?'

Lucy didn't respond.

'We just need to pop out to get some black pudding,' Em said, ushering Jack out the door.

There was an awkward silence after Em shut the front door.

'I can't stand black pudding, can you?' Mark said.

'I like it, actually, but then you'd say it was a northern thing.'

'Oh good god, we're not revisiting the whole "You think

I'm Northern, but I'm really from the Midlands, you soft southern bastard" routine, are we?' Mark looked exasperated.

Lucy bit her lip. *Why did you dig that old chestnut up again, Lucy Thomas? You're the one who needs to say sorry.* She took a deep breath.

'I just wanted ...' They both spoke at the same time.

'Ladies first.' Mark sat down on the chair opposite Lucy.

'I am sorry I didn't believe you last night.'

'And I'm sorry I didn't tell you about Gabriella.' Mark looked directly at her. 'I was in love with you. I didn't want anyone else.'

Lucy noted the past tense. *And you're still in love with him,* her inner voice helpfully pointed out.

'Too late now,' she said aloud.

'Yes. As you said last night, we've both moved on.' Mark was holding her gaze as he said it. She visualised walking over to him and giving him the longest, sexiest kiss.

'Shall we bury the hatchet?' he asked. 'Preferably not in my back?'

'That would be good.' Lucy said.

They both stood up. Mark walked over to Lucy and hugged her. 'No hard feelings,' she said.

Mark pulled away from her slightly, looking flustered. 'No hard feelings. Not that sort, anyway.'

24

Two hours later, Em was driving Lucy to Exeter for their shopping trip while Jack took Mark back to the airport.

'I'm glad you and Mark are friends again,' Em said. 'And not just because it makes the wedding planning easier.'

'I don't know how to feel about it.' Lucy wasn't sure how much to tell Em. They'd all been laughing and joking together earlier like nothing was wrong. But Lucy's emotions were in turmoil.

'What do you mean?'

'I've still got the hots for him.'

'For Mark? But what about Josh?'

'He's attractive as well, but ... I don't know.'

'Spoilt for choice?'

Lucy stared ahead at the countryside, flying by outside the car window. 'Not really. Mark's spoken for. But you know how you used to say Jack made your heart skip a beat? Mark has the same effect on me. He has ever since that first night we met. Even when I was angry with him. And now we're back to being friendly, it's worse. Josh doesn't do that for me. No one else has. Not since Dylan.'

Why did you say that? You mustn't think about Dylan.

Em looked surprised. 'That's the first time you've mentioned Dylan for years.'

Lucy didn't want to reminisce about the man she'd dated nearly ten years ago. It still hurt to think about him walking out on her. Em didn't know the whole story. If she did, she wouldn't have said that.

Lucy wanted to tell Em about it, but today wasn't the day. It would ruin their mood for wedding dress shopping. She needed to shut down this particular conversational cul-de-sac immediately. 'That's all in the past. Right now, I need to work out what to do about Josh.'

'I know I said earlier that Mark was due to leave Hannah, but Jack thinks he seems really content with her.'

'Really? So why was he getting a hard-on when he hugged me earlier?'

Em raised her eyebrows.

'I probably imagined it,' Lucy said. Had she? She was sure she hadn't. 'Tell me about Hannah.'

'Would you like to meet her? You'll be able to judge for yourself then. I bought Jack tickets to see Muse at the O2 in London next Saturday as it's his birthday. Mark and Hannah are coming. Kate was meant to be joining us too with her new man, Andy, but they cancelled yesterday.

'Kate?'

'Jack's sister.'

'Oh, that Kate.'

'Andy snapped his Achilles heel playing football on Wednesday night. He's had to have an operation, so a trip to London is out of the question. Do you and Josh want to join us instead? We're all stopping in Nancy's flat in Bloomsbury. You don't have to worry about booking a hotel.'

Was it a wise idea to spend a weekend in close proximity to Mark and his girlfriend? Probably not. But Lucy hadn't been to London for a while. And Josh had said they should do something together next week to make up for being apart this weekend. Plus, she'd see how Josh behaved with her friends.

'I'll text Josh to see if he's up for it.'

***

'There's the wedding dress shop over there.' Lucy pointed to a window with a dressmaker's dummy dressed in lace and silk.

'Perhaps it's a bit early for shopping for the dress. We haven't settled on a date yet. And the way things were going with finding a venue, it could be two years away.'

'But you'll still have a summer wedding. We're here now. It wouldn't hurt to have a look. As your matron of honour, I insist.'

Lucy had a point. *You're just getting cold feet because it's reminding you of getting married to Connor.*

The shop looked small outside, but as they walked in, there was a sign on the wall advertising the large showroom upstairs.

'Have you booked an appointment?' the haughty woman behind the counter asked. Her name badge described her as 'Julie, Assistant Manager'.

'Yes,' Lucy said. 'It's in the name of Emily Gillespie. I booked it online last week. We're a bit early.'

'Ah yes, here we are,' Julie's attitude thawed, clearly pleased they weren't dropping in for a casual browse. 'Which of you is the blushing bride?'

Lucy pointed to Em.

Julie looked Em up and down. 'Yes, we have lots of dresses that would suit. When are you getting married?'

'We're still finalising the date, but we're aiming for May,' said Em.

'May 2021?' Julie asked.

'No, May 2020.' Em replied.

Julie looked flabbergasted. 'Next May?'

'Yes. Next May.'

'But that's only eight months away.'

'Is that a problem?' Em asked. Clearly, it was, but Em was at a loss as to why.

Julie proceeded to talk to Em as if she were about seven years old. 'Most of our dresses are on a 20-week lead time, and then we have to book you in with our seamstress to get it properly fitted. That often takes several visits as brides have an annoying habit of losing weight between fittings. We normally have customers who are organised enough to buy their dresses at least a year in advance.' Her frostiness had returned. 'However, we do have a few in stock for emergency weddings. I'll check with my colleague. Wait here.'

She went upstairs.

Em looked at Lucy. 'How is planning a wedding eight months in advance an emergency? Honestly, why does every wedding professional I deal with behave as if we're asking the impossible?'

Julie returned before Lucy had a chance to answer.

'Karen is going to see what we can do for you. She'll be five minutes if you'd like to go upstairs.'

'That's very kind,' said Em. 'I didn't realise I was asking so much.'

The upstairs showroom was large and brightly lit. Another bride-to-be was standing on a box in the middle of the room, wearing a complex long-sleeved lace dress and being admired by two women, one of whom was Karen. The other woman, presumably the bride's mother, was sharing her opinion of the frock.

'Darling. It looks lovely, but what about Toby? I can imagine him getting caught in the lace. He's so excitable.'

Em and Lucy exchanged a look.

'Would that be at the altar or afterwards?' Lucy whispered to Em as they sat down on a chaise longue at the far end of the room.

'Toby is perfectly well-behaved, Mum.'

'Is he? He wasn't at your sister's wedding last year. He couldn't keep away from that bitch at the ceremony.'

Em was trying to visualise Toby. He didn't sound like the perfect groom.

The bride turned to look at them. 'Toby's my Jack Russell terrier.'

'Oh,' Lucy looked relieved.

'Though my groom is quite excitable too,' the bride laughed.

'And he was busy sniffing around the other bitch at the wedding,' her mother said disapprovingly.

'Mum! That's no way to talk about Ellie. George was helping her fix a problem with her bridesmaid's dress.'

'Hmm. I know he said he was trying to do up her zip, but it looked the opposite to me. Are you sure you're doing the right thing marrying him?'

'Your dress looks amazing,' Em said encouragingly before the conversation got any worse.

'Thank you.' Judging by the expression on the bride's face, she was grateful for the change of subject as well as the compliment.

Karen looked at Em. 'Ladies, you're welcome to look through some gowns while you're waiting. Not these racks here. That small rack at the back is all we can guarantee to do in time. They're our ex-display dresses.'

'Nice,' muttered Lucy.

'Shall we leave?' Em said to Lucy as they moved to the back of the room. 'I don't feel welcome, and I haven't tried anything on yet. For all they know, I could afford to pay a premium to get one made in time, but instead, I'm relegated to picking over last year's leftovers.'

Lucy looked as annoyed as Em did. 'We may as well see what they've got while we're here. It might give you some ideas.'

Em started looking through the rail. Too small. Too big. A dull beige colour that wouldn't suit anyone. It was obvious why no eager bride had snapped these up already.

George's bride was back in her normal clothes and saying goodbye. Karen turned her attention to Em.

'There is one that we could order in time. And it would show off your lovely figure perfectly.' She pulled a dress off the rail nearest to her and held it up in front of herself.

Em turned to look and took a sharp intake of breath. The pretty diamante belt would emphasise her narrow waist. The plunging neckline covered in thin lace would show off her cleavage without being too revealing. Even the colour would work against Em's pale skin.

Karen was right. It would show off Em's figure perfectly. It was why she'd chosen it for her wedding to Connor.

Lucy must've recognised it too. 'Not that one,' she said, glaring at Karen.

'Oh, but you should at least try it on. You can never be sure until you wear it.'

'It's lovely, but it's not for me,' Em said quietly. 'I don't think any of them are. Sorry.'

She headed down the stairs and out of the shop as fast as she could. When she got outside, she took a deep breath in a bid to calm down.

Lucy appeared behind her. 'That was awful. I'm sorry. It never occurred to me that that could happen.'

'Me neither. What luck!' Em sighed. 'Fate seems to be pushing me not to marry Jack.'

'Don't say that. It's just a stupid dress.' Lucy hugged Em.

'It's not just the dress, though. It's the venue. It's

everything.'

25

'I'm home,' Em shouted as she walked into the living room.

'Hello, you. Lucy caught the train ok, then?' Jack asked.

'Yes, we got there with two minutes to spare.' The local trains had been cancelled due to Sunday engineering works, and the replacement bus hadn't turned up. Lucy had a business meeting first thing on Monday, so Em had had to drive her 50 miles to the nearest mainline station.

'I'm knackered,' she said, flopping down on the sofa.

'Perhaps this will help.' Jack emerged from the kitchen and put a glass of Pinot Grigio on the coffee table in front of her.

'Yes, it will. You're an angel.'

Jack sat beside her with his own glass of wine and pulled her in for a hug.' It's good to be alone again.'

'I suppose so.' Em snuggled into him.

'You don't seem that enthusiastic about it?' Jack sounded concerned.

'I'm sorry. I'm just exhausted. Nothing seems to be going to plan with the wedding. We can't have it on the date we want. We can't get a venue. We've had all the aggro between Lucy and Mark. Then dress shopping was a nightmare yesterday. It's like fate is trying to tell us something.'

'Come on. Things are improving. Mark and Lucy are getting on now. Mark said he was pleased they were friends again. We were talking about it when I took him to the airport. And I might have a solution to the venue issue,' Jack said, looking pleased with himself. 'I was thinking about it while you were being Lucy's taxi.'

'Go on then?' Em was curious now. She'd been pondering how to solve the venue problem all the way back from the railway station, too, but the only solution she'd come up with was to delay the wedding, and she didn't want to do that.

'Why don't we have an engagement party?' Jack suggested.

Was that it? Was he mad? That meant they'd have two celebrations to organise. 'That's going to be even more stressful. I thought we were keeping it low-key?'

'Hear me out first,' he said. 'We invite our friends and family to the engagement party - only the ones we get on with. We'll have no pressure from our families to include Uncle Tom Cobbly and all because it's just an engagement party. But what they don't know is we secretly got married that morning at the registry office in Barnstaple. Just the two of us. We get a couple of the office staff there to act as witnesses. Then we announce it at the party in the evening. What do you think?'

Em grinned. 'I like it. I like it a lot.' It would eliminate the stress and potentially save some money so they could spend that on the new house, but there was one drawback. 'Lucy would be upset at missing out on the ceremony.'

'Ok then. We ask Lucy and Mark to be our witnesses and swear them to secrecy. We only tell them on the day, so there's less risk of it slipping out accidentally. They'll be in Dashford for the engagement party anyway. We won't need to come up with some excuse to get them here.'

'That could work.'

'I'm not as stupid as I look sometimes,' he laughed.

'When are we going to do it?'

'As soon as possible, as far as I'm concerned.'

'Nancy will be disappointed about not hosting the wedding reception here.'

'So we have the engagement party here instead.'

'How are we going to tell her without spoiling the surprise?'

'We tell her the truth, but we leave out the bit about the wedding. We say we can't get a decent ceremony venue without having the reception there, too. And they're all booked for at least 18 months, so we'd like an engagement party in the meantime if the offer of the marquee still stands for that.'

Genius. 'I love you, Jack.'

'I'm glad about that. It will make being married a lot easier if you do,' he laughed.

26

'I have good news,' Jack announced as he walked into the flat the following evening.

'I was just about to say the same.' Em joined him in the hall and gave him a kiss. 'You first.'

He put his laptop bag down and took off his jacket. 'I've managed to reorganise my diary so I can work at home tomorrow, which means we can go straight round to the house as soon as the solicitor lets us have the keys.'

'Lady Luck is on our side at last,' said Em. 'I've been dying to tell you my news all day.'

'Why didn't you text me?' he asked.

'You said you were in meetings all day, and I wanted to tell you face to face.'

'Well?' He looked at her quizzically.

'Nancy's fine with the engagement idea, so I contacted the marquee company. They're fully booked until February, but they'd just had a cancellation for the last Saturday before Christmas. The registrars have a free appointment early that day, too. So I've got them both pencilled in subject to confirmation from you.'

He picked her up and swung her around. 'So I get a new Mrs Jack Campbell for Christmas this year?'

'I'm not sure I like the way you said that, but yes, you and I will be husband and wife in fourteen weeks and five days' time.'

'I'm not bothered if you don't want to be Mrs Carver. You can call yourself Nellie the Elephant for all I care.'

'Sounds good.' Em pretended to give it serious consideration. 'Perhaps I'll go for that. It will make me more memorable when I'm marketing my portrait services.'

'Mrs Elephant Paints would have a certain ring to it,' he laughed.

'Ms Elephant, if you don't mind.'

***

While Em and Jack were celebrating their marriage plans, Lucy was alone in her Birmingham flat. She'd had a busy day at work, which was exactly what she needed to take her mind off the events of the weekend.

Josh was travelling back from France. His flight was due back any minute now. She'd offered to pick him up from the airport, but his friend was giving him a lift home. He said he'd pop around to see her as soon as he was back. She sensed he was desperate for a shag after four days apart.

She'd had no time to look at Instagram all day, but now she was sitting on her sofa, she opened it without thinking and started scrolling through her feed.

Several photos of friends' cats, allegedly looking cute but just staring at the camera, as far as Lucy could tell.

Em's work-in-progress photo of her new Dashford harbour painting. She double-tapped that one. She might buy it for the office.

Kizzy's new nails. Longer than ever. How the hell could

she type with those?

A baby scan photo. Shit - whose was that? Ella. She read the caption.

```
12 weeks. So happy! Baby Wagstaff due
30.03.2020
```

A honeymoon baby. Lucky Ella and Sam.

Lucy felt faint. Tears welled up. She put the phone down on the coffee table.

He'd have been nearly ten years old now, her little boy. Did Dylan ever think about him? Probably not. She wondered if he was a father now. He might have a better understanding of what she'd gone through if he was.

Lucy got up, grabbed a tissue from the bathroom, and blew her nose.

She was in control again now. It was a good job that she'd found out while she was on her own. What if Ella had told her in person?

And Ella was unlikely to be the only friend to get pregnant over the next few years. Lucy needed to come up with a strategy. She'd thought about it before, but until now, it had never been someone in her friendship group announcing their pregnancy. She could get away with excusing herself when it was someone at a networking group or yoga. But close friends would expect her to be delighted for them straight away. If she'd been open about her miscarriage at the time, they would probably tread carefully if they had a baby announcement to make, but they were all oblivious.

Her phone buzzed. A text from Josh.

```
Back on terra firma. Cock raring to say
hello to your vag in approx 40 mins. J
xx
```

Charming, but at least you knew where you stood with Josh. He lacked the finesse of some of her ex-lovers, but he was always keen. How would he handle it if she got pregnant? Not well, she suspected. She needed to think about that, too.

27

Jack pulled the car up on the drive at Octopus Cottage.

Em dangled the keys she'd picked up from the solicitors at lunchtime. 'Who's going to open the door?'

'You do it,' Jack said as they got out and walked up the path to the front door.

'I'm not sure which one's which.'

There were half a dozen keys, all looking very similar, and none of them labelled.

'Try that one,' he said, pointing to one of the Yale keys

Em put it in the lock and turned the key. 'You must have psychic powers. It worked.'

'Just a minute.' Jack scooped her up in his arms.

'I thought you were supposed to carry me over the threshold after we're married.'

'Nothing stopping me from having a practice run now.' He kissed her as he stepped inside. They both went quiet as they looked around the hall.

'You know that renovation plan I made,' Em said.

'Yes.' Jack sounded distracted.

'I think it might need a few amendments.'

Now that all the furnishings had gone, the house looked much worse than Em remembered. She could see dark outlines on the wallpaper where pictures used to hang, and the carpet had more threadbare spots than she'd noticed before.

'We'll be ok. We wanted to strip it right back anyway.' Something about Jack's tone gave Em the impression that he was saying that to reassure himself as well as her. 'Houses always look forlorn when they're bare.'

'Do they? I've never seen any of the homes I've lived in when they're empty.'

'My house felt sad and abandoned when all the furniture was on the removal van. But I'm sure it feels like a home again for whoever lives there now. And this house will be the same. It's not the bricks and mortar and plaster that make a home. It's all the love and laughter and memories you create living there.'

'That's very poetic.'

'It's true. I'm looking forward to making lots of wonderful memories with you here.' He gave her another kiss.

'I think you better put me down. If you put your back out now, we are totally screwed.'

28

Em and Jack were spending Friday evening at his mother's for a pre-birthday dinner for Jack.

'How's your new house?' Olivia asked.

'It's going to keep us busy for a couple of months, at least.' Jack said, putting his cutlery down on his empty dinner plate.

'But we've made a start on the decorating already.' Em added.

'Can't you get a professional in?' Olivia asked.

'Nancy's got the local decorator fully booked for weeks on her cottage makeovers.' Jack said. 'I did try to get some other quotes, but no one came back to me. They're all busy. So it's either do it ourselves or wait until the new year.'

'I can't wait to have a look around. I've obviously seen the photos Jack sent me, but it's not the same as being there in person.'

'No, you don't get the full effect of the mothballs,' Jack said, laughing.

'The smell's improving now we've ripped the carpets out.' Em said. 'When are you next in Dashford, Olivia?'

'Not until your engagement party. Talking of which, are

you inviting Caroline?'

Em looked puzzled. 'Who's Caroline?'

'My niece, Jack's cousin. I take it as you don't know her, she's not on the guest list.'

'No,' Jack said cautiously. 'Mark will be there. I thought it might be awkward inviting Caroline as well.'

'Surely that's not a problem. That was all years ago.' Olivia turned to Em. 'Caroline had the hots for Mark when they were teenagers, but he didn't feel the same way about her. But she's a grown woman now. She won't be following him around like a lost puppy.'

'Not like a puppy, no.' Jack didn't sound convinced. 'More like a fully grown rottweiler on heat based on the last time they met.'

Olivia frowned. 'Mark will be there with Hannah, won't he? Caroline won't bother him if he's got a partner. If you could be a darling and invite her that would solve a problem. Your Aunt Verity will struggle to get to Dashford on her own now she's given up driving.'

'Given up?' said Jack. 'Nancy said it was a two-year ban.'

'What for?' asked Em. Jack had described his mother's sister as the black sheep of the family, but given he came from a long line of overachievers, she assumed that probably meant Verity had scraped a 2:1 degree.

'Driving whilst under the influence of drugs.' Jack said.

Olivia looked embarrassed. 'It was purely for medicinal purposes.'

Jack snorted. 'The ban might have been shorter if she hadn't had a large joint in her mouth when she got pulled over. And being on a call to her dealer with the mobile phone in her hand didn't help either.'

Olivia glared at him. 'I see Nancy filled you in on all the details. I was trying to keep it quiet.'

'It was all in the papers, Mother. It's hardly a state secret.'

'Anyway, if you could invite Caroline, she can chauffeur her mother.'

'I guess it will be fine.' Jack raised his eyebrows at Em.

'Any news on the wedding date?'

'We're still struggling to get a venue. We tried the Bay View Hotel the other day, but that didn't work out.' Jack asked.

'Probably for the best.' Olivia looked sheepish.

'Why's that? It seemed a lovely hotel to me.' Jack caught Em's eye.

'Well, let's just say there's some history there. Nancy wouldn't set foot in the place, not even for your wedding.'

'I'm curious now, Mother. What happened?'

'It's not my place to say. You'll have to ask Nancy. Are you ready for dessert?'

***

'I've got something to show you.' Olivia whispered to Em in the kitchen later. 'Don't tell Jack. Come with me before he notices you've gone.'

Em was intrigued. She followed Olivia up to the first floor and into the large dressing room off Olivia's bedroom.

'A little bird tells me you're having trouble finding a wedding dress.' Olivia said as she shut the door behind them.

'Would that little bird be Nancy by any chance?' It was unlikely to be Jack.

'It might be. I'm about to show you something, and I won't be offended if you don't like it. I want you to be completely honest.'

Olivia pulled a hanger out of one of the wardrobes. Em could tell there was a kingfisher blue, mid-length dress under the clear plastic cover.

'This was my mother's gown.' Olivia unzipped the cover to reveal a taffeta cocktail dress in a classic 1950s off-the-shoulder style. 'She bought it to wear for a film premiere.'

'A film premiere?' Em had realised that Jack's family moved in more exalted circles than her own, but every time she visited his childhood home, she found out a new fact that made them seem even more fascinating. She wouldn't have been surprised if Olivia had casually revealed she was twentieth in line to the throne. It would be intimidating if they weren't all so lovely.

'"A Star is Born", if I remember correctly. The 1954 version. Judy Garland, not Lady Gaga. My mother knew one of the producers.'

'It's stunning.' Em couldn't take her eyes off it.

'It is. Are you sure you like it?'

'I absolutely love it.'

'It's not a traditional wedding dress colour. Are you bothered by that?'

'No. It's perfect. White and cream do nothing for my pale skin.'

'I was nine years old when she wore it, and it enchanted me. I never forgot it, but it was totally out of fashion when I was the right size to wear it. Now vintage is all the rage, and everyone wears whatever suits them, it could do with another outing.'

'Wouldn't Kate like it?' Em didn't want Jack's sister to be upset that Olivia was lending it to her.

'Kate's too much of a bean pole for it to do anything for her. It's the ideal shape to show off your curves.'

Olivia offered up the dress against Em's body. 'I think it's going to fit. Would you like to try it on?'

Em was eager to give it a go. She took off her jeans and shirt. Olivia held the dress so Em could step into it.

'Almost perfect,' Olivia said as she helped Em with the zip. 'You need it taking in on the waist if anything.' Olivia stood behind Em as she looked in the full-length mirror. She pulled the fabric tighter around Em's middle. 'Nancy knows a wonderful dressmaker in Barnstaple who'll sort it out for you.'

'Nancy knows about your kind offer?'

'Oh yes. In fact, she was the one who put the idea into my head.'

Bless, Nancy. It was like having a guardian angel sometimes.

'Well, what do you think?' Olivia asked.

'I think it's amazing. Are you sure you want me to wear it? I'm scared I might drop some food down it or damage it.'

'If you do, you do. It's been hanging in this wardrobe for far too long. It's yours now.'

'Thank you so much.' Em gave Olivia a peck on the cheek.'But perhaps I ought to borrow it? Then it could be my something old, borrowed and blue?'

'What an excellent idea.'

Em smiled to herself. There was only one problem. 'How am I going to get it home without Jack seeing?'

'That's an excellent question. I think I will have to employ my little bird to bring it to Dashford for you. Leave it to me and Nancy.'

29

Lucy led Josh up the stairs to Nancy's apartment. Despite the Saturday afternoon traffic in central London, they'd still managed to arrive on time. Jack was waiting for them by the open door. Lucy gave Jack a hug. 'Happy birthday, professor. This is Josh,'

'Pleased to meet you.' Jack smiled and shook Josh's hand.

'Thanks for inviting us,' Josh said. Lucy could tell he was weighing up Jack.

'No problem.' Jack stood back to let them into the hallway.

'Which room are we in?' asked Lucy.

'You've got the sheep,' Jack pointed down the end of the hall. 'On the left.'

'Sheep?' Josh looked confused.

'There are sheep on the wallpaper,' explained Lucy, remembering the rural scene wallpaper from the last time she'd stayed here when Em received her portrait award last December.

'Em's out food shopping,' Jack said.

'We'll just put our bags in our room, and then we'll be sociable,' Lucy said, walking down the hallway into the bedroom.

Josh followed her and shut the door. 'Very nice. You have some well-heeled friends.'

'Nancy is. I'm not sure about the rest of them.'

'Who's Nancy again?'

'Em's employer, Jack's godmother and Mark's mother.'

'Are you and me the only people she hasn't got a connection with?'

'Yes.' Lucy laughed. 'She's lovely. It's good of her to let us use the flat.'

'Well, if her son's here, it's not much bother if we stay too.'

'Yes, but all the same.'

'Am I going to be the youngest one here?'

Why was he asking that? 'I think so. Though I've not met Hannah yet.'

'Hannah?'

'Mark's girlfriend.'

'Oh yes. You did say. So we're not likely to be out partying all night, then?'

'You and I can if you want. I've never been clubbing with the rest of them. I'm guessing Jack and Em won't want to go. I wouldn't have thought Mark would either.' During the brief time they'd dated, Mark had always preferred to prop up a bar rather than get on a dancefloor, though Hannah might have changed him. She looked like she might enjoy going out to a club based on her Instagram posts. Lucy had spent half an hour yesterday scrolling through Mark and Hannah's feeds to assess how happy they were together. Blissful by the look of it.

Lucy heard the front door open again and Em's voice. 'Shall we be sociable?' she suggested, pulling a gift-wrapped box out of one of her bags.

'If we must.' Josh looked sulky.

'You don't sound that keen.'

'I guess I'd have preferred to stay at home with you.'

'Why didn't you say that before?'

'I didn't think it through. It's going to be a dull weekend.'

'Dull?' Lucy was shocked. 'We're in London. We're off to a concert at the O2. We can go out partying afterwards. How is that dull?'

'They're all old and stuffy. I was hoping I'd make some new friends.'

'How have you jumped to that conclusion? You've only met Jack, and he's barely said two words to you yet. He's not old. He's only six years older than me.'

'He dresses like a typical grown-up public school boy.'

'What does that mean?'

'Open-necked shirt and cashmere sweater with jeans. Not exactly cutting-edge fashion.'

'What were you expecting? You don't exactly look like Mr Unconventional yourself.' Lucy looked Josh up and down, taking in his black cargo trousers and plain grey t-shirt.

'We're here now. I'll just have to put up with it.'

Lucy sighed. It wasn't a good start to the weekend. 'Come on, Josh. You won't make any new friends by stopping in here all afternoon.'

Em and Jack were in the living room.

'Hi, Josh. Nice to meet you,' Em called from the kitchen.

'You too.' At least Josh sounded perkier with Em.

Em got a couple of mugs out of a cupboard. 'The kettle's on. What do you want to drink? Tea or coffee?'

'Tea, please,' said Lucy, sitting down next to Jack on the sofa.

'What coffee have you got?' Josh asked.

'All sorts. It's one of those coffee pod things. The pods are all on the holder next to the machine. I don't like coffee, so it's a mystery to me. Feel free to help yourself.'

Lucy leaned over to Jack and gave him a peck on the

cheek.

'This is for you.' She handed over the present. 'I hope you like it.'

'Thank you. I wasn't expecting anything. I'm too old for presents now.'

'Don't say that,' she said. *Really, don't say that.* She glanced at Josh, who raised an eyebrow as if to say, "I told you so".

Jack carefully removed the wrapping paper, revealing a long, thin black box. He opened the lid. A sleek black fountain pen with silver detailing nestled inside.

'It's beautiful. You're too generous. Thank you.' Jack gave Lucy a peck on the cheek.

'Em said you'd lost yours.'

'Why do you still use a fountain pen?' asked Josh. 'Bit old fashioned, isn't it?'

'Perhaps I'm old fashioned.' Something about the way Jack said it gave Lucy a hint that he'd picked up on Josh's opinion of him. 'I like the way the nib glides over the paper. I write better with a fountain pen than with a biro. I thought someone who created luxury cars for a living would appreciate good design?'

Josh didn't reply.

'So what's the plan, birthday boy?' Lucy asked, slipping her arm through Jack's.

'We'll need to leave here about seven. Would you like takeout first?'

'Yeah. What shall we have?'

'It's Jack's choice as it's his birthday,' Em said.

'The Japanese restaurant a couple of streets away is good,' Jack said. 'We can't get that in Dashford. There's a menu on the fridge door.'

Em passed the menu to Josh, who was grumpily scrolling through something on his phone like a bored teenager.

'Does that work for you, darling?' Lucy asked him, trying

to get Josh to engage.

'Yeah, whatever.' He couldn't have sounded less interested if he tried.

Lucy heard the front door opening.

'Hi!' a woman's voice called out.

Lucy tensed.

'Are you ok?' Jack whispered.

'Yes. This just feels weird.'

He put his arm around her and gave her shoulder a comforting squeeze just as Mark walked in.

'Swapping girlfriends now are we?' Mark looked briefly at Lucy and looked away.

'It is my birthday. I get to pick.' Jack ducked as Em threw a tea towel at him.

Jack got up and gave Mark a hug. 'Thanks for coming.'

'I've missed your last two birthdays. Thought I better not miss this one. Hannah, you know Jack and Em. This is Lucy and?'

'Josh.' Josh said as he walked over to Mark to shake hands.

'Pleased to meet you, Josh.' Mark appeared to be sizing Josh up.

And so did Hannah. Devouring him with her eyes would be a better description.

Josh perked up, too. 'We're having Japanese for dinner,' he said to Hannah. 'Can I help you choose? I spent a year in Japan, so I know my way around the cuisine.'

'That's so helpful. I don't know my sashimi from my sushi,' she said. They huddled together over the menu on the kitchen island, Josh asking Hannah what she liked to eat.

Lucy was gobsmacked.

'I'm sure Josh will help you next.' Em seemed as surprised as Lucy at Josh's sudden improvement in mood.

Hannah took the hint and went off with Mark to their room.

'So, are you going to help me?' Lucy asked Josh, her arms folded.

'You work opposite a Japanese restaurant. You know exactly what it all means,' he said, passing her the menu as he headed out of the room. 'I'm off to the bathroom.'

Josh closed the living room door after him. 'I'm sorry I bought the man-child with me,' Lucy said sadly to Em and Jack.

'Is he always like that?' Em didn't look impressed.

'No. He's usually good fun. He seems to have made up his mind to be a complete arsehole today.'

***

Lucy went back to their room.

Josh was sitting on the bed, scrolling on his phone again.

'What's your problem?' she said, hands on hips.

Josh looked defiant. 'What do you think? Draping yourself all over Jack. I thought I'd play you at your own game with Hannah.'

'Why not Em if you're jealous of Jack?'

'I don't fancy her.'

'But you do fancy Hannah?'

'Nice long legs. Natural blonde. Big smile. Yeah. She's hot.'

'And what about Mark?'

'He's not my type.'

'Haha. Very funny.' *Don't lose your rag. Josh might genuinely be jealous.* 'I'm sorry I've upset you. Jack's a natural hugger. We're always like that. Em doesn't get jealous. She knows it means nothing.'

'Natural hugger? Creepy old man, more like.'

'Well, I don't think so. Are you going to be like this all weekend because that's not fair on everyone else if you are?'

'Just don't make a play for the professor, ok?' Josh got up off the bed and gave her a hug. 'Friends again?'

'I suppose so. Look, Josh. These are my friends. I enjoy their company. If you don't get on with them, our days are numbered.'

He looked thoughtful for a moment.

'I better be on my best behaviour then. Don't suppose there's any chance of a fuck?'

30

'Are we standing?' Josh asked.

'No, we're up in the seats.' Jack was working out which gangway they needed to use.

'Too old to stand up then,' Josh muttered.

Lucy scowled at him. 'I thought you were going to behave,' she whispered.

'Sorry! It slipped out.' He didn't look that sorry.

'Come on. We're going to miss the first song at this rate.' Jack led the way up the steps.

They found their seats just in time.

About three songs in, Lucy felt her phone buzz in the pocket of her jeans. A text from Em. Why was she texting when Lucy was standing next to her?

`Josh not a Muse fan?`

Lucy replied.

`He said he liked them.`

Em nudged her. Josh was texting.

Another text from Em.

`He's been doing that since we got here.`

Lucy leaned into Josh and slipped her hand through his arm. He clicked the screen off on his phone. Interesting that he didn't want her to see what he'd been texting.

Lucy looked along the row at the rest of their party.

Jack and Mark were next to one another, singing along. Hannah was at the opposite end of their group, leaning forward to look around Mark towards Josh.

Em texted Lucy again

`Hannah's been texting, too`

Lucy:

`I can't see who or what Josh is texting.`

Em:

`Are they texting each other?`

Lucy:

`Let's watch.`

Josh started typing again. She saw him put his phone down. Hannah checked her phone and started typing. The pattern repeated several times. Josh always had a slight smile each time he read a new text.

Another text from Em:

`They are!`

She'd added a scream emoji.

Time to ask Josh what he was up to. Lucy to Josh:

`Not enjoying the concert?`

Lucy glanced across at him. She could see him read a text, but he didn't smile this time.

Josh replied:

`Its good`

Lucy:

`You're doing a lot of texting.`

He replied straight away:

    Its work

What a bullshitter! Lucy texted Josh again:

    At 9 on Saturday evening???

She noticed Hannah look over at Josh. Waiting for a reply to her latest text, no doubt.

Josh was typing again, presumably replying to Hannah as he had that soppy grin on his face again. Hannah started replying as soon as he'd sent it.

Lucy to Em:

    What do I do?

Em to Lucy:

    I don't know.

Em started typing again. No three dots on Lucy's phone, though.

Lucy to Em:

    Who are you texting?

Em to Lucy:

    Jack. He wants to know why everyone's
    texting

Lucy to Em:

    Mark isnt.

Em to Lucy:

    He is now.

Lucy got a new text, this time from Mark:

    Why do you keep texting? Can't you at
    least pretend to enjoy the concert for
    Jack's sake?

What a cheek! Especially considering his girlfriend had sent far more texts than Lucy. Lucy replied:

    I didn't start it!

Lucy looked at Mark. He mouthed "Sorry" at her and then started typing:

I thought you were Hannah.

Lucy to Mark:

Because we look so similar??

Mark to Lucy:

I picked the wrong name from my contact list

He added a sad emoji. Odd. It wasn't like Hannah's name would be next to Lucy's on his list. Had he thought "girlfriend" and selected Lucy without thinking? No, don't be ridiculous. But at least he'd noticed that Hannah was texting someone. Should she tell Mark who was on the receiving end of Hannah's texts?

Lucy to Mark:

Em and I think Hannah and Josh are texting one another

She could see Mark watching Hannah and Josh surreptitiously now.

Mark replied a minute or so later.

They are.

Lucy to Mark:

Can you see what they're saying

Mark to Lucy:

No. Can you

Lucy to Mark

No

Em to Lucy:

I'm feeling left out now.

Lucy to Em:

Mark's confirmed that Hannah and Josh are texting one another.

Em to Lucy:

Does he know what they're saying?

`Quick.Josh`

What did that mean? Lucy looked across at Josh. He was distracted by the giant robot moving around the stage, and he'd left his phone unlocked in his hand.

Lucy turned her head to see his texts better.

'Are you ok?' Damn, he'd spotted her looking.

'I've got a crick in my neck.' Lucy rubbed her neck with her hand to make it seem more authentic.

He put his phone away, but she'd already caught sight of some of the words on the screen. "Show you later". It might be innocent, or it might not.

Josh slid his arm around Lucy's waist. 'I'll give you a massage later,' he whispered in her ear, giving her his best seductive look. Perhaps she'd misjudged him. She snuggled into his shoulder. *You are getting paranoid in your old age, Lucy Thomas.*

***

'Fancy going on somewhere?' Josh suggested as they stood in the long queue for the tube.

'Not me,' said Jack. 'I'm exhausted.'

'Me neither.' Em snuggled into him. 'We got the keys to the house last week. We've spent most of the week cleaning and stripping wallpaper. I'm worn out.'

Josh pulled a face at Lucy, clearly not impressed with Jack and Em's answers.

'Count us out as well,' said Mark, putting his arm around Hannah.

Lucy noticed Hannah roll her eyes at Josh. No, she wasn't being paranoid. There was something going on.

'Lucy?' Josh looked at her hopefully.

Three hours ago she'd have said yes, but the way he was behaving with Hannah again was pissing Lucy off. 'No. I fancy a hot chocolate in front of a warm fire.'

'Seriously?' Josh looked disgusted.

'Yes, seriously. It's cold now.'

'It was 24 degrees earlier.'

'Not now though, is it? In fact, the atmosphere is feeling positively chilly.'

31

Lucy, Josh, Mark and Hannah were all in the kitchen, having breakfast the following morning. Jack walked in on his own.

'Where's Em?' Lucy asked.

'She's gone out for a paper. She'll be here in a minute. I'm going to make some tea. Anyone else want one?' Jack offered.

'Yes, please.' Lucy joined him by the sink.

'Is Hannah making eyes at Josh?' Lucy whispered to him.

'Not sure,' he said. He did glance in their direction, but she sensed he didn't want to get involved.

Hannah was sitting between Mark and Josh at the dining table, ignoring her smashed avocado and looking more animated than ever. Em had told Lucy that Hannah rarely laughed at anyone's jokes, but it was noticeable that she found Josh absolutely hilarious. She was telling a story about a client while keeping her hand unnecessarily on Josh's arm. Josh was enjoying being the centre of attention.

Mark, on the other hand, looked deeply uncomfortable. He got up and joined Jack and Lucy by the sink.

'Are you ok?' asked Lucy.

Mark sighed. 'I feel like I've slipped into an alternative

universe where you're being nice to me, and Hannah's dating Josh.'

'She was all over him last night as well.'

'Yes, and not me,' Mark mused. Lucy felt sorry for Mark. He wasn't used to being second best where women were concerned.

'Tea?' Lucy asked.

'Please.'

She topped up the teapot and poured him a cup. Josh and Hannah were still flirting. Lucy had had enough.

'Josh, we ought to set off back to Birmingham soon.'

He glared at her. 'We're not in a rush. Hannah's suggested we go for a walk. She wants to make the most of the sunshine.'

'Because there's so little of that in Spain,' Lucy muttered under her breath.

Jack raised his eyebrows.

'We'll it's true,' she whispered to Jack.

'What are you two plotting?' Em asked as walked in.

'I'll explain later.' Lucy said.

'I'd love to see the statue of Virginia Woolf in Tavistock Square. I adore her writing,' Hannah enthused.

Mark looked amazed. 'You've never mentioned that before.'

'Haven't I?' Hannah barely took her eyes off Josh as she answered.

'You and Josh can sample the delights of Bloomsbury,' said Mark. 'I fancy a trip to Spitalfields market. I need to get Mum a birthday present. Anyone else want to join me? Lucy?'

'Thanks. I'd like that.' Spending time with Mark would be far more enjoyable than watching Hannah and Josh together.

'Jack? Em?'

Lucy's heart sank. Please don't say yes.

'I'm happy reading the Sunday supplement and chilling

here with Jack, thanks,' Em said, giving Jack a look. Thank god for Em.

Jack raised his eyebrows. 'I'm fine stopping here, apparently.'

***

Ten minutes later, the front door closed behind Mark and Lucy, leaving Jack and Em alone in the apartment. Em was washing up the breakfast things.

Jack leant back against the kitchen island and folded his arms. 'What are you up to?'

'I don't know what you mean.' Em looked at him with her best innocent face as she passed him a tea towel.

'I wouldn't have minded going to the market. We could look for some things for the house. But I got the distinct impression that would've been the wrong answer.'

'Now Lucy and Mark are talking again. I think they need some time alone.'

'In case you haven't noticed, they're both in relationships.'

'With people who seem more interested in each other than their partners.'

'You don't like Josh then?'

'I don't like him openly flirting with another woman in front of Lucy. I thought he was alright until he started doing that. What do you think?'

'He's a good match for Lucy. And to be fair to him, Hannah's the one who started the flirting.'

'But he didn't have to encourage her. Or are you saying flirting with other people's partners is acceptable?'

'Lucy flirts with me occasionally.'

'But not seriously. I wouldn't have been surprised if Josh and Hannah had started snogging one another's faces off the way they were looking at each other this morning.'

'I just think you should lay off the matchmaking. Be less

Nancy!' He said, putting down the towel and pulling her into an embrace.

Em sighed. It wasn't worth arguing.

'They're all grown-ups,' Jack said. 'They can do as they please. What do you want to do now?'

'We've got at least an hour's peace and quiet.'

'We could try out that roll-top bath you're so obsessed with?'

***

'Aren't you bothered by Hannah flirting with Josh?' Lucy had been biding her time to ask Mark. They'd casually chatted about work, business, the weather - everything but relationships - on the way to Spitalfields. Now they were walking side by side around the market, it didn't seem intrusive to bring up the subject.

'Are you bothered by Josh flirting with Hannah?' he asked.

'Yes. Does that make me a bad person? Or batshit mental?'

Mark laughed. 'An interesting choice of phrase.'

'It is, isn't it? I think Em shared that one.'

'I'll have to have words with Jack later.' He didn't seem too put out that his comments had got back to her.

'You didn't answer my first question.' Lucy said.

'No, I didn't.' He paused. 'The answer is not as much as I should be.'

'Why? Has she reached her fuck by date?'

He looked amused. 'Do your boyfriends have those?'

'Some of them. Others were already well past theirs when I met them - the discarded food bin around the back of the supermarket sort of boyfriends. I'm avoiding that type of man now. I didn't think Josh had reached that point.'

'But you're thinking he might be passed his fuck by date now?'

'After his behaviour this weekend, possibly.'

'Did I have a fuck-by date?'

How should she answer that? She decided to be honest. 'No, you didn't. That's why I was so upset when I thought you were two-timing me with Gabriella.'

They walked on to the next row of stalls. Lucy wasn't paying much attention to what was on sale. And Mark didn't seem to be either.

'You didn't answer my question about Hannah?'

'I don't think I should discuss that with an ex-girlfriend.'

Ex. He wasn't thinking about getting back together, then.

'No, probably not. I wouldn't like you discussing me with Hannah.'

He looked uncomfortable. Had he been discussing her with Hannah? 'Does Hannah know we went out for a while?'

'No. I haven't mentioned it.'

'I did wonder if the flirting with Josh thing was some weird sort of revenge.'

'I don't think so. She has no idea we were together. I feel guilty about not telling her.'

'Does she do it a lot? Flirting with other people?'

'No. That's what's interesting. What about Josh?'

'I don't know. We've only been going out for a couple of months. This is the first time we've been anywhere with other people. It's just been the two of us until now.'

'Why were you happy for him to spend the morning with Hannah?'

'What was I supposed to do? He clearly wanted to. Have you ever been cheated on?'

'Not that I know of. My exes tend to get fed up with me not paying them enough attention and walk away.'

'I have been cheated on - several times. If someone's going to cheat on you, they'll go ahead and do it. You can't spend your whole life keeping them away from temptation. It's better to find out sooner rather than later when you're saddled with a mortgage and kids. Why didn't you go along with Hannah and Josh?'

'Because I suspect she thinks I've reached my fuck by date, as you so delicately put it.'

'What makes you say that?'

'She doesn't enjoy my company as much as she used to, even when Josh isn't around. I'm beginning to feel like an inconvenience. Nothing I do is right.'

'I'm sorry.' Lucy wasn't sure what else to say.

They walked in silence for a few minutes. A vintage jewellery stall caught Lucy's eye. She stopped to look at the necklaces and pendants.

The woman on the stall gave them both a smile. 'Are you looking for a gift for your beautiful girlfriend?' she asked Mark.

'We're not together,' Lucy jumped in. *But you wish you were.*

'Something for yourself, then?' she said to Lucy. 'That one would go with your colouring perfectly.' The woman pointed to a silver filigree pendant with a green stone in the centre. She picked it up. 'Would you like to try it on?'

Lucy knew the tactic. Once she'd worn it, if she liked it, it would be hard to say no. But it was beautiful.

'It's Victorian.' The seller walked round to the front of the stall and placed it around Lucy's neck. She held up a mirror so Lucy could see it.

'It goes with your eyes,' Mark said.

Lucy felt a warm glow. She wasn't sure if it was the hot air in the market or the way Mark was looking at her in the mirror.

Concentrate on the pendant. The chain was the perfect length. She could wear it for work or evening. 'How much is it?'

'£155. It's Sterling Silver. You'd be paying a lot more if it were new.'

'That's more than I've got available to invest just now. I'll have to think about it.' Lucy took the pendant off and looked at it in her hands.

'I don't think I'll have it for long,' said the seller.

'I'm sure you won't. It is lovely, but I do need to leave it for now. Thank you.' Lucy handed it back.

'Come on, Mark. We haven't got anything for your mother's birthday yet.'

'Did you really like that pendant?' he asked as they walked down the next aisle.

'I did, but I can't justify buying it this month. Sometimes you can't always have what you want.'

'No, you can't,' he said distractedly.

32

'Mind if I put the football on the radio? Everton are playing away.' Josh said as he manoeuvred his car out of the parking space.

'No. Carry on.' Lucy hated football, but if Josh were concentrating on his team's performance, he wouldn't want to talk to her, which suited her perfectly. She needed to confront him about Hannah, but not until they got home when she could gauge his reaction properly.

She distracted herself with tidying up her email inbox while Josh navigated the Sunday afternoon traffic, shouting at the radio whenever the opposition scored, which, sadly for him, was twice more than Everton.

The game finished as they joined the M6. Josh turned off the radio. 'That was a pretty crap match.'

It wasn't the only crap match. After getting her unread message count down to zero, Lucy had been reflecting on her future with Josh. She decided they didn't have one. It wasn't only the length of time he'd spent with Hannah today that was bugging her. It was the sulky way he'd behaved yesterday. If he was like that when they'd only been going out for a couple of months, what would he be like after a few more months or even years? And then there was his laddish attitude, which was beginning to annoy her.

'What did you get up to with Mark this morning?' Josh casually asked. She was surprised he was bothered.

'We went to the market. Then we stopped at a cafe for a sandwich and came back to the flat.'

'He's probably too old for anything more exciting than shopping after a late night.'

A sneery thing to say. Josh was showing his true colours today. But Lucy was conscious she was stuck in a car with him. She didn't want to get into a row now. 'He's not much older than me, but if that's what you think.'

'Past his physical peak. Unlike me.' Josh glanced at the satnav. 'And in 30 minutes' time, I'll give you a reminder of what an excellent physical specimen I am.'

Cocky sod. He was going to be disappointed. She should've taken the train home.

Josh must've sensed her mood. His next sentence was more conciliatory.

'I'm sorry I went off with Hannah. I'd have rather spent the time with you. It got fucking boring after an hour. You wouldn't have given me chapter and verse on Virginia Woolf's life.'

Josh put his left hand on Lucy's leg and slowly moved it up her thigh, pushing her skirt up higher.

'I'd prefer it if you kept both hands on the wheel,' she said.

He took his hand away. 'You didn't say that the other day.'

'You weren't driving at 90 miles an hour in the outer lane of a busy motorway then.'

Lucy concentrated on her phone again, hoping it would discourage Josh from chatting.

He took the hint. She opened Instagram. Perhaps her friends and family had had more successful weekends. She paused over the latest post from Mark. A selfie of him and Hannah embracing in front of an airport departure board, both of them smiling at the camera as if they were the happiest couple in the world. Lucy read the caption.

> Heading back home with my darling H
> #missingspain #couplegoals

It didn't look like Mark was upset with Hannah. So much for him being passed his fuck by date. She put her phone away and watched the suburbs of Birmingham whizz by.

Twenty minutes later, Josh pulled up on the double yellow lines outside Lucy's flat. 'I'll drop you and our bags off, then find somewhere to park.'

They both got out of the car.

Josh opened the boot and passed Lucy her case.

'You can leave yours in there,' she said.

'But I'll need it for tonight.'

'That's why you better take it home.' She smiled. 'Bye, Josh,' she said as she walked towards the entrance.

33

'That should help.' Kizzy put a steaming mug of tea down on the conference table in front of Lucy.

They'd just finished the latest in a series of tricky meetings with Lucy's newest clients, the two directors of a company that imported artisan coffee from obscure locations around the world. After enduring their continuous bickering for two hours, Lucy could understand why their previous marketing company had ended their contract.

'Thank you! You're an angel.' Lucy leant back in her chair. 'I wish they were more willing to listen to our advice instead of point-scoring against one another. We've been in this room most of the morning, and all we've agreed on is a change of font for their logo.'

'Perhaps we should bin them off?' Kizzy suggested.

Lucy laughed. 'If we got rid of every client you suggested we binned off, I'd have no business, and you and Flynn would be looking for new jobs.'

She looked through the glass wall where Flynn was beavering away on a new ad campaign on his Mac. 'If we can make this account work, we can afford to take on another member of staff, and then you and Flynn won't have to work so hard. I'm giving up on Swanky Grinders just yet.'

'Do you think they fancy one another?'

'Who?'

'The Swanky Grinders - Michael and Aaron.'

'What makes you say that?'

'I'm sure there's some sexual tension between them. You know how good I am at sensing it.'

'I don't even think they're gay, despite the name,' Lucy said as she got up to photograph the notes on the whiteboard.

'If they're not out, they should be. I can imagine them ripping one another's clothes off when they get back to their office.'

'Thank you for putting that lovely image in my head.' Michael and Aaron were always smartly turned out, but neither of them had the sort of physique Lucy wanted to see naked. 'I think you've been reading too many male-on-male romances.'

'Talking of romance, how did your weekend in London with Josh go?

'About as well as the meeting we've just had! I dumped him.'

'Why?'

'We discovered we wanted different things.' Other people's partners, but Lucy didn't mention that.

'How did he take it?'

'He called me a boring cow.'

'Nice - you're well shot of him. What's Mark's new woman like?'

'She ignored me for most of the time. She was too busy making eyes at Josh.'

Kizzy looked appalled. 'What about Mark?'

'He wasn't making eyes at Josh.'

'You know what I meant!'

'Mark is still as attractive as ever, unfortunately.

***

That evening, Lucy was on her own in the office, trying to come up with a marketing strategy that neither Michael nor Aaron could disagree with. Flynn and Kizzy had gone home hours ago. She ought to do the same.

Her phone buzzed. A phone call from Em. Good. She could get Em's opinion on the weekend's events. Lucy clicked the green button.

'How's things?' Em asked. She sounded on edge. Not her normal bright and breezy self at all.

'Where do I start?'

'How about how you managed to keep your cool with the man child making a play for the ice maiden?'

Lucy laughed. 'Sounds like a synopsis for a new video game. He said he was sorry. He went off with Hannah as revenge, and he didn't enjoy it.'

'Oh, he did, did he? Or was he just trying to get back in your knickers after Hannah rejected him?' Em sounded angry.

'What do you mean Hannah rejected him?'

'Jack overheard them talking outside the front door of the building when they came back on Sunday. He was in the basement, putting our rubbish in the communal bins. Their voices carried through the open window. They had no idea he was there.'

'What did they say?'

'Hannah told Josh that it had been fun, but she wasn't leaving Mark. Then Josh had a go at her for using him. Jack said he sounded really cut up about it.'

Lucy was trying to take it all in. So Josh hadn't been bored by Hannah at all. He'd wanted to carry on seeing her, and when she'd refused, he'd tried to mend things with Lucy.

'Jack's only just told me. I don't know why he sat on that information for a day. We've had a discussion about that.'

From the agitation in Em's voice, it sounded like the discussion might have been a row. 'Are you ok?'

'Yes, just slightly annoyed with him. Is Josh with you now?'

'No. The good news is he didn't get back in my knickers. As Kizzy would say, I've binned him off.' Lucy gave Em a summary of what had happened in the car on Sunday evening.

'Thank god for that.'

'Has Jack told Mark what he overheard?

'No. He didn't want to interfere. But it turns out he didn't need to anyway. Mark phoned him a few minutes ago. Hannah's left him.'

Lucy's heart skipped a beat. *Don't be so selfish! Poor Mark.* 'But I thought you said that Jack said that Hannah said that she wasn't leaving him?'

'Do you have to use such complicated sentences at this time of night?'

'Hannah told Josh she wasn't leaving Mark.'

'Yes. But she must've changed her mind. Or she only said that to get rid of Josh? Either way, Mark said she was quiet on the flight back to Spain. Then they had a massive row when they got back home, and she slept in the spare room. When he got up this morning, there was a note on the dining table.'

Lucy realised her heart was beating faster than normal. She took a deep breath to get her emotions under control. 'A bit dramatic. What did it say?'

'She was fed up with being ignored, and she realised she'd be happier with someone else.'

'Who?'

'She didn't say. It's unlikely to be Josh.'

But none of that made sense after Mark's Instagram

update. 'Mark posted a photo of the pair of them at Heathrow yesterday afternoon. She looked happy enough with Mark then.'

'Easy enough to put a smile on your face for a photo. That doesn't mean it was genuine. Perhaps she wanted him to publicly show his commitment to her after he'd spent a good chunk of the day with you?'

It was as good an explanation as any. Not that it mattered now. 'How's Mark taking it?'

'Jack said he didn't seem surprised. It solved a problem, which Jack thought was an odd thing to say.'

Bearing in mind her conversation with Mark yesterday, it didn't seem that odd to Lucy.

'You've gone quiet,' Em said.

'I was just thinking.'

34

After Lucy finished her call with Em, she walked home, poured herself a stiff vodka and tonic and sat on her sofa. Her apartment had a large picture window with spectacular views over Birmingham city centre. Em always said the view was mesmerising, but Lucy rarely had time to enjoy it. For the first time, she knew what Em meant. Focussing on the lights reflecting off the office block windows in the distance was helping to stop her brain from going around in circles thinking about Josh and Mark.

She'd not heard from Josh since she'd walked away from him yesterday. Her ego might have enjoyed the spectacle of him trying to win her back, but in reality, she was happy to be rid of him. Not that she was angry with him. He'd actually done her a favour.

If he hadn't flirted with Hannah, she wouldn't have been able to spend time with Mark yesterday. She'd forgotten how easy it was to be in Mark's company compared with most other men, including Josh.

There was probably another Lucy and Josh happily sharing dinner somewhere in a parallel universe. Or a Lucy and Mark who'd been together for a year already because that Lucy had let Mark explain who Gabriella was instead of jumping to conclusions and fleeing home upset.

But there was still a chance of improving her current reality. Lucy found Mark's contact details on her phone. It was midnight in Spain, but Mark was a night owl. He might still be awake. If not, he could reply in the morning.

Her thumb hovered over the message button, wondering how to play it. *Stop overthinking!* She tapped the button and started typing.

    Em told me about Hannah. So you were
    right. You are past your fuck by date.
    Hope you're ok.

What about kisses at the end? Perhaps one.

She took another gulp of her drink. What was the worst that could happen? She clicked the send arrow.

Three dots appeared. She hadn't expected him to respond so quickly.

    I thought you liked men who were past
    their fuck by date x

One kiss back. And he was trying to be amusing. It was looking promising.

    I didn't say that. I said I seemed to
    pick them x

Three dots again.

    Could you pick me? Xx

Two kisses. Was that significant, or had it just been a slip of his thumb? But the request to choose him made it look deliberate. Did she really want to give Mark another chance? She took another gulp of vodka. Absolutely.

    I could but you're 1500 miles away xx

Should she have been more enthusiastic? She was thinking about sending another text when a new message appeared.

`Can I call you? Xxx`

Three kisses now. She smiled to herself.

`I suppose so. You're going to wear that x button out otherwise xxxx`

Another speedy reply from Mark:

`Give me two minutes and technically it's not a button xxxxxxxxxx`

Lucy smiled to herself:

`Picky xxxxxxxxxxxx`

No dots this time. But he had said to give him two minutes.

Exactly two minutes later, her phone rang.

'Why did I have to wait two minutes?' Lucy asked as soon as she answered the call.

'I needed to get comfortable,' Mark said.

'What does that mean?'

'We could be talking for a while. We always used to.'

'Where are you?'

'Lying in bed. Where are you?'

'Sitting on the sofa enjoying the view.'

'Are you on your own?'

'Yes, just me. You?'

'Yes. There's no one else here. It's eerily quiet.'

His voice had a slight slur to it. 'Have you been drinking?' she asked.

'I've had a couple of beers. Actually, three. I wouldn't have been brave enough to phone you otherwise.'

'Am I that scary?'

'No, you're not scary at all now you've stopped being angry with me. I love talking to you. It's just I don't know if I should be calling you.'

'You can talk to me anytime.' Lucy said.

35

Lucy yawned. She needed another caffeine hit. She hadn't slept well thinking about Mark. They'd stayed on the phone talking until nearly 2 am, but she had still been too energised to relax.

Her mobile rang. Mark. She wasn't expecting him to call back so soon.

'Hi,' she said.

'Are you ok?' He sounded worried.

'Yes, of course I am. Why wouldn't I be?'

'I'm really sorry about last night. I shouldn't have kept you talking so late.'

Her heart sank. Why did he sound regretful now? 'I enjoyed talking to you.'

'And I enjoyed talking to you, too. But what about Josh?'

'He wasn't there.' It was odd. Despite being on the phone for the best part of two hours last night, Josh's name hadn't come up at all.

'I knew that. I meant ... I know how I'd feel if my girlfriend had spent hours on the phone with her ex.'

'Josh and I have split up. I realised he wasn't for me in the car on the way home from London.'

'That's good. Oh shit, I'm sorry you've split up. I'm making a mess of this.'

At least he was pleased that Josh was a goner as far as Lucy was concerned. 'It's ok. I knew what you meant.'

'Can we still be friends?'

Friends. Lucy tried to hide her disappointment. 'Yes, we can still be friends.'

She could hear voices in the background.

'I've got to go,' Mark said. 'I need to get the business open. Can I phone you again tonight?'

'Yes, I'd like that.' Lucy leaned back in her chair and sighed.

Kizzy looked up from her desk. 'That wasn't Josh, was it?'

'No, Mark.'

Kizzy pulled a disapproving face. 'He's friend-zoned you?'

'Yep.'

'You need to send him a clit pic.'

'A what?'

'You know, like a dick pic, but your bits.'

'And you think that will work, will it?'

'It has for me when they're getting cold feet. Reminds them of what they're missing.' She winked. 'The lighting in our office toilet is perfect for it.'

36

Em sat outside Mary's cafe watching the waves crash onto the sand. The wind was strong today. Apart from one lone dog walker, the beach was empty. It was so lovely just to sit quietly and do nothing for a few minutes.

'I haven't seen you down here for weeks,' Mary said, bringing Em a mug of hot chocolate and sitting down next to her.

'I've been busy with work and painting and now the house.' Em nodded in the direction of the cliffs.

She'd spent most of the day clearing out the bathroom and putting a base coat on the walls ready for the plumber to make a start on the refit tomorrow. But she also had an errand to run that gave her the perfect excuse to take a break.

'Jack and I have got you a present to say thank you for tipping us off about the cottage.' Em reached down to pick up the large brown paper carrier bag that was leaning against her chair.

'I wasn't expecting anything,' Mary said, taking the bag and peering inside. 'Ooh. Is it what I think it is?'

Hopefully, it was. It was covered in bubble wrap, but Mary

should be able to identify it. One of Em's paintings of the view out to sea from the cafe. Phil had mentioned she'd been admiring it.

'If you don't like it, Phil says he'll swap it.'

'I will do no such thing.' Mary looked thrilled. 'Thank you very much. I'll have to tip you off about more houses in future.'

'One's enough.' Em laughed.

'How are the wedding plans coming along?'

'The Bay View Hotel was our last hope for next May, but that didn't work out, so it's all up in the air.'

Mary raised her eyebrows. 'I'm surprised you went there.'

'Really?' It suddenly dawned on Em that Mary was bound to know what happened with Nancy. 'Why's that?'

***

It was hard work walking up the hill to Dashford Grange that evening. All the muscles in Em's legs ached. She shouldn't have sat with Mary for so long.

Her phone buzzed. She hoped it was Lucy replying to the WhatsApp message she'd sent her earlier, but it was just a spam text.

Em was itching to know whether anything was going on between Lucy and Mark. After the way Lucy had reacted to the news of Hannah's departure, Em suspected that Lucy was planning to get in touch with him straight away. She wouldn't blame her. After all, Lucy had admitted she still had the hots for him.

But that was two days ago. Surely she would've told Em by now? Em decided to text this time.

`You've been quiet. Everything ok?`

Lucy started replying.

`Yep all fine`

Em was going to have to be more direct.

`Have you spoken to Mark?`

Another three dots

`Yes a lot`

The perfect excuse for a phone conversation. Em pressed the call button.

'So you're talking to Mark?' Em said as soon as Lucy answered.

'Yes. We've spoken every night this week. At this rate, I'm going to have to take out an international phone tariff.'

'And?'

'It's going well.'

'Which means?'

'It's just like when we were together last year, but without the sex.' She sounded disappointed.

'At least you're taking it slow.'

'Sort of. He's invited me over to Spain for the weekend.'

'That's great. You'll still get some decent sun in September. Better than the biting wind we've got here.'

'For god's sake, Em. The weather is the last thing on my mind!'

'I don't see the problem. You get on so well. Just enjoy it.'

'While it lasts? That's how that phrase usually ends.'

'I didn't say that. I hope it will last.'

'I don't want to screw things up.'

'How would you do that?'

'What if I can't stick to the friends-only rule when I see him in person, and it ruins everything?'

'He might not want to stick to being friends when he sees you, either.'

'I'm hoping not. But if he does want more, I don't know how it would work long term with him in Spain and me here.'

'Other people manage long-distance relationships. Jack and I had to cope with living 200 miles apart for months. I know he wasn't in another country, but he was a five-hour drive away. You can probably fly to see Mark quicker than either of us could drive up and down the M4.'

'I guess.'

'You're doing that overthinking thing you do when you're about to go on a first date. But it's not a first date. You both know each other already. Go and enjoy his company.'

'Hmm.' Lucy went quiet.

'Were you hoping I'd say something else?'

'I was hoping Jack might have said something. If I had a clue how Mark really feels, it would help. You couldn't ask Jack to sound him out, could you?'

'He hasn't mentioned anything. They talk about all sorts of weird stuff. I don't think they discuss emotions unless one of them is seriously upset.'

'Ok.' For someone who was about to spend a weekend with the love of her life, she still sounded depressed.

'I'll ask Jack if he'll sound Mark out.'

***

'You're late.' Em was in the kitchen looking at the instructions on a microwave lasagne.

'I got stuck in traffic.' Jack slipped his arms around her waist and kissed her. 'I'm starving. I had to skip lunch. Is that what we're having for dinner?' He frowned.

'If I'm cooking, yes.'

He let her go and headed to the fridge. 'I could whip up a carbonara instead?' he said, grabbing a pack of bacon.

'If you insist.' The threat of a ready meal usually prompted him to offer to cook.

'How was your day?' he asked as he started chopping the bacon.

'Good. I got the bathroom ready for the plumber, and I went to see Mary.'

'Did she like her picture?'

'She loved it. She was very grateful. And very informative, too.'

Jack stopped chopping. 'What does that mean?'

'She knows why Nancy's banned from the Bay View.' Em couldn't help looking smug.

'We shouldn't be talking to Mary about that.'

'Don't pretend you aren't interested. You tried to get your mother to dish the dirt last week. Anyway, I didn't bring it up. Mary did when I mentioned we'd looked at the Bay View for our wedding ceremony. But if you're not bothered ...'

'I didn't say that,' he grinned. 'What's the story then?'

'It's all rumour, of course. But she reckons the owner had a drugs racket going on, smuggling them in via the harbour. Nancy sussed her out.'

'Her?'

'Yes, Silvia Moretti. She's Italian. She moved back to Italy. But she still owns the hotel.'

Jack looked puzzled. 'But Nancy would've gone to the police if anything illegal was happening.'

'That's exactly what I said. Apparently, the rumour is that Silvia was having an affair with Xander.'

'You've lost me now. That would be even more of a reason for Nancy to report her, I would've thought.'

'Xander asked Nancy not to grass Silvia up, so she didn't.'

'I don't recall Nancy being subservient to Xander.'

'I can't imagine she was, but that's the story that did the rounds in Dashford in 1989. Whether it's true or not, who knows?'

'Only Nancy,' he said thoughtfully as he put a saucepan of water on the hob. 'What did you say the name of the Italian hotel owner was?'

'Silvia Moretti. Why?'

'Mark's half-sister Gabriella is a Moretti.'

'Really? So they could be related?'

'Probably not - Moretti's not an unusual surname in Italy.'

'And Gabriella's too young - she must've been born in the late 90s.'

'Yes. Just a coincidence then.'

'In other news, I also spoke to Lucy.'

'Oh yes?' Jack was concentrating on cooking now. He didn't sound quite as interested as he had in Mary's gossip.

'Has Mark said anything about her?'

'What makes you ask?' He seemed cagey.

'So he has said something?'

'I know he's invited her to stay with him this weekend.'

'Are his intentions honourable?'

'That sounds like a question from one of your Jane Austen novels.'

'You're avoiding answering.'

Jack sighed. 'He's looking forward to spending time with her. He doesn't want to rush things as she's only just split up with Josh. He says he's happy that they're friends for the time being.'

'For the time being? That sounds hopeful. I think Lucy would like to be more than friends too.' Should she have said that? If Jack told Mark, that might make things easier for Lucy - or not.

'You're not matchmaking again, are you?'

'No, I'm not being manipulative. Lucy told me she wants him back.'

'We better see how it works out then.'

'You're not prepared to ask him.'

'Ask him what exactly? "Hi Mark. Are you planning to fuck Lucy this weekend?"'

'You could be a bit more subtle.'

'But that's what it boils down to.'

'Well, yes.'

'No, I'm not going to ask him. Leave them to work it out themselves.'

37

The Friday evening flight from Birmingham to Malaga was packed with a mix of regular commuters who quietly sat wearing headphones, keeping themselves to themselves, and several stag and hen parties, who were doing the complete opposite.

Lucy was trying to work while a member of Daz's Dirty Dozen on her left leaned across her laptop, flirting with Naughty Natalie's Maid of Honour in the opposite aisle seat.

Once upon a time, Lucy would have flirted with him herself, but now it just irritated her. She agreed to a seat swap so the love birds could sit next to one another. She suspected they'd be taking it a lot further as soon as they landed. Which got her thinking about Mark. Em said Jack had hinted the "friends only" rule could be shortlived, but she wasn't 100% sure. Lucy would have to play it by ear.

A couple of hours later, she emerged from security into a sea of drivers in the arrivals hall, all standing around with pieces of paper or iPads with names written on them. The Smith family, Mr Mahmoud, Jo & Sonja, everything but Lucy Thomas. She kept walking. Mark must have forgotten to order her a taxi. She was nearly at the exit doors when she heard a familiar voice.

'Luce!'

There he was, Mark himself, looking hot in every sense of the word. There was a sheen of sweat across his forehead, and he was out of breath but smiling.

'I managed to get someone to do my bar shift this evening. Sorry, the traffic was bad. Have you been waiting long?'

'No. I've only just got here. Are you ok?'

'Yes, but I need to get to the gym more often. Running across that car park has creased me.'

They looked at one another for what seemed like an age. Mark put his arms out. She happily walked into them.

'I'm so glad you're here,' he said as they embraced.

She felt Mark inhale deeply. 'Hmm'

She pulled back. 'Were you sniffing me?'

'No. Well, possibly. Your hair always smells amazing.'

'Weirdo!' she laughed. 'I'll leave my bottle of shampoo for you to sniff when I leave.'

'Don't talk about leaving yet.' He looked serious. Was he about to go in for a kiss? If he was, it looked like he thought better of it. He pulled away. 'Give me your bag,' he said, heading towards the exit.

The hour-long drive to Nerja was going to drag.

***

Mark had moved since she last visited him. Instead of a modern house, he was in a spacious apartment in the old town.

'Bit of an upgrade after my last place,' he said as he rolled her suitcase along the winding pedestrianised street. 'Handier for the beach, and it has a pool.'

'You've got your own pool?'

'I share it with the three other apartments. But most of the time, I'm the only one here off-season. We can go for a dip later. None of the other flats are occupied this weekend.'

From the outside, number 8 looked like a traditional Spanish house. White painted walls, two-storey, heavy wooden shutters across the windows. But inside, it had a whole different vibe. White minimalist furniture, with a sleek modern kitchen to match. The only thing that wasn't minimalist was the sofa. The huge squishy cushions looked very welcoming after a long day at work, and the hard seats on the cheap flight.

'Do you mind if I sit down?' Lucy asked.

'Be my guest.'

'This is bliss.' Lucy shut her eyes and sank back into the comfortable upholstery.

'The sofa or being here?' He smiled.

'Both.' She grinned mischievously back at him. This was heaven. It was too nice. What if he did just want to be friends? Now he was within touching distance, she realised it was going to be even more of a challenge sticking to the friends only rule than she originally thought.

'You look worried,' he said.

'I'm just tired. I've had a full-on day at work. And I'm no good at snoozing on the plane.' Her stomach rumbled loudly.

'When did you last eat?'

'I grabbed a sandwich at lunchtime.'

'There's a great bar three doors down. They serve traditional tapas until late. Do you want to get a bite there?'

***

'That was delicious.' Lucy finished the last mouthful of patates bravas.

Mark picked the wine bottle out of the ice bucket. 'It's empty. Fancy another?'

'I really shouldn't.'

'Last year, you could drink me under the table.'

'That was last year. I'm far more mature now.'

He didn't look convinced.

The waiter appeared. 'Can I get you anything else?'

'It was lovely, but I'm full now, thanks,' Lucy said.

Mark said something in Spanish. She suspected he'd asked for the bill.

'Si señor,' the waiter replied and walked away.

'Impressive. Whenever I speak in my school girl Spanish, they look pityingly at me and respond in perfect English.'

'When you've lived here a while, it starts to come naturally.'

'Do you think you'll stay?'

He seemed unsure how to answer. 'I considered it. When I was seeing Hannah, we talked about building a holiday let business together. But now ... Sometimes I miss the rain and snow. And my friends.'

He looked at her like he used to when they were going out. She'd missed that look and the kisses that usually followed it. 'What are you thinking?' she asked.

'I wish the waiter would hurry up with the bill.'

Right on cue, he appeared. 'Señor.'

'Gracias.'

'Going halves?' Lucy reached for her handbag.

'No way. You flew out here. Put your purse away.'

Mark got out his card and paid.

'Let me leave the tip then,' she said, putting a few euros on the plate.

'How about a walk on the beach?' Mark said.

'Don't you see enough of it during the day?'

'I do, but it's the first time you've been here. Well, for more than an hour.' He grinned.

'Don't remind me.'

They walked outside onto the street. The warm air hit her

after the pleasant chill of the air-conditioned bar. It would be cooler down on the beach, but Lucy was feeling tired again. 'I'd be happy to go back to yours. The beach can wait until tomorrow.'

'Suits me,' he said. He led the way back through the crowds.

'Fancy a dip in the pool?' Mark asked as he unlocked the door to his apartment.

'Straight after we've eaten? You like living dangerously.'

'The jury is out on whether you get cramp if you swim straight after a meal. But if you so get in trouble, the pool's not that deep. I promise I'll rescue you.'

'I might enjoy being rescued,' she grinned. *Shut up, Lucy! A friend wouldn't say that!*

'Let's see, shall we?' A friend wouldn't look at her like that, either. Perhaps he was feeling the same way.

Mark had put her suitcase in the guest bedroom before they went out earlier. She went in there to get changed. She started rifling through her suitcase. Where was her swimsuit? She went through the case again, more methodically this time. Definitely no sign of it. She must've left it on the bed at home. How bloody annoying. She'd invested in a new one as well, one that emphasised her cleavage.

'Sorry, I forgot my cossie,' she shouted.

'Is that so?' He didn't sound like he believed her.

'Seriously, I have. I must have left it at home.'

'You'll have to skinny dip. I promise not to look. We're the only ones here this weekend.'

She wasn't sure how she felt about that. But it wasn't as if he hadn't seen her naked before. And she'd spent a good few hours in the gym since then. What did it matter? She wanted to convert him from friend to lover, and this might speed things up. She wrapped herself in a towel and walked into the living room. Mark was already waiting for her. Her eyes were drawn to his tight swim shorts that didn't leave much to the imagination.

'If I'm skinny dipping, you are too,' she said.

'I suppose it's only fair.' He went back into the bathroom and emerged with a towel around his waist.

'Not like you to be shy?' she said.

'I don't normally parade naked in front of my friends.'

So they were still friends as far as he was concerned.

They went outside onto the deck. The pool looked inviting, the water glowing turquoise in the dark. But she'd been caught out by enticing-looking swimming pools before.

'It is heated, isn't it?' she asked.

'Yes, at this time of year,' he said as they walked to the edge. 'Ladies first. I'll be a gentleman and turn my back.'

Lucy threw her towel onto a sun lounger and jumped in.

She screamed. 'You told me the pool was heated!'

'It is heated. Just not that much,' he grinned. 'You'll soon get used to it.'

'Ok, smart arse. Your turn.'

'You're looking.'

'I'll look away.' Lucy shivered. 'Not that there'll be anything left to see with water this cold.'

He laughed. She heard a slight splash. 'I'm in,' he said.

'Do you have to say that to all your women?'

'I don't remember you complaining before. I'm going to make you pay for that.'

'You'll have to catch me first.' She gave him a cheeky grin, then started swimming towards the other end of the pool.

She could hear splashing as he followed her. She giggled as his hands slipped around her waist.

'I don't think you were trying very hard to escape,' he said.

'Why would I want to do that?'

He was staring at her intently now. No more "friends only"

by the look of it. He was as turned on as she was. He pulled her close to him. The feel of his damp skin against hers made her shiver, but not with cold this time.

'Do you need warming up?' he whispered in her ear.

'Depends what you mean by warming up. Parts of me are very warm already.'

He lifted her up easily. She instinctively wrapped her legs around him.

'I've missed you, Mark Farnham,' she murmured, brushing her lips lightly against his cheek.

'Mummy, there are two naked people in the swimming pool,' a child's voice echoes round the pool area. They both instinctively looked up to the apartments. Mark held Lucy tighter and dipped down so only their heads were above the water.

'I thought you said no one else was here,' Lucy whispered in his ear.

'I didn't think there was. There must be someone stopping in the penthouse.'

The floodlights on the building burst into life, and someone stormed out onto the top balcony. The silhouette looked like it belonged to a woman standing with her hands on her hips.

'Don't look, Noah,' she said. She leaned over the balcony. 'This was advertised as a family-friendly accommodation.'

'We're family, we're friendly, and we're very accommodating,' Lucy yelled back.

The silhouetted woman disappeared, and the upstairs door slammed.

'What did you say that for?' Mark laughed. 'She'll think we're indulging in some weird incest thing.'

'It sounded good when I said it in my head.'

'I think your comedy routine needs a bit of work,' he whispered.

'Does it? Shall we go inside and discuss it?' Lucy said hopefully.

***

Lucy lay in Mark's arms.

'So much for just being friends,' he said.

'You're not complaining, are you?' She didn't think he was.

'No.' He smiled. 'But promise me one thing. If you're ever thinking of dumping me again, talk to me about it first.'

'Ok. As long as you promise to keep me up to date with any extra female relatives you discover.'

'I'll try. Seriously though, you can trust me.'

'I'm not very good at trusting men.' Lucy turned away.

'Why?' He rolled on his side and looked at her.

Was it too soon to mention Dylan? She was going to have to bring it up sometime.

'There was someone I trusted completely at uni.' She hesitated.

'Did he cheat on you?'

'No.' She took a deep breath and looked deep into his eyes. She wanted to know how he would react to what she was about to say. 'I got pregnant. Accidentally.'

He didn't recoil in horror. That was a relief. She carried on. 'I worked out how we could afford to live. I was just about to start my first proper job. He was a PhD student. He was doing some lecturing so we wouldn't have been destitute. But he didn't want to know. He told me to get an abortion, and when I refused, he walked out. He never came back, not even to pick up the few things he kept at mine. I ended up taking them around to his flat, but his flatmates said he'd moved. He'd gone to London. No forwarding address.'

'What happened to your baby?'

'I had a miscarriage.'

Here we go again. The tears started and wouldn't stop. Was she ever going to be able to say those words without breaking down? He scooped her up in his arms and cradled her until the sobbing eased off.

'The doctor said it was unlikely the stress had caused it. Probably a genetic abnormality. Nature taking its course. Nothing to worry about. "You're young. I'm sure you'll have more babies, Ms Thomas." He was trying to be reassuring, but it felt so callous.'

'Oh, Luce,' he kissed her forehead.

'I got it so wrong with Dylan. It was a complete shock. I thought we'd stick together regardless of what life threw at us. I've not trusted my judgment about men since then.'

'So you keep everyone at arm's length?'

'Except when I'm shagging them,' she said with a half laugh through her sniffles. 'It's safer that way. I can brush it off when they inevitably hurt me. Not a recipe for long-lasting happiness, is it?'

'No,' he said thoughtfully.

'You won't tell anyone, will you, not even Jack? I haven't found a way to tell Em yet. She'd be horrified that I went through all that and didn't confide in her.'

'I won't tell a soul. It's your secret. Thank you for trusting me with it.'

'What about you? How have you got to 36 and not had a long-term relationship?'

He lay on his back, looking at the ceiling.

'It's simple. I haven't prioritised the women in my life. That's why Hannah left. It's why they always leave. When I was a solicitor, I was expected to work long hours. So there were lots of missed dates, and girlfriends sat at home feeling neglected. And then, after Isabella, I didn't trust my instincts about women. So I carried on neglecting them even when I had a job that meant I didn't have to. Not a recipe for long-lasting happiness, either.'

Em had told Lucy ages ago about Mark sleeping with Jack's wife. 'I thought you and Isabella were a one-night stand?'

'We were, but we'd been having an emotional affair for weeks. Well, I thought we were. It turned out she was manipulating me. She completely fooled me.' He looked at Lucy again. 'I'm not proud of any of that. It really hurt Jack. Who does that to their best friend? But I thought I loved her so much it was worth it.'

'So you're going to have a lonely life, too.'

'Yes. We've both got to change our ways.'

He was looking at her intently now. 'I did prioritise you above work last year. I wanted to. I thought I'd found someone I could trust again. That's why I was so hurt when you ghosted me.'

'I'm sorry. Are you willing to give me a second chance?'

He leaned in and kissed her. A long, slow, gentle kiss that made her whole body come alive again.

'Was that a yes?' she asked.

'Of course it was.'

38

Em walked into the kitchen in Dashford Grange. She made a mug of Earl Grey, grabbed a biscuit from the tin, and sat down next to the Aga. The next guests were due to arrive for another half an hour. Time to catch up with Lucy. She got out her phone and sent a text:

    How's Nerja?

Lucy replied immediately.

    Warm

Em:

    And how's Mark?

Lucy:

    Hot!

She'd added a wink emoji. It looked like Lucy's visit was going well.

    How long did his resolve to be just good
    friends last?

Lucy:

    2 hours

Em:

`I'm surprised he resisted you that long.`

Lucy:

`The first hour was in the car on the way from the airport. Limited scope for serious flirting. Got to run. We're going paragliding.`

Em:

`I thought you said you'd never do that.`

Lucy:

`Mark can be very persuasive.`

Em smiled to herself.

Nancy walked in. 'What's amused you?'

'You're back.'

'So it would seem.' Nancy headed for the laundry room and put her suitcase down.

'Your youngest son is a bad influence,' Em said as Nancy returned to the kitchen. 'He's got Lucy to go paragliding.'

Nancy looked thrilled. 'I assume that's not in Birmingham. You didn't say Lucy was visiting Mark.'

'I've not seen you since I found out Lucy was going. It was all very last minute.'

Nancy had spent half the week in Berlin visiting one of her friends. 'Mark didn't mention it to me either. Probably wanted to keep me out of the loop on that one.'

'How was Berlin?'

'Very interesting. I haven't been there since 1989.'

'When the wall came down?'

'Yes, an exciting time one way and another.'

The same year as the Bay View Hotel incident. Perhaps she could get Nancy to spill the beans on that. 'Yes, 1989 was an eventful year.'

Nancy paused for a second. Did she suspect Em knew

something? If she did, she ignored it. 'Is Jack around?'

'He's up at the Cottage, stripping wallpaper, hopefully. He won't be back for a couple of hours yet.'

'Excellent. I have something in the car for you,' she said, heading outside to the courtyard. Em followed her.

Nancy popped the boot lid on her car. Em spotted a flash of kingfisher blue fabric inside.

'The dress! Thank you so much.'

'Olivia said you were keen to get it here, so I made a detour on the way back from the airport to collect it. Have you and Jack set a date then?'

'No, I just wanted to see it again.'

'We can keep it in one of the wardrobes upstairs so Jack doesn't see.'

'That would be lovely.' And easy for Em to sneak it over to the flat before the actual wedding.

'Do I need to book you in with the dressmaker quickly as well, or will that wait until next year?' Nancy was fishing for info. 'She gets booked up on the run-up to Christmas. You'll need to visit her soon if you want it altered for the festive season?'

'It will wait.'

39

Lucy and Mark were standing on the beach after their paragliding session.

'That adrenaline rush has worn me out. I could do with a lie-down. Was that your cunning plan?' Lucy asked.

'Possibly.' He grinned and put his arm around her shoulder. 'Let's go home.'

They headed up to the main road in silence.

'You've gone quiet,' Lucy said.

Mark stopped and pulled her into a hug. 'About what you told me last night about your um …' He hesitated.

'Spot of bother?' she said. Referring to it like that avoided triggering the crying. Why was he bringing that up?

'Yes.' He looked at her, concerned. 'I think you should tell Em as soon as possible.'

'What do you know that I don't? Em's not pregnant, is she?'

'No, but Jack's keen to have some little Carvers running around that new house of theirs. I have a feeling it won't be long before she is.'

He had a point, but the thought of telling Em brought her

out in a cold sweat. 'I have tried to tell her lots of times, but I always chicken out.'

'What are you afraid of? I'm sure she'd be sympathetic. Jack would too.'

'I know, but dropping it into a conversation is difficult. It's a bit of a mood killer.'

'Not as much of a mood killer as you bursting into tears if she tells you she's pregnant. She won't understand why you're upset. And if you tell her at that point, it will put a real damper on their excitement.'

He was right. 'I don't want to do that to them.'

'I know you don't.'

'You're a wise man, Mr Farnham.'

'Sometimes. If you need my help, just ask. Though I have no idea how I could help.'

'Thank you.' She kissed him.

'There's one more thing,' he said, looking directly into her eyes. 'If you were pregnant with my child, I'd stand by you.'

Lucy so wanted to believe that, but it was an easy thing to say, not quite such an easy thing to do. 'That's a big promise. You might feel differently if it happened.'

'No,' he said. 'I thought about it last night. I promise I wouldn't abandon you.'

***

'When have I got to get you back to the airport?' Mark murmured in Lucy's ear.

She rolled over to face him, pulling him close under the sheet. 'A couple of hours yet. I wish I didn't have to go.'

Sunday had been bliss. They'd spent most of the day in bed, apart from half an hour or so in the pool when Mark heard Noah and his mother go out.

'I wish you'd stay.'

'I can't. I've got a meeting tomorrow and I can't cancel it.' Lucy sighed. 'How are we going to make this work? You living here and me living in Birmingham? It's not like I can get a job over here.'

'You could.'

'I sound like someone chewing a wasp when I speak Spanish, and I'm used to being my own boss. I couldn't work for someone else again, and I can't run the marketing business from Spain. Clients expect me to see me face to face. I'd have to sell up and start afresh over here.'

He kissed her. 'We'll think of something. I've had a few ideas.'

'Such as?'

'I need to do some asking around. Can you come to see me again next weekend?'

40

Lucy FaceTimed Em on Monday evening after work.

'You don't look that brown.' Em was looking closely at Lucy on her screen.

'I didn't get an opportunity to sunbathe. Mark had other ways of keeping me occupied.'

'I can tell. You've got a glow about you that I've not noticed in years. When are you seeing him again?'

'I'm flying back out there on Thursday evening.'

'Taking time off work? It must be serious.'

'I can catch up with a few emails and documents while Mark's at the beach.'

'Are you going to fly out to Spain every weekend?'

'For the next few weeks. Mark can come here when the season's finished at the end of October.'

'Planning ahead. That's a good sign.'

'Yes, it is.' Lucy beamed. 'Anyway, enough about me. How are you and your lovely new house?'

'I'm not sure how lovely it is at the moment. It feels like half of the old fixtures and fittings are in the skip now. And Jack can't help much as he's working long hours getting up to speed on his new job. It feels weird without him here all the time. I was spoilt over the holidays.'

'Sounds like you need cheering up.'

'I'm ok. Just tired. By the way, have you heard Ella and Sam's big news?'

Lucy took a sharp intake of breath. 'What news?' she asked, just in case it wasn't what she thought it was.

'They're having a baby.'

So it was that. 'That's nice,' she said, trying desperately not to cry.

'Are you ok?'

Remember what Mark said. She took a deep breath. 'I've got something I need to tell you.'

***

'I did it,' Lucy said as soon as Mark answered her FaceTime call.

'Did what?' he asked.

'I've just told Em about my spot of bother.'

'And?'

'It was ok. She was upset. But not with me. We both cried. But I think it will be alright now.'

'I'm proud of you,' he said. 'Sorry, that sounded patronising, but you know what I mean.'

'Yes, I do. Thank you for being supportive.'

'My pleasure.' He smiled.

'I love you.' It was the first time she'd said those words to any man since Dylan.

'Oh, Luce. I love you, too.'

41

Em and Jack stood on the landing at Octopus Cottage, admiring their newly refurbished bathroom. It looked exactly how Em had hoped. Shiny new modern white suite with turquoise tiles on the main wall and matching cupboards. The plumber and his tiler had done a superb job.

'We should've kept the avocado suite,' Jack said, looking serious.

Em dabbed white emulsion paint on his nose. 'It's all outside in the garden if you're missing it. Come on. The sooner we get this painted, the sooner we can move in. We need to finish in here today. That's what it says on the plan. Then we can start on the dining room.'

'I never realised you were such a slave driver.'

'And I never realised you were such a procrastinator.' Em handed Jack his roller and a newly filled paint tray. 'Your furniture's coming out of storage in three weeks. We've got to keep the momentum going.'

'Can we have the radio on?' Jack asked.

Em rolled her eyes. 'If it will help you work faster, yes.'

Jack disappeared into his new office and returned with an

old transistor radio.

'How long have you had that?' Em asked. Her dad had kept a similar one to listen to in his shed, but it hadn't worked for years.

'Since I was a child. My grandfather gave it to me.' He extended the aerial and twiddled with the dials. 'The signal's not great here. I can only get local radio.'

The current show was a phone-in, and today's topic was the state of the main road through Dashford, with various callers complaining about the big pothole at the entrance to the harbour car park.

'Is this the best we can do?' Em asked.

'The news will be on in a minute.' Jack picked up the roller.

'Oh, before you start that, could you be an angel and fetch that new tin of white paint from the garage? I'm going to finish this one any second else.'

Jack sighed. 'Anything else?'

'Could you put the kettle on, on your way back? I'll need some warm water to wash the brushes.'

Fortunately for Em, Jack's reply was interrupted by the radio announcer. 'Welcome to North Devon FM. Here's the one o'clock news on Sunday 29th September.'

'Shit!' Em said.

'What's the matter?'

'It's Lucy's birthday on Tuesday, and I haven't got her anything. All this decorating knocked it out of my head.'

'You could send her some flowers.'

'She's my best friend. I have to do better than that. I'll see if there's some jewellery I can get from the gallery tomorrow. I hope Mark's doing something for her birthday.'

'He's not mentioned anything.'

'He does know, doesn't he? Could you remind him?'

'Would that be before or after I shove the broom up my backside so I can sweep the floors as well?'

42

Lucy sat on her sofa, looking out over Birmingham. 31 years old. She didn't like the sound of that. It hadn't felt like her birthday today. She hoped this wasn't how birthdays were going to be now she was in her fourth decade. Neither Kizzy nor Flynn had remembered at work. Em had texted her to apologise for forgetting to post her present on time. And she had no girls' night out to look forward to, either. Everyone was either away or, in Ella's case, suffering from raging morning sickness that was so bad it extended into afternoon and evening sickness as well.

The lights on top of the BT Tower flickered in the twilight. Not a bad view, but she'd much rather be watching the setting sun from Mark's garden in Spain, preferably cosying up to a semi-naked Mark on his comfortable double sun lounger and sipping a generous glass of sangria.

Cheer up, Lucy. Only three more days before you'll be back on the plane to Malaga and spending the weekend doing exactly that.

Lucy had been disappointed when there was no card or present from Mark in the post this morning. But they'd only been officially back together for just over two weeks. He might have forgotten it was her birthday. She'd dropped it into the conversation at the weekend, but he had been half asleep at the time. And even if he had posted something then, it probably wouldn't get to Lucy for a few days.

Stop being maudlin. Phone him. She checked the clock. It would be 7.30 pm in Nerja now. Mark should be back in his apartment. He might be in the mood for a chat or perhaps more. She picked up her mobile and called his number.

Mark answered straightaway.

'Hey sexy,' she said, putting on her best sultry voice.

'Happy birthday, darling,' he said.

At least that's what she thought he said. It was difficult to be 100% certain because the traffic noise in the background was unusually loud.

'Where are you?' she asked.

'Um. Just walking along the road.'

'I didn't think any road in Nerja was that noisy?'

'Um. I'm in town.'

'Malaga? What are you doing there?' Mark had told her he rarely ventured into the city. He preferred the relative peace of Nerja.

'I'm visiting a friend.'

'Ooh, which one? Have I met them?'

'Yes, you know them quite well. Look, I'm going to have to go. Speak to you later.'

He cut off the call before she had a chance to say goodbye.

"You know them quite well." The phrase was playing on repeat in her head. Lucy didn't know anyone in Spain quite well, apart from Mark, of course. The only other person she knew, even vaguely over there, was Hannah. Mark had mentioned she'd moved to Malaga. Could that be why he was being cagey?

Shit. She wished she'd never phoned him. *Don't be ridiculous - it's better to know the truth.*

She phoned Em instead. 'I think Mark's cheating on me with Hannah.'

'And good evening to you, too! Why on earth would he do that?'

Why would he do that? 'Probably to have someone to fuck during the week until I obligingly fly over to serve his sexual needs at the weekends.'

'How many glasses of prosecco have you had?'

'Just two. What's that got to with anything?' Em wasn't usually that interested in Lucy's drinking habits.

'And have you eaten anything this evening?'

'No. Why is my level of food intake suddenly important?'

'You do have a tendency to get paranoid on prosecco, particularly on an empty stomach.'

'I do not!' Lucy was indigent. 'What are you trying to imply?'

'See what I mean!'

'No, I don't.'

'Ok then. What about that poor woman you accused of stealing your coat in that pub we went to last year until Charlotte reminded you that you'd left your coat at home?'

'Hmm.' Lucy sighed. 'I'm just feeling down because I'm on my own on my birthday. '

'I'm sorry. Happy Birthday, by the way.'

'Thanks. And I wasn't having a dig at you. How is the dining room looking in ditzy magnolia or whatever colour you went for?'

'It's Alluring Lily, and it's looking great. Just one more coat to do. Look, if you're concerned about Mark, why don't you phone him back and ask him outright who he's visiting? You don't want a repeat of the Gabriella incident.'

'Ok. I will in a bit. I better have something to eat first after your diagnosis. I'll leave you to your painting.'

Lucy hung up and walked over to the fridge. It wasn't

exactly bursting at the seams. The rest of the bottle of prosecco was in the fridge door next to a half-full bottle of milk and a dried-up lump of cheese well past its use-by date. A punnet of slimy mushrooms lay in the salad drawer. They must be left over from that recipe she'd failed to find time to make three weeks ago. She binned the mushrooms and decided to get a takeout.

Lucy plucked the Chinese menu off the fridge and phoned through her usual order. Half an hour to wait.

It was getting dark outside. She drew the curtains, put on the television and started channel hopping.

She skipped past a soap with a couple arguing about the man's affair with another woman and a documentary about promiscuity among chimps. She settled on a quiz. No reminders of potential infidelities there. The camera focused on the host. 'Our final question of this round is "What did 17th-century actresses Nell Gwyn and Moll David have in common?"' A bespectacled man who looked like a much older version of Josh pressed his buzzer. 'They were both mistresses of Charles II.'

For God's sake! Lucy switched off the television just as the doorbell rang.

Great. The takeout delivery was early for a change. She pressed the intercom button.

'Delivery for Lucy Thomas.' The driver spoke in what sounded like a poor impression of a Black Country accent. Something about his shape looked familiar, but he had his hood up, and the video feed was never that great at dusk. He was carrying a food order, though.

She buzzed him up and opened the door.

The man who appeared at the top of the stairs was instantly recognisable.

'Adam!' What was the hell was he doing here? 'How the mighty have fallen,' she said. 'From senior accountant to takeout delivery man in less than four months.'

'I'm not being paid for this!' He sounded outraged, then tried to look pleasant. 'I thought I'd surprise you on your birthday. I bring food and flowers.' He handed over a bag of take-out containers and produced a small bunch of red carnations from behind his back.

'Well, you've definitely surprised me,' Lucy said. 'Isn't your wife going to be wondering where you are?"

'No. We've split up.'

'She found out about your cheating ways, did she?'

'She was having an affair with the scoutmaster while I was away during the week.'

Lucy couldn't help smirking. Karma. 'Good for her.'

'Thanks for the sympathy.'

'You were seriously expecting me to be sympathetic? And your Tuesday woman? What happened to her? Let's face it, Tuesday wasn't my night when we were together.'

'She moved to London.'

'Has she really? Or have you promoted her to Wednesdays?'

'I thought you might be pleased to see me now I'm single again.' He seemed genuinely surprised that she hadn't welcomed him with open arms. 'I'm really sorry about lying to you. My marriage was a nightmare. I needed to find solace in another woman's arms.'

He grabbed her hand and looked imploringly at her like a puppy in an RSPCA advert. 'Lucy, I love you. I'll do anything you want if you'll take me back.'

'Anything?'

'Yes, anything.'

'Adam. The only thing I want is for you to disappear from my life. I could never love you, not after all the deceit.'

She was interrupted by the doorbell. Hopefully, the real takeaway this time.

'Adam. Please go.' Lucy shoved the flowers and takeout bag into his hands and opened her front door.

The doorbell rang again. Longer this time. The delivery driver must be getting impatient. She buzzed them up. Adam was still standing in her hallway.

Lucy put her hands on her hips. 'I've asked you to go, so go,' she said loudly.

A familiar voice came from the stairwell. Someone who was definitely not the usual Chinese delivery man was running up the stairs. 'You heard what she said. You should leave.'

Lucy beamed at him. 'Mark! You have an impeccable sense of timing.'

He put his arm around her and gave her a long, lingering kiss.

'Why are you still here?' he said, scowling at Adam.

'I recognise you.' Adam turned to Lucy. 'If you're working your way through your exes, I guess it will be my turn in a couple of months. But don't expect me to wait for you.' He stormed out.

'What was all that about?' Mark asked.

'That was Adam.'

'The one with a family and another woman as well?'

Lucy nodded. 'Apparently, he has neither now.'

'My heart bleeds for him. Why was he here?' There was a hint of concern in his tone.

'Are you jealous?'

'Slightly. But as you were in the process of throwing him out, not much.'

'He wanted to surprise me on my birthday. He was hoping we could get back together.'

'I'm glad you said no.'

'And I'm glad you're here. Why didn't you tell me you were coming?'

'It wouldn't have been a surprise if I'd phoned ahead,' Mark laughed.

'Am I the friend you were visiting?'

'Yes. Who else would it be?' He looked puzzled.

She didn't answer but kissed him instead.

The doorbell rang again.

'Is that another ex?' Mark murmured in her ear.

'I hope not. With a bit of luck, it'll be the Chinese.'

'What? All 1 billion of them?'

***

'What's that?' Lucy looked at the jewellery box on her pillow. It hadn't been there when she went to the bathroom a few minutes ago.

'Your birthday present.' Mark smiled from the pillow next to it.

It was too big to be a ring box, so he wasn't about to do something stupid.

'I thought you turning up was my present.' She got back into bed, picking the box up as she leaned back against the headboard.

'It was one of them. I thought you'd appreciate an actual present as well.'

Lucy undid the red ribbon that was neatly tied in a bow around it and opened the lid. Inside was the pendant she'd admired at the market all those weeks ago.

'When did you get this?'

'The day you saw it at Spitalfields. I sneaked back and bought it when I went off to the toilet while you were in the cafe.'

So she hadn't imagined it. He had been thinking about them getting together again even then.

'You're full of surprises.'

'All good ones, I hope. Happy birthday, darling.'

43

'I almost missed the plane.' After five weeks of travelling backwards and forwards to Spain, Lucy had got the journey from home to the airport down to a fine art, but she'd almost cut it too fine this week. At least Mark was in the arrivals hall at Malaga already. She guessed there was less traffic on the coast road now the holiday season was over.

Mark gave her a passionate kiss. 'I've missed you.'

'I can tell,' she grinned. 'I miss you more each week.'

'Let's get home.' He grabbed her suitcase. 'How was work today?' he asked as they walked hand in hand out to the car park. He didn't need to ask about the previous days. They'd talked every night this week as usual.

'Sitting in my little office, concentrating on drawing up marketing plans for coffee beans was hard this morning. Somehow, my mind kept wandering back to you.'

'I'm glad I'm more interesting than coffee.'

'How's your day been?'

'Quiet. I had a business meeting over lunch. Oh yes, and a complaint letter from the owners of the penthouse, saying we'd upset his guest the other week.'

'Noah's mother?'

'Yes,' he said, putting her case in the boot of his car. 'The way she described it in her email, you'd think we were partaking in a full-blown orgy.'

'Perhaps we should have invited her to join in.'

'God, no. I want you all to myself,' he said, pulling her in to kiss her again.

'Your wish is my command.'

***

Lucy woke up to the sound of crockery clinking together. For a split second, she was confused about where she was.

'Good morning, darling.'

She remembered now. She was lying in lovely, sexy, easy-to-get-on with Mark's king-sized bed.

'Morning.' She rubbed her eyes and yawned. 'Why are you so bright and breezy at this ungodly hour?'

'It's 10 am. Even on British time, it's not early.' He kissed her. 'I bring you a croissant, some tea, and good news. At least, I hope it is,' he said, getting back into bed with her.

Lucy sat up and sipped her tea. 'I'm intrigued.'

'I've got someone interested in buying my business. The chap who owns the bar. He mentioned it last year, but I wasn't looking to sell it then. I paid him a visit yesterday. He's just emailed me, offering a higher price than I expected.'

'And that means?' She hoped it meant he was free to come back to England, but she didn't want to jump to conclusions and then be disappointed.

'If it all goes through, I'm not tied to Nerja any more.'

'And where would you like to be tied?'

'I love the way you bring everything around to sex,' he laughed.

'I don't know what you mean. It's that filthy mind of yours. When will you know?'

'Hopefully, we can get it all signed and sealed in the next few weeks.'

'You could be home that quickly? No more flying backwards and forwards to Spain?'

'No more 3000-mile round trip every weekend.'

That would be amazing. She loved being with Mark, but the journey was tedious. But there was one thing she needed to clarify. 'Where are you going to live?'

'I haven't worked that out yet. Do you know anyone who's got room for me?' He looked at her expectantly.

She pretended to think. 'I might do. There's space in my flat. Well, there isn't, but I'm sure I could squeeze you in.'

'Or we could get somewhere bigger?' He was serious about living together then.

'What would you do for a job? I can't keep the two of us.'

'The sensible thing would be to re-register as a solicitor. I've checked the process. It shouldn't take long. And I've still got a few contacts. I've already sounded one of them out. I should be able to get a job in Birmingham.'

'But is that what you really want? I thought you didn't enjoy office life. I want you to be happy.'

'I could get some locum work to try it out again. Or I could get into property development. I was planning to do it here. No reason I couldn't do it in Birmingham.'

'Are you absolutely sure? Swapping all this for living in the middle of a busy city?'

'Yes. Home is where the heart is. And my heart is with you.'

***

Mark left after breakfast to sort out the jet skis for the day. Lucy went outside on the terrace. It was warm for late October but not warm enough for a bikini. She went back inside to put on her shorts and t-shirt, then headed out again to lay on the sun lounger by the pool. She wanted to make the most of the Spanish sunshine before Mark sold up and moved to Birmingham.

She'd brought a book with her, but she couldn't concentrate on reading. Her inner voice insisted on haranguing her about how stupid she was to agree to move in with Mark so soon. But it felt right. What was so wrong with wanting to see him more often? He could cook, he didn't snore, he made her laugh and feel wanted, he respected her, and he was a generous lover. Why wouldn't she want to spend as much time with him as possible?

She needed to speak to Em. Not that Em would discourage her. She'd not exactly been subtle with her matchmaking as far as getting Lucy and Mark together was concerned. But explaining what was going through her mind to someone else usually made Lucy see things more clearly.

She FaceTimed Em. Come on, pick up. It didn't usually take her this long to answer.

Just as she was about to give up, Em's face appeared on the screen. 'You pick your moments.'

'What do you mean?'

Em waved a toilet brush in front of the camera.

'Eugh!'

'You did ask.'

'Sorry, I forgot you'd be in the middle of a changeover.'

'Lavender Cottage had a particularly feral family in it this week. Two under fours and a shaggy dog the size of a small horse. They've brought half the beach back to the cottage. It's taking me twice as long as normal to get it clean.' Em sighed.

'I can phone back later?'

'No, I could do with a break. Your location looks more bougie than mine! Is that a palm tree?'

'Two, actually.' Lucy turned the phone around to show Em the garden and the view of the Mediterranean.

'Not too shabby. Do you want to see my view?'

'Go on, then.' Lucy wasn't that keen after the glimpse of the toilet brush.

Em panned around the cruddy bathroom, then walked onto the landing, showing off the muddy marks up the stairs.

'What's that phrase? Take only memories, leave only footprints,' Lucy said.

'Well, they've certainly done that. I think you win the prize for the most luxurious FaceTime location this week.' Em grinned. 'How are things going with Mark?'

'Fast.'

'What does that mean?'

'He's selling up his business so he can come back to England and live with me in Birmingham.'

'Seriously. When?'

'Hopefully, in the next month or so. He's found a buyer already. '

'Wow! A man who's willing to commit.'

'I know. It's a bit of a shocker. A complete first for me. That's why I phoned.'

'How do you feel about it?'

'Surprisingly ok. Ecstatic even.' She sniffed.

'Luce. Are you crying?'

'I might be.'

44

'I'm sure you told me this was going to be fun,' Em said as she pulled her coat tight around her body, trying to win her fight with the wind to keep the hood in place. 'When I agreed to be your assistant, I had visions of sunny days sitting under a parasol watching you film in southern Europe with blue skies and calm seas. And here we are in a force nine gale 40 minutes drive from home. Why did I say I'd do this again?'

'Because you were worried Clara would want to get naked with me,' Jack said.

'I'd admire any woman who'd take her clothes off in this weather.'

Em, Jack and the crew were standing on the end of a harbour in Devon, grimacing in the driving wind and rain.

'Where is Clara?' Em asked.

'She's back in the hotel. She's got a bad headache.'

'That's convenient.'

Jack scowled at her. Probably not very charitable, but Clara was in a warm dry room, not feeling like she could be swept out to sea at any moment. Right now she was in the better position, even allowing for the headache.

'Jack! We're ready for you,' Ian, the director, shouted.

'How is anyone going to hear you in this wind?' Em shouted.

'It all helps to conjure up the sense of peril that seafarers have to endure.' Ian shouted.

Em turned to Jack again. 'As your assistant, I think it's time I got you a coffee.'

'But the cafe's five minutes' walk away,' said Jack.

'It's probably only three minutes with this wind blowing me along. And it will be warm and dry.' She didn't wait for a reply.

***

Em had grabbed a seat by the cafe's heater. She'd just about thawed out by the time Jack and the rest of the crew appeared.

'That looks cosy,' Jack said, giving her a peck on the cheek.

'It is. But I think your need is greater than mine.' She got up and offered him her seat.

Normally, Jack would be gentlemanly and refuse, but not today. 'I'll let you have it back in a minute.' He rubbed his hands together and held them out near the heater.

'Did you get it all done?' Em asked.

'Yes, after three takes. It's not perfect, but it will have to do. I can do a voiceover in the studio for the rest.'

'What about Clara? I thought you were going to do a piece to camera together?'

'Her assistant texted Ian. She's out of action for the rest of the day. She thinks she's got flu.'

Perhaps Clara was genuinely ill, or she'd taken one look at the weather forecast and decided a warm hotel bed was the better option.

'Shall I get you a fresh cup of coffee?'

'Yes, please. You're an angel.' He shivered.

While Em was at the counter, she noticed Ian slide into the seat next to Jack. They were in deep conversation when she returned.

'Ian's got a proposition for you,' Jack said.

Ian got up and offered Em his seat while he perched on the edge of the table. 'You've done television before, Em.'

'Only when I won the Unity Portrait Award. That was just the interview with Clara, then a few shots of me working in my flat and walking across the beach.'

'Yes, and you were very good, particularly on the beach. I remember watching it at the time because Jack said his portrait might be featured.'

'I hadn't thought about putting "walks well across a beach" on my CV,' she laughed.

'Perhaps you should,' Ian said. 'It's certainly a skill we'd appreciate now, as well as staring off into the distance, looking deep in thought.'

'I thought that was Jack's speciality?'

Ian laughed. 'A good sense of humour helps as well.'

'Sorry, where is this conversation going?' Em had a good idea, but she couldn't quite believe it.

Jack chipped in. 'What Ian's trying to get round to asking is, will you co-present with me?'

'But I don't know anything about pirates.'

'Yes, you do. You know more than Clara. You proofread my book. And you've had to listen to me talk about them for weeks on end. I've written the scripts, so you only need to learn the information in those. You don't have to be word-perfect. I have every faith in you, and so does Ian.'

Ian nodded. 'Why don't we record the piece Clara should've done today with you now? See how you feel about it then.'

'Ok. If you think I'm good enough.'

'Of course, you're good enough. Angie!' Ian called to the

makeup artist who was sitting at another table. 'Sort Em out, will you? The rain's easing off a bit, so there's a fighting chance some of her make-up will stay on.'

***

'And cut. Brilliant.' Ian sounded pleased.

'Really?' Em thought it had gone reasonably well. Much better than she had expected, to be honest. But she wouldn't have said brilliant.

'Yes, really. You had a natural conversation with Jack. You asked him all the right questions. Your voice was clear. You sounded genuinely interested. It looked great on camera. You can watch it back if you like.'

'Oh no! I cringe seeing myself on screen.'

'I'm not going to force you to watch it. Just one last piece to camera, and we are done for the day.'

'Which one's that?'

'You're talking to camera, contrasting a female pirate's life to a sailor of today. We're going to record that with the beach in the background.'

The crew started moving their equipment.

'Jack, I feel really nervous. It's one thing them filming us having a chat. This is more like a performance.'

'Just imagine you're talking to me like you did earlier.' Jack hugged her.

'But you know all this stuff. Why would I be explaining it to you?'

'Imagine you're explaining it to Lucy, then.'

'She'd be taking the piss out of me.'

'How about Nancy? She would listen attentively.'

'Ok. Nancy.' She could see Jack was getting exasperated.

'Don't overthink it. Take a deep breath. You can do this.' He pulled her in closer. 'If you get this right, we'll be able to work together again,' he whispered in her ear.

'I thought you were supposed to be encouraging me.' She laughed nervously.

'Charming. At least you've relaxed now.' He kissed her.

There was a cough behind them. Angie, looking annoyed. 'Can you keep your hands off the talent? I need to touch up Em's lips now.'

'You're doing great,' Angie said as she applied a fresh coat of lipstick.

Jack moved behind the camera.

'Action!' Ian shouted.

'As you've heard already, women pirates in the 17th and 18th centuries were treated no better than their male counterparts.'

She continued with Jack's script. Somehow, the adrenaline rush helped her do a faultless first take. The crew gave her a round of applause, relieved to be finished for the day.

'Excellent. You're a natural.' Ian patted her on the back. 'Now all I have to worry about is breaking the news to Clara.'

'I've got the job then?'

'You most certainly have.'

45

Tuesday evening. Lucy was relaxing with a glass of wine after a particularly stressful day, arguing about the best way to market her toilet seat client's latest innovation, the vibrating loo seat. She'd declined an offer to try one out at home. This account wasn't working out quite how she'd planned, but she couldn't afford to say goodbye to them just yet.

She massaged her neck, trying to ease the tension in her muscles. Perhaps the vibrating loo seat would have helped with that. They'd probably have more success marketing it as a neck massager or a sex aid.

But what she needed was to come home to Mark in person. She imagined his strong fingers gently working on the knots in her neck muscles. A few more weeks, and that ought to be happening for real.

Her phone rang. Talk of the devil.

'Luce.' Mark sounded so deflated.

'What's wrong, darling?'

'I don't know where to start.'

'Has the business sale fallen through?'

'No, that's all going well. Lucy. Um. Hannah came to see

me this morning.'

Hannah? Lucy was sitting bolt upright now. Why was she back on the scene? Surely, she hadn't seduced him after all he'd said about being in love with Lucy.

'Are you still there?' Mark asked.

'Yes.'

'She's pregnant.'

Fuck. Lucy remembered what he'd said about not abandoning her if she ever got pregnant with his child.

'How far gone?'

'Ten weeks.'

When was ten weeks ago? No, it was eight weeks because of the mad way they calculated pregnancy lengths. She tried counting back in her head, but she couldn't concentrate.

'I can't abandon her.'

'A child in the womb is worth one in the mind.'

'I'm sorry?'

She wasn't surprised he was confused by that statement. She wasn't sure it made sense herself. 'I know you want kids. Of course, you'd choose a woman who's already pregnant over one who doesn't know if she can carry a child to full term.'

'It's not like that! Lucy, I love you. I wanted to be with you more than anything.'

Wanted. Past tense. So that was it then. He'd decided to go back to Hannah.

'I feel like a complete shit doing this.' It sounded like he was trying not to cry. 'I have to stay here. Try to make it work. For the child's sake.'

'Not many men would do that. It's 2019, not 1919.'

'I know. But I can't leave her to do this on her own.'

'Are you sure she wants you back?'

'Yes. She wants us to bring our child up together.'

'And it's definitely your baby?'

'Yes. It must've happened just before our London trip.'

So that was it then. She may as well get this over and done with now, like ripping a plaster off in one quick pull.

'I wish you and Hannah a long and happy life together. I really do. Goodbye, Mark.' Lucy ended the call before he could say anything else.

46

'Hello, you,' Jack said as he walked into Em's studio at Octopus Cottage. It was his usual greeting, but he hadn't said it in his normal cheery tone.

'I wasn't expecting you till lunchtime,' Em said, descending the stepladder. 'I need another twenty minutes to finish painting the ceiling, then I can take a break.'

The work on the house was nearly done, so Em had finally started work on decorating her studio.

'Have you spoken to Lucy in the last 24 hours?' Jack still sounded concerned.

'No. I haven't spoken to her since the weekend.' Lucy's calls had been less frequent since she'd started seeing Mark again, but Em had seen that as a sign that things were going well.

'I've just spoken to Mark. They've split up.'

'Again? They were deliriously happy last week. What happened?'

Jack filled her in on the Hannah situation.

'Oh my god.' Poor Lucy. She'd had plenty of shitty luck with men, but this was a whole new level of crap.

'Mark's worried. Lucy put the phone down on him. And now she won't answer.'

'I'll try.' Em picked up her phone from the windowsill and dialled Lucy's number. The phone rang out.

'How's Mark feeling about the baby?' Em asked while she was waiting for Lucy to pick up.

'All over the place.'

Lucy's familiar voicemail message kicked in.

'She's not answering me either. I'll try again in a few minutes. It's definitely Mark's baby?'

'I know you don't like Hannah, but she always seemed loyal to Mark. I never got the impression she played around.'

'Except for making eyes at Josh in London.'

'Except for that. But Mark said the dates worked out. It must've happened just before London.'

Em tried to get in touch with Lucy several more times that morning. She texted, tried WhatsApp and left voice mails. No reply to any of them. She checked Lucy's location on Snapchat. No sign. She must've turned location services off.

She could be in a client meeting. Em phoned her office number. Kizzy answered.

'We don't know where she is. I even popped around to her flat, but there was no answer. She had two client meetings this morning that I've had to cancel. I've just told them she's been taken ill.'

Em was really worried now. Lucy was always 100% professional when it came to her business. 'Did you go inside the flat?'

'No, I haven't got a key.'

Em used to have a spare key in case Lucy ever got locked out, but Charlotte had agreed to have it when Em moved to Devon.

Em called Charlotte and explained.

'I'm working in town today. I've got Lucy's keys on my

key fob. I'll go round there right away.'

Half an hour later, Charlotte called Em back from Lucy's flat. 'No sign of her. Everything looks neat and tidy. Her electric toothbrush is missing from the bathroom, though.'

'Is her suitcase in the hall cupboard?' Em asked.

She could hear Charlotte's heels clicking across the floor. 'Yes, the big one's here. But there's no sign of the overnight one. There's a gap where I guess it should be. Do you think she's gone to Spain to talk to Mark face to face?'

'I'm not sure she'd do that. She usually has a "screw 'em attitude" when someone splits up with her.

'But she's really in deep with Mark. We went out for a drink after work the other night. She was so happy he was moving in with her.'

'She might try to fight for him, I suppose.'

'I better get back to work. I've got a meeting in twenty minutes. I don't think there's anything else I can do here.'

'No, thanks for checking. I don't know what we do now.'

'We'll just have to wait until she turns up. I'll let you know if I hear anything.'

'I'll do the same.' Em said.

***

Em heard a car pull into the courtyard. She looked out of the window. Lucy. Thank god!

She ran to the front door and opened it. 'Hi. Where the hell have you been? We've all been worried sick.'

Lucy looked awful. No make-up. Red, puffy eyes. She'd clearly been crying - a lot. Em had never seen her looking this bad, even after a heavy night's drinking.

'You'll never guess what's happened,' Lucy said quietly as she walked into the flat.

'Hannah's pregnant and Mark's gone back to her.'

'He's spoken to Jack then.'

Em nodded. 'Mark's worried about you.'

'Is he? A bit late for that. Can I stay on your sofa tonight?'

'Of course you can. Jack's at his taekwondo session, but he'll be back soon. I'll put the kettle on.'

Lucy sat down on the sofa. She sniffed.

Em went into the bedroom and grabbed a box of tissues. 'Here. These might help.'

Lucy blew her nose loudly.

'I can't slag him off, can I? Normally they leave me because they're shits. But he's doing the honourable thing, standing by his pregnant girlfriend. How can I hate him for that?'

'Ex-girlfriend.'

'Not now. She's already moved back in. '

'Has she?' Jack hadn't mentioned that.

'Yes, I went to see him. I thought I could talk to him. See if he was really happy going back to Hannah. '

'You've been to Spain today?'

'I got the early flight. Then I came back this afternoon. I couldn't face going home after I arrived back at the airport, so I just drove and found myself here. Sorry, I didn't call ahead.'

That explained the lack of replies.

'What did he say?'

'He didn't. I thought he'd be at the jet ski hire, so I went there first, but his assistant Carlos said he was having a day off. So I went to Mark's apartment, but there was no reply. I ended up sitting in the bar opposite to see if he came back.'

'And did he?'

'Yes, after I'd worked my way through five coffees. He was with Hannah, pulling along a big suitcase. She'd got a small box with some plants in it. They were laughing and joking with one another. Mark didn't look too distressed. I sat back so they couldn't see me. I watched him go into his apartment with her.'

'Did you knock on the door?'

'What was the point? I know I misinterpreted things with Gabriella last year. But there is no way this could have been anything other than Hannah moving in with him. It would only have caused more upset. What are you doing?'

Em had picked up her phone. 'Texting Charlotte to say that you're alright.'

'Why Charlotte?'

'Because I got her to go round your flat to see if you were there. I think you should text Kizzy as well. We've all been concerned about you.'

'I thought I emailed the office to say I'd be away for a few days?'

'Kizzy didn't get it if you did.'

'Shit. Sorry.'

Jack walked in. 'Lucy! I thought it was your car outside.'

'Hi. I'm borrowing your sofa for the night. Hope that's ok?'

'We could ask Nancy if you can sleep over there if you want a proper bed.'

'I'm sorry if I'm in the way.'

Jack sounded concerned. 'No, it's not that. I thought it would be more comfortable than our rickety old sofa bed.'

'Stopping with my recent ex's mother?'

'I hadn't thought of that. I don't know if Mark's told her yet. I don't think he'd even mentioned he was moving back to England. You sleep in with Em. I'll take the sofa.'

'No, I'm not going to sleep much. Your sofa will be fine.'

'Are you ok if I tell Mark you're here?'

'I guess. Not sure it's any of his business now.'

'He's been trying to get hold of you. He's worried about you.'

'I've blocked him again. I can't deal with it. There's nothing to say.'

'It's a no-win situation. It's awful. He's so upset, too.'

'I wish him well. I really do.' She looked like she was

going to cry again. 'I guess I'll get over it, eventually. You'll have tough old Lucy back in no time.'

***

'Are you sure you're ok to drive? You look exhausted.' Em was standing next to Lucy's car in the courtyard the following morning.

'I'll be fine. I did get a bit of sleep last night. And I'm fuelled up with caffeine thanks to Jack's excellent coffee-making skills. I'll take it steady. I need to get back. I don't want to screw up my business as well.'

'What do you mean "as well"? You didn't screw this relationship up.'

'No. For once, I picked a decent man. And look how that's turned out. I must've been some homicidal despot in a previous life.'

They hugged. 'Don't worry, I'll get over it somehow. I'll see you again in a few weeks for your engagement party.' She gave what looked like a forced smile. 'I'm looking forward to that.'

'Are you?' Em wasn't convinced.

'Yes, I'll put a brave face on it. It will be good to see Mark again, even if Hannah is with him. I presume you'll be inviting her now?'

'I guess so, assuming she wants to travel.'

'I'm sure she will. It'll be months before she's too far gone to get on a plane. Make sure Mark knows I don't mind them both being there. I thought about it last night. It's not fair on Jack if he thinks he should stay away. '

'Thank you. As long as you're sure.'

'I'm going to have to get used to it. I'm friends with you. Mark's friends with Jack. Our paths are going to keep crossing.' She opened the car door. 'I better get going before Nancy sees me.'

Em waved her off.

It was odd that Nancy hadn't popped over. She usually saw everything that was going on at Dashford Grange. She must know something.

Em had admin work to do this morning. She went over to the kitchen. Nancy was already there, drinking a cup of tea. 'I've just made a pot of Earl Grey. Do you want one?'

'Thanks, I'll pour it.'

'Was that Lucy's car in the courtyard?' Nancy had seen it then.

'Yes. She popped in to see me and Jack.'

'You don't have to be cagey. Mark's told about Hannah and the baby.'

'Are you looking forward to being a grandmother again?'

'I should be, though why both my sons have to reproduce with women who don't live anywhere near me, I don't know. But I can't help feeling that something's not right with this.'

'In what way?'

'Hannah was unhappy enough with Mark to leave him. But now she's in a bind, she decides he's good enough to live with. You know me. I'm usually an optimist, make the best of everything and all that. But I can't see it working out well. "You'll do" isn't the basis for a happy relationship. How is Lucy taking it?'

'As you'd expect. It's a difficult thing to bounce back from. She thinks the world of Mark. I think he's the first man she's truly loved. For a long time anyway.'

'Poor girl.' Nancy tidied the tea things away. 'But neither of us can do anything about it. We just have to be there for both of them and pick up the pieces later.'

47

Jack and Em had finished their final day's filming yesterday in Malaga and were tacking an extra day onto their Spanish trip so they could catch up with Mark and Hannah in Nerja. Mark topped up Em's glass of wine as they sat on his terrace, watching the sunset.

'So you're going to be a TV star?' Mark smiled at Em.

'I wouldn't say that,' she said, blushing.

'I'm sure the marketing team are going to capitalise on us being husband and wife,' Jack said.

'Mr & Mrs History?' suggested Mark.

'Except we're not yet,' Em said.

'We will be by the time it's aired.' Jack grinned.

Em frowned. The scheduled broadcast date was April next year. As far as everyone else knew, they weren't getting married until May. She gave Jack her best "shut the fuck up" look.

'Did you enjoy being in front of the camera?' asked Hannah, who seemed willing to engage with Em as an equal this time.

'Yes, I did in the end. It was a shock initially, being put on the spot. But I'm glad it happened that way because I would've said no if I'd had time to think about it. And it was lovely to be with Jack, of course.'

'So working together can be fun,' Hannah said pointedly.

'That's a dig at me,' Mark grinned. 'We're thinking of setting up a holiday let business, but I said I wasn't sure working together as a couple was a good idea.'

'Would you keep the jet ski business as well?' Jack said. 'I'm not sure Em and I would survive working together 100% of the time.'

'No, I've had enough of jet skis. I've agreed to sell it to the guy who owns the bar next door. Once the paperwork's all sorted, it will be all his. Time to move on.' Mark swirled the ice around in his drink thoughtfully.

'I'm going to bed now, darling,' Hannah got up and kissed Mark on the cheek. She turned to Jack and Em. 'Sorry to be anti-social. I'm feeling so tired these days. Pregnancy is exhausting. Good night.'

They sat in silence until Hannah was safely indoors and out of earshot.

'Everything ok?' Em asked Mark.

'Yeah, mostly. It's difficult learning to live with someone. But I guess we'll manage. How's Lucy?'

Em didn't know what to say. Distraught. Still sobbing over you if I so much as mention your name. The truth wouldn't help. 'She's keeping busy, throwing herself into her work.'

'I thought she'd have a new man in tow by now.'

Em shook her head. 'No.' She left it at that. 'I'm feeling tired as well. It's been a busy few days. I think I'll head to bed and leave you two boys to catch up.'

***

Jack came to bed about half an hour later. Em was awake, reading her book. He looked puzzled. 'You said you were tired?'

'It was an excuse to leave you two alone to talk.'

'Thank you.' He got undressed and climbed into bed beside her.

'How is Mark really?' Em asked in a low voice, unsure of how much sound carried around the apartment.

'He asked me how we managed to live together,' Jack whispered back.

'What did you say? By buying a bigger home?'

'That's one solution. I think Hannah's hard work at the moment, judging by what he said. She likes everything just so. She's pressuring him to get rid of a lot of his things.'

'They need to make room for their new addition.'

'It sounds like it's more about imposing her taste rather than fitting in the baby equipment. Compromise doesn't seem to be in her vocabulary. If it wasn't for the baby, I think he'd have suggested they call it a day.'

'Poor Mark. Poor Hannah as well.'

Jack raised an eyebrow. 'Are you warming to her?'

'Well, it's a difficult situation, and she has been pleasant to me this holiday. Perhaps now I'm a fledgling TV presenter, I'm far enough up the food chain to warrant some respect.'

'You won't say anything to Lucy about any of this, will you?'

'No. It wouldn't help either of them, sadly.'

Jack turned out the light. 'I'm very lucky to have you.'

'Yes, you are,' she laughed.

48

Lucy phoned Em for a catch-up. She'd been so wrapped up in the Mark disaster that she'd forgotten to ask Em how Jack's documentary filming was going. And she vaguely remembered one of their locations was Malaga. There might be some news about Mark.

'How's everything?' Em asked.

'All work and no play,' said Lucy. 'But I'm okay with that.'

'Are you sure?'

'Yeah. It's November. It's cold and the nights are longer. Time to snuggle down for the winter. I'm sure I'll feel more outgoing in the spring. If I keep telling myself that, I'll believe it eventually.'

'You sound like an old bear.'

'Thanks!' Hibernating sounded like a good idea. The thought of sleeping for four months and then emerging again when the heartache had gone away was appealing. But she still needed to know what was going on with Mark. 'Enough about me. I want an update on your foreign travels with the monkey puncher.'

Em laughed. 'Strictly speaking, it was an ape.'

'Does it matter? The poor thing still ended up with a swollen eye from her bloody enormous diamond ring. So come on, what happened? Any new bruised and battered mammals to report?'

'Clara had flu, so I never even saw her, and neither did Jack.' Lucy was relieved. She didn't want Em to lose her partner to his annoying ex as well.

'So Jack's presenting on his own again?'

'Not exactly.'

'What do you mean?'

'I joined him on camera.'

'Seriously? OMG, you're going to be famous again!'

'I'm not sure I was famous the first time.'

'You were on telly. We can't have been the only people that watched. Am I going to have to book an appointment a year in advance to see you from now on?'

'Not quite. Though I do have my own agent now. She's Jack's agent as well. She's seen some clips and thinks I may be able to get other presenting work.'

'Wow! Will I be able to come with you to the BAFTAs?'

'I don't think we're in that territory yet.'

'How was it in Italy and Spain?'

'Nice and warm. The hotels were OK. You can tell it's not a big budget production, but they were clean and comfortable.'

Lucy took a deep breath. 'Did you see Mark?'

Em hesitated.

'You did then. How is he? And Hannah?' It sounded less desperate if she asked about Hannah as well.

'They're fine. Working out how to live together.'

It was an odd way to put it. Still, what did she know? She hadn't properly lived with anyone since she'd left her flat share five years ago. But it confirmed Mark and Hannah were still together. *How evil are you for hoping they had broken up?*

'Are you still there?' Em asked.

Lucy felt like she needed to cry again. Time to end the call and wallow in self-pity for a few minutes.

'Yes. I've got a report to finish for tomorrow. I better go. I'm glad the filming worked out so well. Speak soon.'

Part Three

December 2019

49

Lucy's hairdresser, Poppy, was mixing the dye for Lucy's new highlights. 'Are you sure about this? Red's a drastic change. It will look fabulous, though. Very Christmassy.'

'I'm absolutely sure. I need a new look. New everything. I'm in a rut. I want to knock 'em dead at Jack and Em's engagement party.'

'Anyone you've particularly got your eye on?'

'Not after Mark, no.' Lucy sighed. She'd stuck to her plan of not dating anyone since Mark had gone back to Hannah, but the novelty of not having to epilate her legs on a regular basis had worn off now. She was bored of being single, and she wasn't looking forward to spending Christmas alone. Her original plan had been to go to Italy to visit her parents, but her mother had scuppered that when she announced they were going on a last-minute trip to Goa. 'I'm sure Em will take you in, sweetheart,' Lucy's mother had said.

Em would probably take pity on her and invite her round to Roger and Cynthia's for Boxing Day, but Christmas Day was going to be a dud this year.

Poppy's voice brought Lucy back to the present. 'Will Mark

be there with what's her name?'

'Hannah. Yes.'

Lucy had practised being pleasant to Hannah in the bathroom mirror. She hadn't quite mastered hiding the look of contempt in her eyes, but as Hannah didn't seem to pay much attention to other women, she was unlikely to notice.

'So you want to make Mark see what he's missing?'

Lucy hadn't thought of it like that, but perhaps subconsciously, that was what she hoped would happen. 'Possibly,' she said.

Poppy started applying foils and chatting about her family.

Lucy's phone buzzed. A text from Kizzy with another query from her new branding client.

'You need a new job as well,' said Poppy. 'How many interruptions is that today? It must be at least five, and you've only been here ten minutes.'

Poppy had a point about the number of interruptions. After the success of their rebranding, Aaron from Swanky Grinders had recommended Lucy to a friend whose business distributed hand-fired clay tiles made in the foothills of the Andes. The new client was eager to get their marketing plan signed off as soon as possible. It wasn't going to be an easy wind down to the Christmas holidays for Lucy, Flynn and Kizzy this year.

'I can't get a new job. That would mean selling my business, and I'm not ready to let it go just yet. There's no way I could work for anyone else again.'

'I thought you sold your business a couple of years ago?'

'That was my social media one. But now I'm building up a high-end marketing agency, I'm planning to keep it for a lot longer.'

'You need more staff. A woman should be able to go to the hairdresser without being pestered by the office every 30 seconds.'

Lucy had been thinking about her business a lot lately. It tied her to Birmingham, which hadn't worried her before, but when she was with Mark, it would have been a lot easier if she earned her living doing something that she could do anywhere. Not that it mattered now that he'd left her, but someone else might come into her life who wanted to put down roots away from Birmingham or go travelling for months. She might even like to go travelling for months herself. Eventually, she'd get to the point where she could afford to get another senior member of staff to run it on her behalf but, at this rate, she wouldn't be in that position for years yet.

'And what if you decide to have kids?' Poppy continued. 'You'll have to take time off, then. What you need is a business coach.'

Someone who could give her a fresh point of view on where to take the business next. Not a bad idea. 'Do you know anyone?'

'Funny you should ask. One of my other regulars is a business coach. Petra. I don't know how good she is, but she can afford to have a blow-dry every week, so she can't be doing that badly. I'll get you her details when I've finished your foils.'

50

A week later, Lucy was sitting in her favourite coffee shop at a table at the back, working on her laptop. It was pouring with rain outside, but she felt warm and cosy thanks to the festive decorations, the warm glow from the vintage-style light bulbs, and the Christmas songs playing quietly in the background.

'Have you been stood up again?'

Lucy recognised the voice. Josh. She looked up from her laptop. She was surprised she hadn't bumped into him before. He must've been avoiding coming in here since they split up.

'No. I'm waiting for a client.'

'Charging for it now?' He gave her a stupid grin.

'Ha ha. Very funny. So you're back on the market?'

'I might be.'

'I'm sure the single women of Birmingham can barely contain their excitement.'

'If my date doesn't arrive, could we get together again?'

Was he serious? 'Why would you think I was that desperate?'

'It wasn't that bad, was it? We had some fun.'

She considered telling him to go forth and multiply, but then she spotted an attractive woman making her way between the tables to where Josh was standing. Probably his date. Lucy could have some fun with this.

'Let's see.' She made sure that she was speaking loudly enough for anyone in the vicinity to hear. 'Blatantly flirting with my friend's girlfriend in front of me and then trying to gaslight me into thinking you didn't fancy her just so you could get back in my knickers. And, the sad news, Josh, is it wasn't that exciting most of the time when you did get past my underwear. You reminded me of a cross-channel ferry.'

'What do you mean?' he said, clearly affronted. The woman stopped walking towards him.

'Roll on, roll off.'

The occupants of the table next to Lucy's appeared to be choking on their drinks.

'So no, I don't want to go out with you again, Josh.'

The attractive woman turned round and beat a hasty retreat towards the door. Mission accomplished. Lucy smiled as she watched her go outside.

Josh followed Lucy's gaze.

'Shit. Scarlett! Scarlett!' he shouted as he weaved his way back through the tables and charged out of the door, nearly knocking over the person who was walking in. Hopefully, that would stop Josh from drinking in here again.

Lucy went back to actioning emails on her laptop.

'Hi. You look pleased with yourself.'

Lucy looked up. Someone else was standing by her table now, someone Lucy was much happier to see.

'Harry! I successfully scared off an annoying ex.' She gave Harry a hug. 'It's so good to see you. Take a seat.'

51

'We've run out of pigs in blankets for the turkey, but everything else is available.' The barman at the Kingfisher sounded bored as he handed Jack six menus.

'Thanks,' Jack said and headed back to Em and Lucy, who were sitting at a table by the roaring log fire.

'Life's going to be a lot easier with Harry around,' he heard Lucy say as he sat down next to Em.

'Who's Harry?' Jack asked.

'My new partner,' she said with a smile. Em hadn't mentioned Lucy was dating again, but she must've been for a man to reach partner status already.

'I've been bumbling along without a clear plan since Mark left me. And then I met Harry again, and everything slotted into place. I'm hoping 2020 will be my best year yet.'

It was good to see her so upbeat again. Although she drove him mad sometimes, she was a good friend to Em. She deserved some luck with her love life. He hoped Harry was more like Mark than Adam or Josh.

'When do we get to meet Harry?' Em asked.

'At my New Year's Eve party. You're still coming up to

Birmingham, aren't you?'

'Yes. We'll be there,' Em said.

'Great. Who are we waiting for?' Lucy looked at the empty chairs. 'Mark and Hannah?'

She seemed a little apprehensive as she mentioned the two of them.

'No, Dad and Cynthia, and they're bringing Nancy with them.

'Mark and Hannah won't be here till later. They're getting the last flight out of Malaga.' Jack looked at his watch. 'They should be in the air right now.'

'What's the plan for tomorrow's party?' Lucy asked.

'We need a hand with a few things. That's why we were so pleased you could get here early.' He caught Em's eye. Hopefully, she could pull this off without giving the game away about the wedding ceremony.

Em smiled at him. 'Yes. We were wondering if you wouldn't mind coming with us first thing. We've got an errand to run in Barnstaple. It's a legal thing. We've got some papers to sign, and we need someone who knows us to witness our signatures. We need to leave Dashford Grange by 9.15. We'll be back here by 11.'

'That's fine. Do you need new wills or something?'

'Yes, we do,' Jack said. It wasn't a lie. They would need new wills after they were married, but they weren't going to worry about that tomorrow.

'I thought you said you wanted me to help with prepping for the party?'

'Oh, we need that too.' Jack grinned. 'We're going to fully exploit you while you're here. Make you work for your supper.' *Don't get carried away. She might smell a rat.*

'There's just one thing about this appointment,' Em said. 'Do you think you could dress up a bit? I don't think they'll appreciate it if we turn up in joggers.'

'What sort of solicitor cares what their clients are wearing?' Lucy looked suspicious. Em might have just screwed this up.

Jack tried to rescue the situation. 'Well, they're slightly old-fashioned. It's not like Birmingham.'

'I thought Devon was all laid back and casual.'

'Not for everything.' Em said.

'So, meeting a new client level of smart?'

'Yes, exactly,' Em said.

'Good job I packed a dress then.'

Lucy's phone buzzed.

'Ooh, it's Harry. I need to take this,' she said, excusing herself.

'That went well,' Jack whispered to Em.

'Yes, I don't think we told a single lie.'

'No, you were very good. Too good. I'll have to bear that in mind in future.'

52

'Will I do?' Em walked into the middle of the living room in the flat and did a twirl in her vintage dress.

'You look gorgeous,' said Jack. He frowned.

'Everything ok?' Surely he liked her outfit.

'Your dress seems oddly familiar, that's all.'

'It was your grandmother's. Your mother loaned it to me.'

Jack raised his eyebrows. 'You're honoured. Kate and I were never allowed to so much as touch it.'

'Old, borrowed and blue all in one. And this is my something new.' Em picked up the faux fur shawl she'd bought to go with it. 'Lucy will be suspicious as soon as she sees me dressed like this.'

'It won't matter. We're going to tell her as soon as she arrives. Is my tie straight?'

'Not quite.' Em adjusted it. 'There. Perfect. She smoothed the lapels down on his jacket.'

He kissed her. 'I'm so happy we're doing this.'

'So am I. I can't believe it's finally happening.' As soon as she'd put on the dress this morning, Em had felt all the stress and anxiety evaporate. Everything felt right at last.

There was a knock on the door. 'Ready?' Jack said.

Em took a deep breath. 'Yes.'

Jack went into the hall.

'Why are we wearing suits on a Saturday morning?' Mark asked as he walked into the flat. 'Hi, Em. You're all dressed up, too.'

Mark narrowed his eyes. 'Anyone would think we're going to a wedding?'

'Would they?' Jack said with an innocent expression on his face.

'Yes, they would. Are we?'

'Possibly,' Jack grinned.

'Oh, come on. Really? You devious pair.'

Jack handed Mark the ring box. 'Look after those, will you? Lucy will be here in a minute.'

'Does Hannah mind us borrowing you for the morning?' Em asked.

'No. She's in Spain.' Mark was interrupted by another knock at the door. 'I'll explain later.'

So Hannah couldn't be bothered to turn up for their wedding either. Charming.

Jack opened the front door, and Lucy marched in. 'This had better be good, Emily Gillespie. I hate getting dressed to the nines at this hour on a Saturday. Oh, Mark, you're here.' She seemed taken aback.

'Lovely to see you too,' he said, equally on edge.

Lucy regained her composure. She looked him up and down. 'A red shirt. An interesting choice. It goes with your eyes. Are you ok?'

'Late night flight. Not much sleep.' Mark suddenly seemed on edge.

Em interrupted, worried Lucy might snipe at him again. 'Are we ready to go?'

'You're eager to get to the solicitors,' Lucy said. 'This all feels very odd.' She narrowed her eyes. 'That frock is rather over the top for a visit to a sign a will.'

'Work it out, Luce,' said Mark. 'I guessed.'

'I've got a headache, and my brain shuts down on a Saturday morning when I've had a busy week. Will someone please put me out of misery?'

'We're off to Barnstaple registry office,' Em said.

'But you aren't getting married till next year.'

Em could see the penny drop as soon as Lucy finished the sentence.

'Oh my god!' She ran excitedly towards Em and hugged her. Then she backed away and stared at Em's waistline. 'Are you pregnant?'

'It must be the cut of the dress,' she said, smoothing it over her stomach.

'I'm sorry. I didn't mean it like that. You look absolutely amazing. I just wondered why the sudden change of plan.'

'We got fed up with all the grief with the wedding arrangements,' Jack said. 'We wanted a quiet ceremony.'

'Followed by a party tonight. Clever.' Lucy nodded in approval.

'Will you two be our witnesses?' Em asked.

'It's a bit late for saying no,' Mark laughed.

'Come on. We don't want to be late.' Jack shepherded them all outside and down the steps into the courtyard.

'Shall I be chauffeur?' Mark offered.

'Do you drive like your mother?' Em didn't want to spend the last half hour of her single life clinging to the car seat in terror.

'Yes, he does,' Jack said before Mark could answer. 'I'll drive.'

53

The four of them sat in the waiting room at the Register Office, Em tapping her feet and Jack drumming his hands on the arm of his chair.

'Will you two relax? This is supposed to be a joyous occasion,' Lucy said.

Mark got up and peered through the door into the ceremony room. 'No one in there. You must be the first ceremony of the day. I thought you were supposed to be late for a wedding.'

'Not at a register office. They expect you to be on time,' Em said. 'And we have to be interviewed to make sure we're not being coerced into doing this.'

'Isn't your dad going to be upset that he's not here?' Lucy asked Em.

'No, I sounded him out. I said I was so fed up with the venue situation, would he mind if we disappeared somewhere and got married on our own? He said it would be a relief - he hates giving speeches.'

Two smartly dressed women emerged from one of the office doors. 'Ms Gillespie, would you like to come with me?'

one of them said. 'Mr Carver, my colleague will interview you.'

Em and Jack disappeared down a corridor, leaving Lucy alone with Mark for the first time in weeks. She sneaked a looked at him. Despite her jibe about the red shirt earlier, it did suit him now his summer tan was fading.

'Where's Hannah?' she asked.

He took a deep breath. 'In Spain. Moving her stuff out of my apartment.'

Had she misheard him? 'What did you just say?'

'She's moving out.' He looked as if he were gauging Lucy's reaction.

She stared back at him. 'I don't know what to say.'

Mark looked away and focused on the floor. 'It's not my baby.'

'Oh my god.' She resisted the urge to hug him. 'How do you know?'

'We had a massive row last week. She said I was rubbish in bed. Not like Josh.'

'Josh?! When did those two get an opportunity to do the deed?'

'In London, after we all went to bed on the Saturday night. On the sofa in the living room and then again on the kitchen island, so she delighted in telling me.'

Lucy was speechless. Josh had fucked Hannah, then got back into bed with Lucy like nothing had happened. She remembered waking up when he walked through the bedroom door in the small hours of the morning. She'd assumed he'd been to the bathroom. She'd tried snuggling up to him, but unusually, he'd resisted her attentions. She'd thought he was still pissed off with her because they hadn't gone clubbing. 'I ate my breakfast on that kitchen work surface. How come none of us knew? The flat's not that big.'

'It must've been those martinis that Jack whipped up after

we got back from the concert. I thought he was heavy-handed with the vodka.'

Lucy tried to process the information. 'How do you know the baby's not yours?'

'You can get pre-natal paternity tests that analyse the mother's blood against the prospective father's DNA. Some of the baby's DNA crosses the placenta into the mother's bloodstream. So I paid for a test, and the result said there is a 90% chance that I'm not the father.'

'And Josh is?'

'I assume so. Unless she's been playing away with someone else as well. I don't know what to believe now.'

'But there's a 10% chance it could still be yours?'

He nodded. 'We're going to get another test when the baby is born. Then we can be 100% certain.'

'And if it is yours?'

'I guess I'll have to pay child maintenance and negotiate access.'

'You wouldn't go back to her?'

'Absolutely not. She cheated on me and lied about it. She must've known Josh could be the father the whole time.'

Poor Mark. 'So you're single again?'

'Looks like it.'

'I'm sorry.'

'Are you?' He looked crestfallen.

'About the baby, I mean, not you being single.'

'It's a relief. I do want children, but not like that. It would never have worked.'

He gave her a long look. 'What's happening with you?'

She didn't have time to answer as Em reappeared in the corridor, quickly followed by Jack.

***

The ceremony flew by. Lucy found it odd watching her best

friend and Jack share their vows with hardly anyone else in the room. It made it more emotional somehow. But she couldn't help feeling they deserved to be bathed in warm sunshine on a tropical beach somewhere rather than in this converted office on a grey December morning. And then there was Mark.

'Lucy?'

Em's voice snapped her back to reality. 'Sorry. What am I meant to be doing?'

'Sign here.' The registrar pointed to a line at the bottom of the register page.

Mark's signature was already on there. Lucy carefully wrote her name next to his.

'Would you like me to take a photo?' the registrar offered.

Jack handed over his phone. She took one of Jack and Em pretending to sign the register and another with Lucy and Mark in the background.

And that was it. Lucy's best friend of 28 years was now Mrs Jack Carver.

'You're next,' Em said, handing her the bouquet of roses.

'Perhaps.' She caught Mark looking at her.

'Aren't you supposed to throw that?' Mark asked.

'After the last bouquet throw we took part in, this way is far safer.'

'What are you doing for the rest of your wedding day?' asked the registrar as she tidied up the desk.

'We're having a surprise party with all our friends this evening,' said Jack. 'We better head back home to make sure everything's organised.'

'No need to rush.' Mark smiled. 'Mother dearest has it all under control. She's in her element. She's so thrilled your engagement party is at her house. She'll be ecstatic when she finds out it's your wedding do as well. It will make up for Nigel having all his celebrations in America. Which means we've got time to have a swift half. The pub over the road looks open.'

Jack looked horrified. 'It's only 10.30 in the morning.'

'Wouldn't have stopped you once upon a time,' Mark grinned.

'I'm a respectable married man now.'

'Oh, come on. As your best man, I insist we've got to raise a toast to you and Mrs Carver. We won't be doing that until this evening otherwise.'

'I wouldn't object,' Lucy said.

'I better consult my wife,' Jack said.

'Your wife could do with a drink too!' Em put her arm through his and led him to the exit.

54

Em and Jack were sitting in a booth in the pub while Mark had gone to the bar to get drinks. Lucy had excused herself, saying she was going to help him.

'At least they're talking to one another,' Jack said. 'Odd about Hannah though.'

'Is it? Probably using her pregnancy as an excuse. I'm sure she finds Spain much more appealing than Devon on a cold December day. Anyway, we've got to get going with sorting out the party. What are we going to do with our wedding rings?' Em waved her hand at Jack.

'I didn't think about that. No one's going to notice, are they? They're used to seeing your engagement ring, and I had a ring for years until I split with Isabella. I don't want to take mine off.' He looked concerned.

'Would that be bad luck?'

'No. But let's not risk it. I don't want to lose it. Or you, Mrs Carver.' He kissed her. 'Are you sure you want to change your name?'

'I'm quite enjoying being Mrs Carver.'

'Good.' He kissed her again.

'Do you think Lucy's alright? She seemed very quiet at the Register Office.'

'I'm sure being in Mark's company is upsetting after all that's gone on.'

'Yes. It must be.' Em looked across at them, standing by the bar. 'I don't like their body language. It's looking like it might go downhill. Let's do our best to keep them apart today. We don't want any arguments. I'll help with the drinks.'

***

Mark placed their order at the bar. He was very aware of Lucy standing next to him. It wasn't the ideal spot to talk with the barman within hearing distance, but he needed to know where he stood. He looked over at Em and Jack, who were deep in conversation. Would he ever be that close to someone emotionally? He thought he'd had that with Lucy, but she seemed distant today, even now she knew he'd split up with Hannah. Hopefully, it was because the implications of his news hadn't sunk in yet.

The barman went to the other end of the bar to fetch something. Now or never.

Mark looked at Lucy. 'So about us?'

'It's not about us today, is it?'

'That will be £12.50, please.' The barman was back. Why did he have to be so bloody efficient?

'Yes, sure.' Mark got out his credit card. The barman walked to the other end of the bar again to get the card machine.

'Lucy?'

'Shall I help with those?' Em had walked up to them. Lucy wasn't going to answer now.

Mark sighed. 'Thank you,' he said with an air of resignation.

'Come on, Luce,' Em said as she picked up their drinks.

'Tell us all about Harry. You didn't get a chance last night. Cynthia didn't let you get a word in edgeways. '

Harry. Who the hell was Harry? Mark picked up his drink and followed them.

But Lucy still didn't get an opportunity to say anything about Harry because at that moment a loud woman in every sense of the word burst through the pub doors.

'There you are. The registrar said she thought you were coming over here to celebrate. When were you going to tell us?'

'Cynthia,' Jack said.

Jack's new stepmother. Jack had mentioned she had a big personality.

'I told Cynthia we should leave you alone.' Roger followed Cynthia over to the table.

'It's alright, Dad. We just wanted to be on our own for the ceremony.'

'Congratulations! I'm so happy for you both.' He shook Jack's hand and then hugged Em. ' You're not expecting me to do a speech tonight, are you?' he added nervously.

'No - no speeches. But how did you know we'd be in Barnstaple?'

'Cynthia is something of a Miss Marple. She heard a car start up this morning. So she looked out of the cottage window, and there were the four of you heading off all dressed up. She guessed what might be going on. And this is the nearest register office, so here we are.'

There was no chance of getting Lucy to talk about Harry now. Mark may as well do his duty as best man. He forced a smile. 'Can I get you both a drink?'

55

Jack was going to drive the four of them back home while Roger and Cynthia followed behind in Roger's sports car.

Mark settled into the back seat. Lucy got in next to him. Good. He might get a chance to find out whether Harry was a serious love interest. But Em insisted on chatting. She wasn't normally this talkative. Or perhaps she was and he hadn't noticed before.

He heard a ping. A text on Em's phone, judging by the direction it came from. That would distract her for a minute or two.

'Is Harry joining us today?' he asked Lucy.

She looked puzzled. 'No. It would be awkward. No one knows Harry here. Apart from me, of course.'

Em turned round again.

'That was the caterers. They're going to get everything set up half an hour earlier than we planned. So we need to get the marquee decorated before 5 pm. Lucy, can you give me a hand after we've got changed?'

Em turned to Mark. 'Jack needs to pick up the drinks and glasses from the wine merchant. Would you be an angel and help him?'

'I might be more helpful with the decorating. I'm taller than you and Lucy?'

'We've got step ladders. We'll be fine.'

So no chance to speak to Lucy for the rest of the morning and most of the afternoon as well, probably. Damn it. Hopefully, Jack knew something. Mark would have to ask him when they went to the wine merchants.

***

Mark went to his room to get changed into his casual wear, ready for the trip to the wine merchants. There was a knock on the door.

'Are you decent? I've brought you some tea.' His mother never waited on him normally. She must be after something. He opened the door for her.

'Have you spoken to Lucy yet?' she asked as she walked in.

'Only briefly. I had time to tell her what happened with Hannah, but nothing else.'

'Are you wearing that shirt again tonight?' Nancy nodded towards the red shirt that Mark had just taken off and hung on the wardrobe door.

'Yes. Why?'

'It could do with ironing. I can't believe you went to the solicitors dressed in a creased shirt.'

Something about the way she said it, implied she didn't believe the story about this morning's trip to Barnstaple. He needed to be careful what he said. 'I don't think anyone noticed.'

'Do you want me to iron it for you?'

'Are you feeling alright, Mother dearest? You've never offered to iron a shirt for me before.'

'I'm feeling absolutely fine, and that's simply not true.'

Nancy looked indignant. 'What about when you had the interview for Cambridge?'

'Ok, I exaggerated slightly. You only offer to iron for me once every 18 years. Why are you suddenly concerned about my shirts?'

'We don't want Lucy thinking you've lost pride in your personal appearance, do we?'

'Are you matchmaking again?'

She put her hands on her hips. 'Are you objecting? You told me Lucy was the love of your life.'

'She is.'

'So why the glum face? You're single again. She's not been out with anyone since you broke up. This should be as easy as pushing at an open door. She's not exactly a Vestal virgin.'

'What about Harry?'

'Who's Harry?'

'That's what I'm trying to find out. I take it you know nothing about him?'

'No, it's the first I've heard about any Harry as far as Lucy is concerned.'

'He's a complete mystery. No one seems to know anything about him. Even Em.'

'You know how you could find out?'

'How?'

'Ask Lucy.'

'Thank you for that excellent advice. That's what I've been trying to do. But there seems to be a conspiracy afoot to keep us apart.'

'Don't be paranoid. Everyone's busy getting ready for the party, that's all. So what about that shirt?'

***

'How's it feel to be a married man again?' Mark asked as Jack drove them both out of Dashford Grange.

'A lot better than last time.' Jack had barely been able to keep the smile off his face since he'd signed the marriage register, lucky bastard.

'Does this mean you're expecting me to conjure up a best man's speech for this evening?'

Jack laughed. 'No. After your last attempt, that's one of the reasons I suggested a surprise wedding.'

'The stories of our escapades didn't go down too well with bride number one, did they?'

Mark remembered Isabella's face when he was recounting a few of the scrapes that he and Jack had got into over the years. She'd looked particularly sour when he'd described them drunkenly trying to get back into Jack's student digs after a late night out when Jack had forgotten his keys. The backyards of the terraced houses had all looked very similar in the dark. They'd climbed through an open window into the wrong house. Mark had flaked out on the sofa while Jack had gone upstairs and clambered into bed with his neighbour, who, after her initial surprise, had been very accommodating.

'So when are you going to make an honest woman of Hannah?' Jack asked.

'I'm not.'

Jack looked shocked. 'What's changed?'

'We've split up.' Mark filled him in on Hannah, Josh and the paternity test.

'When did you get the results?'

'Yesterday.'

'How do you feel?'

'Honestly? Relieved.'

'I don't know what to say.'

'Congratulations on a lucky escape will do.'

'Does Lucy know?'

'Yes. I told her while you and Em were in with the

registrars. I was hoping she'd want us to get back together again, but she still seems distant.'

'It's probably a shock. She was seriously upset that you broke up with her. She's been different since then. Quieter. Concentrating on her business, according to Em.' Jack looked at him with a look of concern on his face. 'And then there is this new partner.'

'Harry?'

'You've heard about him then.'

'Only when his name was mentioned in the pub earlier. I suppose I shouldn't have expected her to be sitting at home alone, pining for me. What's he like?'

'I don't know. He only came up in conversation last night when we were having dinner in the Kingfisher. I didn't even know she was dating again. Em doesn't know any more than I do. We get to meet him in Birmingham at New Year.'

At least it sounded like Lucy hadn't been dating Harry until very recently. He might be able to win her back if she wasn't too deeply involved with him. But Lucy referring to Harry as her partner was worrying. It didn't sound like a casual affair. Perhaps he shouldn't try to win her over. Not today, anyway. He didn't want to spoil Em and Jack's celebrations.

'You have reached your destination,' the satnav announced. Jack pulled into a car park.

'This isn't the wine merchants,' Mark said, looking at the sign welcoming them to the local garden centre.

'Correct. We're going there next. Right now, I need a Christmas tree.'

56

'Do you want this Union Jack bunting?' Lucy was in the marquee with Em, rifling through a mixed box of decorations that Nancy had given them.

'No. We're not royalty.'

'Some of this stuff is vintage. It must date back to the queen's coronation. And this string of flags has got 1977 Silver Jubilee on it.'

'Nancy dug it out from one of the attics in case it was any use.'

'Did you get any new stuff?'

'These fairy lights. We're after a cosy Christmassy feel, not a summery bake-off tent vibe.'

'Stick to the lights, then. You've got plenty.' Lucy packed the bunting back in the box.

Em started laying the lights out on the bar. 'There should be enough to string them around the tent. We've got an LED curtain for the wall by the dance floor, and I bought these jars with lights inside. They can go on the occasional tables.'

'Where is everyone going to eat?' Lucy looked at the sofas, bar stools and occasional tables dotted around the tent.

'It's a buffet, not a formal meal. There should be enough space for everyone to sit somewhere. There are only 60 of us. We went for the nightclub configuration.'

'Complete with a sticky floor and a random groper?'

'No, those were optional extras.'

Lucy had to admit, it looked good. Far less fussy than most of the wedding receptions she'd been to. Perhaps one day she'd do the same for her own wedding. *What are you thinking, Lucy Thomas? You're never going to get married at this rate.* She grabbed a string of lights and handed them to Em, who was now at the top of a stepladder by the side of the bar.

'How are things with Mark? I've not had a chance to talk to him properly today,' Em asked as she clipped the lights to one of the marquee fittings.

'I'm not sure. He seems very low.'

'Perhaps he's worried about Hannah and the baby,' Em suggested.

'Less than he was 24 hours ago, I'm guessing.'

'What do you mean?'

'You've not heard then?' Lucy filled Em in on Mark's latest news.

'That's awful. But it means he's single again.' Em raised her eyebrows encouragingly.

'Yes. I want to know what he's planning to do next, but it's been very difficult to speak to him. Ever since you emerged from your interview with the registrar, we've not had any time alone to talk about it.'

'Ah.'

'What do you mean "ah"?'

Em looked sheepish. 'I thought you were getting a bit tetchy with one another, so I've been on a mission to keep you apart to avoid a row.'

'That explains the verbal diarrhoea in the car earlier.'

'Verbal diarrhoea? I was just trying to keep everyone

talking.'

'Or not talking,' Lucy sighed. *Don't get cross with Em. It's not her fault.* 'Your next mission, should you choose to accept it, is to use your matchmaking skills to get me five minutes alone with Mark. I need to know where I stand. I don't know if he wants me back or not. I'm suspecting not.'

Don't cry. She took a deep breath and counted to ten to fight back the tears. It would've been easier to deal with him being all lovey-dovey with Hannah than with the current weird situation.

Em descended the ladder and hugged her. 'It will all work out, I'm sure.'

'It's just I've been so lonely without him. And I don't mean the lack of sex. I used to be self-sufficient emotionally, but he was such a good sounding board when I needed to talk. I know you are as well, but it's not the same as having a partner.'

'I know what you mean. It's the same with Jack. Isn't Harry any good?'

What was Em bringing Harry into this for? 'Harry's excellent on the business side of things, but that's as far as it goes. I understood what a soulmate was for the first time in years when I was with Mark. I know we weren't together for that long, but what is it they say? "When you know, you know." I'd like that feeling back again.'

Lucy went back to the box of lights and picked up another set for Em to hang. 'Sorry. I sound like a lovesick teenager. This is your special day. You shouldn't be worrying about my love life.'

'Don't be daft,' Em said. 'I'll text Jack to see if he can help.'

***

'Mark!'

Mark was walking across the courtyard to Em and Jack's

flat. He froze. He knew that voice. The gods were not on his side today.

'Caroline. Hello.' He forced a smile. 'What are you doing here?' He hadn't seen her for years and he'd wanted it to stay that way.

'Same as you, I guess. Apparently, there's some form of party going on.' She laughed with that annoying squeak at the end that set his teeth on edge.

'Yes, apparently.'

Caroline's mother emerged from the passenger side of the Range Rover. 'Darling, help me with my suitcase.'

'Coming, Mummy.' Caroline headed to the rear of the car.

'Staying here tonight?' She called to Mark as she opened the boot.

He couldn't lie. It was obvious he would be stopping in his family home.

'Yes.'

'Catch you later,' she said. She gave him a wink as she headed towards the main house.

She was in a flirtatious mood. That was all he needed. Mark ran up the steps to the flat. Jack answered the door.

'Why have you invited Caroline?'

'Because my mother wanted to see her sister. And the easiest way for her to get here is for Caroline to drive.'

'What's her marital status these days?'

'In the middle of divorcing husband number two. '

'Don't tell her I'm single again.'

Jack laughed. 'She might work it out for herself.'

'It's alright for you. She leaves you alone. It's me she makes a beeline for.'

'You're a grown man. If she makes a pass at you, tell her you're not interested.'

'I try every time. She's not good at taking no for an answer.'

Jack's phone buzzed. He read the screen and looked thoughtful. 'Why don't you ask Lucy to pretend to be your partner today? That would kill two birds with one stone. Caroline will keep away from you if she thinks you're with someone and you get an opportunity to talk to Lucy properly about Harry.'

It would mean he could talk to Lucy. But what if she told him she and Harry were serious? Mark didn't think he could cope with that today. 'I'll think about it. Let's get the last of these glasses over to the marquee.'

***

'Mark's definitely avoiding me,' Lucy said sadly. She and Em had finished getting the marquee ready, and now they were having a drink in the kitchen.

'I texted Jack about getting the two of you some time alone, but he hasn't replied yet,' Em said. 'He's probably still trying to keep you apart.'

'But it wasn't Jack who was keeping us apart. I saw Mark in the marquee earlier helping Jack with the glasses for tonight, and he made an excuse to leave. He said he needed to check if there were more glasses in the house. No prompting from Jack. In fact, Jack looked at him, completely baffled.'

Lucy took another gulp of her tea. 'Then I bumped into him in here alone just before you came in, and he said he had to go to the toilet. We're like the couple on that German weather chalet thing your mum used to have. If I go in, he goes out and vice versa.'

Em looked thoughtful. 'He's probably nervous about talking to you, and he doesn't want it to turn into a scene on our wedding day. You'll just have to be patient. He's bound to feel like he's on an emotional rollercoaster after Hannah's revelations.'

This was so frustrating in every sense of the word. 'You know I don't do patient.'

57

Em stood outside the marquee on her own, feeling nervous. Their guests should have started arriving five minutes ago.

'Em!' Ella appeared through the gate into the courtyard, Sam casually strolling behind her.

'You made it!' Em hugged her. 'I was beginning to think no one was coming.'

'There are temporary traffic lights on the main road. We were sitting in the queue for ages. I wouldn't have missed your party for the world.'

'Bar?' Sam asked.

Ella glared at him. 'You could at least say hello first.'

'Sorry. Hi, Em. Where's the bar?' he grinned. 'One big advantage of having a pregnant wife is she can't drink, so I get to be chauffeured everywhere. And I like to make the most of it.'

'I've got another three months of this.' Ella rolled her eyes.

'More if you breastfeed,' Sam said gleefully.

'Jack might be at the bar already.' Em pointed to the back of the marquee.

'Excellent. Your usual, El?'

'Yes, still water, please.' Ella called after Sam as he headed inside. She turned to Em. 'Even fizzy drinks make me feel sick.'

'Do you want anything to eat?' Em offered.

'Oh god, no. I can't face proper food. I've got a pack of custard creams in my bag if I get peckish. Where's the loo?'

'There's one to the left of the back door.'

'Sorry to abandon you, but I'm desperate.' Ella tottered off towards the house.

Jack came out to join Em.

'On your own again?'

'Yes, your mum and Nancy have disappeared, and Ella's gone to the toilet.'

'I've hardly seen you today.'

'Our first day as man and wife, and we've spent most of it apart.' She shivered. Jack pulled her into his arms and kissed her.

'Steady on you two. You're not married yet.'

Jack and Em exchanged a glance. The deep voice came from a tall man in his seventies walking purposefully towards them down the path. Well groomed, white hair. Handsome for his age. Eyes like Jack's.

'Good of you to turn up, Dad,' Jack said.

So this was Peter. There was something appealing about him. She could see where Jack got his looks from.

'Your mother said she would make my life hell if I didn't. And even though we live 600 miles apart, I know she doesn't make idle threats.'

'Good to know you came for Mother rather than me.' Jack sounded pissed off already.

'Don't be so sensitive. And you must be Em. I hope so, anyway. Otherwise, Jack's going to have some explaining to do later.' He gave a hearty laugh. 'Don't start cheating on them, my boy, not until you've married them. That's what my father advised me.'

Charming. Em could see why Jack hadn't been that keen to put him on the guest list. She wished she hadn't persuaded him now. Peter hugged her.

'I hope you're keeping him under control.'

'I don't think he's ever out of control.' Em felt the urge to defend Jack. Was his father always this gladiatorial?

'Get a bottle of single malt down him, and you'll see a different side.'

Em tried not to show her annoyance.

'No Catherine today?' Jack asked.

'No. Your stepmother had to stay at home to look after the pigs.'

'I imagine she has plenty of experience of dealing with pigs,' said Em.

Peter ignored her.

'How's that television programme of yours doing, Jack? Has anyone watched it yet?'

Em could feel Jack's body tense. Amazingly, Jack's voice sounded calm when he answered. 'We've got good enough viewing figures for them to commission a third series. So, yes, people are watching.'

'I found the first series dreadfully dull, personally. I only managed to watch ten minutes of the first episode.'

'We had a five-star review in The Guardian.'

'I don't read that left-wing rag. Waste of paper.'

Peter nodded towards the group of people walking into the garden. 'You've got more guests to greet. I'll say hello to Olivia. I can see her waving to me from the bar.'

'Is he always so rude? I counted at least four insults in that one exchange,' Em whispered to Jack.

'Yes. I told you he doesn't believe in praise. I'm not allowed to get too big for my boots. And, just to be clear, I have no intention of cheating on you, regardless of how long we're married.'

'I never thought you would. I think you take after your mum rather than your dad.'

'I hope so. I really do.'

***

'Not like you to be in the kitchen,' Ella said to Lucy.

'I'm trying to make myself useful.' And hanging around to see if Mark made an appearance, but she wasn't going to share that with Ella. She didn't want to sound like some sad schoolgirl with a crush.

'No one with you today?'

'No. I meant it when I said I'd given up men.'

'Where is the man who put you off men for good? I was looking forward to meeting his pregnant girlfriend. I thought we could swap notes on coping with fat ankles.'

'I can't imagine Hannah permits her body to develop fat ankles. But she's not here. They've split up.'

'Ooh, Mark is here on his own, then?'

'Yes. He's somewhere in the marquee, I think. He was propping up the bar earlier.'

'All our menfolk are.' Ella sounded pissed off.

'Are you and Sam ok?'

'Yeah. Take no notice. I'm just fed up with not being able to have any alcohol while Sam's drinking more than enough for both of us. I'm looking forward to meeting Charlotte's new man.'

'Which one's that?'

'Claudio, the hot Italian banker, or I may have misheard.' Ella chuckled.

Em walked in. 'A hot Italian what?'

'You didn't tell me Charlotte was bringing a new man tonight,' Lucy said.

'I didn't know she was. What's he like?' Em was eager to

get the latest gossip.

'That,' said Ella, nodding towards the door where Charlotte was walking in with a George Clooney lookalike.

'Hi! I hope you don't mind. I brought Claudio along.' Charlotte looked very pleased to have Claudio on her arm.

'Ladies. It's lovely to meet you all properly at last. I've heard a lot about you all.' Claudio had a hot voice to match his looks. Lucky Charlotte.

Charlotte introduced everyone before announcing she needed the toilet. 'I'll show you where it is. I'm always needing a wee,' said Ella.

'I should find Jack,' Em said. 'See you later.'

'Was it something I said?' Claudio asked Lucy.

'I don't think so. Can I get you tea or coffee? That seems to be my job this evening.'

'Coffee would be lovely.'

'You couldn't get that bag of beans down, could you? I can't quite reach.'

'Of course,' he said, handing her the bag from the shelf above Nancy's fancy coffee maker.

'Is there a problem?' he said as Lucy stood looking at the machine.

'Yes. A big one. I don't know how to work this thing.'

***

'What's up with you?' Jack asked. Mark was leaning against the bar, nursing the remains of a pint of beer and looking like thunder. 'You'll make the milk turn sour, as your mother would say.'

'Harry's here.'

'Is he? Where? We didn't invite him.'

'He's in the kitchen with Lucy, helping her make coffee. I was going to fetch something from my room, but I caught sight of them together. He had his arm around her shoulder, showing her how to load the coffee beans. It all looked very cosy. '

'Are you sure it was Harry? Claudio was in there earlier.'

'Who the hell is Claudio?'

'Charlotte's new man. He's just walked in now.' Jack nodded towards the marquee entrance.

Mark looked up. 'That's him. Jesus, she's making a play for her own friend's boyfriend.'

Jack raised his eyebrows.

'Ok. I've not been entirely innocent on that front. I thought we'd put that incident to bed?'

'An unfortunate choice of phrase.' Jack looked less than impressed.

'I'm sorry.' Mark put his head in his hands. Nothing was going right today. 'I may as well become a monk. I'm a lousy judge of women. If Lucy's that fickle, I've had a narrow escape with her too. Did you invite any single women tonight?'

'Charlotte, but she's got Claudio now, assuming Lucy hasn't snaffled him. There's always Caroline, of course.'

'Don't even joke about that situation.'

'Do you want another pint?'

'I'll get them. When are you and Em making your announcement?'

Jack looked at the time on his phone. 'The band should finish any minute now. Looks like the caterers have got the buffet ready. So in about half an hour, after everyone's got their food.'

'Would you be upset if I went to the pub afterwards?'

'Are you seriously going on the pull?'

'No. I need some space. And I don't want to see Lucy with someone else.'

'I'd offer to join you, but leaving your own party on your wedding night is not the done thing.'

Mark looked baffled. 'Why do you want to escape?'

'So I don't have the embarrassment of seeing my father chatting up my mother.' Jack looked over to the sofa on the other side of the bar, where Peter was cosying up to Olivia.

'For fuck's sake, is no one faithful any more?' Mark said.

58

The bar manager nodded to Jack. 'Everyone's got a drink,' he said.

Jack turned to Em. 'Ready?'

'As I'll ever be. I hate being the centre of attention.' This felt worse than the awards ceremony last year.

'I'll keep it short. Are you sure you don't want to say anything?'

'Absolutely. I'm happy to play the subservient wife,' she said. 'For the next five minutes, anyway.'

Jack turned off the music, took his glass and tapped it with a spoon. Em held his arm.

'Sorry to halt the festivities, everyone. We won't keep you long. Em and I would like to thank you for joining us today to celebrate our engagement.'

Ella started a ripple of applause.

'We do have something else to celebrate,' Jack continued.

'Is she pregnant?' Sam drunkenly yelled from the back of the marquee. Ella shushed him.

Em felt herself going red.

'Ladies and gentlemen, we got married in Barnstaple

register office this morning.'

Cheers and clapping all around.

'Are you sure she's not pregnant?' Sam shouted.

'Will you shut up?' Ella hissed at him.

'Thank you,' Jack said when the noise had died down. 'Can I ask you to raise a glass to my wonderful wife, Em?'

'What about you?' Mark raised his glass. 'To Mrs and Mrs Carver.'

'Mr and Mrs Carver,' everyone chorused.

'Thank you. We'll let you carry on now.'

'Not so fast,' Olivia shouted from the marquee entrance. Lucy appeared from the house, carefully carrying a large white cake complete with a model of a couple on top. They looked remarkably like Jack and Em. She put it on the side table nearest to the bar. Nancy followed her, carrying a sword.

'Time to cut the cake.' Nancy passed the sword to Jack.

'Did you tell her?' Jack asked Em.

'No!' Em turned to Nancy. 'How did you know?'

'My darling girl, I know everything.'

***

Mark sat down on the sofa at the far end of the marquee. He was going to finish his drink and then head up the hill to the Kingfisher. He had a lot of thinking to do, and sitting on his own in his favourite corner by the fire would be preferable to forcing himself to be sociable here.

'That was a wonderful surprise.'

He nearly jumped out of his skin. Caroline! She sat down next to him on the sofa and put her arm along the back, right where he was sitting. 'I love a secret wedding. So romantic. And what about you? How does it feel to be back in Blighty?'

'Cold,' he said, instinctively sliding away from her into the corner of the couch.

She moved nearer to him, grabbing a blanket off the back of the sofa. 'We could share this. That should help warm you up. Unless you've got any other ideas?'

The look she gave him implied she already had other ideas, most of which couldn't be actioned in public. He could smell alcohol on her breath. She'd always been more touchy-feely after a few drinks. This must be how a male tarantula felt as the female tried to seduce him.

She was attractive, well dressed, had a high-flying job in London, she was only a year older than him and single. He ought to enjoy her attentions, but the way she'd enthusiastically pursued him over the years had turned him off. Even when Lucy had been openly aggressive to him, she had never made him fear being eaten alive.

Lucy. Mark hoped he'd misjudged the Claudio situation. He'd made Lucy promise to talk to him if she ever thought he was with someone else. He ought to give her a similar opportunity to explain about Claudio - and Harry, for that matter. He looked around the marquee, but there was no sign of her.

'Mark?' Caroline was staring at him.

'Sorry, I was miles away.'

'What's worrying you, honey?'

'Oh, this and that.' My whole life being turned upside down. The woman I love having a new partner and possibly even cheating on him. You coming on to me again. He didn't want to discuss any of those topics with Caroline.

But she wasn't going to be fobbed off that easily. 'You can tell me. We could go into the house where it's quieter.' She leaned over and whispered in his ear. 'We've got a lot of catching up to do.'

That was precisely what he didn't want. 'Sorry. I need to talk to my girlfriend about something,' he said, getting up.

'Girlfriend? I thought you'd split up with Hannah. That's

what my spies told me.'

'I'm back with Lucy. Em's friend.' *Why did you say that? If she sees Lucy with Claudio, she'll want to comfort you or, worse still, confront Lucy.* He would have to find Lucy now to warn her if nothing else.

Caroline looked suspiciously at him. 'I'll keep your seat warm for you just in case she's unavailable.'

59

Lucy was standing at the kitchen island with Nancy, helping her cut up the wedding cake.

'One thing is baffling me, Nancy. How did you know you'd need a wedding cake today?'

Nancy leaned over to her conspiratorially. 'I had my suspicions when Em was keen to get her wedding dress here as soon as possible. Then I spotted her looking at fur stoles on a wedding blog a few weeks ago. You don't need one of those for a summer wedding. So I bought an extra large Christmas cake with plain white icing, just in case. I'd already ordered the custom bride and groom topper. Then, when I saw you all sneaking out first thing this morning, with Em wearing her wedding dress, I got it prepped and hid it at the back of the pantry.'

'Nothing gets past you.'

'No,' Nancy laughed. 'You'll find when you turn 60, everyone thinks you're deaf and blind. It's incredibly annoying, but sometimes it can be quite useful.' She looked towards the back door as it opened.

'Mark, darling.'

'Mother dearest.'

Lucy's heart skipped a beat at the sound of his voice. She looked around and gave him her best smile. 'Hi, Mark. Come to help?'

'Actually, I need to have a word with you.'

Promising, but he looked serious. *Don't get your hopes up.*

'I can finish this,' Nancy offered. 'My study is empty if you want somewhere private.'

'Thanks.' Mark still seemed apprehensive. 'It's this way,' he said to Lucy as he headed into the hallway.

'What can I do for you?' Lucy asked, shutting the study door behind her. Mark was sitting on the edge of Nancy's desk. He avoided making eye contact. He looked so fed up. She resisted the urge to hug him.

'This will sound odd,' he said. 'But could you pretend that we're together?'

Pretend? That wasn't what she was hoping for at all.

He must've sensed her confusion. 'I know it's awkward,' he continued. 'But it would help me out. Jack's cousin Caroline likes me. A lot. And she's not very good at taking no for an answer. But she never makes a move if I'm with someone, so I accidentally implied we were together again. Sorry. It was the beer talking. If you could play along, if she asks you, that would help.'

Interesting that he'd instinctively cast her in the role of girlfriend.

'Ok, then.'

'Thanks. I really appreciate it.' He headed for the door before she could say anything else.

Lucy sighed. He was acting so weird. What the hell was going on in his head? She went back to the kitchen. Only Em was in there now.

'Any news?' Em asked eagerly. Nancy must've tipped her off.

'Mark wants me to pretend to be his girlfriend.'

'Pretend?'

'Yes, pretend. To ward off Caroline.'

'But you were in there on your own with him? Why didn't you ask what was going on with him?'

'I was so stunned by the pretending suggestion that I didn't have time to get my words out before he disappeared again.'

Em looked thoughtful. 'Well, pretending is better than nothing. How far does he want to take the pretence?'

'He didn't say.'

'I think you should ask him.'

***

Mark stood outside the entrance to the marquee, working out what to do next. The pub plan was still appealing, but he couldn't stop thinking about Lucy. *You stupid bastard! You should have asked her about Harry when you'd got her alone in the study!* But the truth was he'd been scared to, in case she confirmed she and Harry were serious.

He heard the tap tap tap of someone walking up behind him in stilettos. Out of the corner of his eye, he saw a flash of green. Lucy. He turned around.

She stood next to him and smiled, her beautiful green eyes looking even more appealing in the warm light of the fairy lights. He noticed she was wearing the pendant he'd bought her for her birthday, which naturally led his gaze to her plunging neckline. *No, don't think about the contents of her bra. Harry has first dibs on those now. Lucky git.*

She glanced inside the marquee. 'Caroline's watching us,' she whispered in his ear. 'What do you want me to do?'

Come with me around the back of the stables and I'll show you how much I've missed you. *You don't want to do that if she is with Harry or Claudio. Get her a drink and then talk to her.* 'Can we walk in together and go to the bar?'

'Ok.' She slipped her hand in his. He turned to look at her, noticing that tiny birthmark she had on the side of her neck. Kissed her there always turned her on and … *Stop thinking about fucking her*. This was going to be much more difficult than he'd anticipated.

***

'That's a very sad face for a new bride,' Nancy said as Em walked into the kitchen with the leftover cake slices. 'What's happened?'

'It's Jack.'

'What's wrong with Jack?' Nancy made a beeline towards the tea caddy. Em must look seriously worried if it warranted Nancy making a brew already.

'He's upset with his dad.'

'Most people get upset with Peter. He's the most obnoxious arsehole I've ever met. Never understood why Olivia married him. At least she can see through him now.' Nancy got the milk from the fridge.

'Can she? It doesn't look like that tonight. They were snuggled up together on the sofa earlier on, and now they're slow dancing. Jack's worried they'll get back together.'

Nancy smiled. 'Tell Jack to stop worrying. I know exactly what his mother's up to.'

Em looked quizzically at her. 'What is she doing, then?' she asked as Nancy put a mug of tea in front of her.

'Her house needs a new roof, and technically, Peter owns a quarter of it. So she's leading him on to get him to hand over his share of the repairs. Simple, really.'

'Couldn't she just send him the bill?'

'He ignores those. Getting him drunk and randy is far more effective.'

'Doesn't he realise that?'

'No, he's far too arrogant. He thinks he's irresistible. Falls for it every single time. He funded 100% of the replacement orangery two years ago. I didn't like to ask how far she had to go to get that signed off.'

60

Mark led Lucy to the bar.

'I'll get this,' he said. 'Your usual?'

'Yes, please.'

'A vodka and slimline tonic with lemon, no ice, please,' he said to the barman. Lucy looked happy that he'd remembered.

He glanced over at the sofas. Caroline was sitting next to her mother now but staring directly at him. Lucy must've noticed, too. She slipped her hand around his waist and moved in closer. It felt good. Too good.

'Mark!'

Caroline's voice came from behind him. How had she got that close to him so quickly without him noticing? She moved with the speed of a vampire.

'Are you going to introduce me?' Caroline asked.

'Lucy, this is Jack's cousin, Caroline.'

'Nice to meet you, Caroline.'

'Lovely to see the two of you together,' Caroline had an expression on her face that said exactly the opposite. 'Are you spending Christmas here?'

'Umm.' Mark wished he'd stopped drinking after the third pint of beer. His brain wasn't functioning quickly enough to continue the lie.

'That's under discussion.' Lucy said. 'But I'm afraid you'll have to excuse us. Mark's promised to show me his train set.'

What was Lucy talking about? He hadn't had a train set since he was ten. The barman offered him the card machine. He tapped his credit card.

'Mark? Your train set?' Lucy asked.

Just play along. 'Oh yes, my train set. I think you'll find the tunnel is particularly interesting.'

'How fantastic. I'd love to see it,' Lucy said, grabbing her drink and leading him out of the marquee.

***

'What was all that about train sets?' Mark asked as they walked into his bedroom.

'It was the only excuse I could think of to get away from Caroline. What's so interesting about your tunnel?'

'I don't know. It was the first thing that came into my head.'

'I'm sure a psychiatrist would have a field day with us,' Lucy said, trying to lighten the mood. He smiled slightly.

She tried a different approach. 'So how long do we have to stay here to convince Caroline we're lovers? Five minutes?'

Old Mark would have given her a witty reply. New Mark sat down on the bed and said, 'Probably.'

What did she expect? He'd had a massive shock. Em had told Lucy to be patient. But she needed him to know that she was there for him when he was ready.

She sat next to him. 'Do you want to talk?'

'Yes and no.' He moved slightly away from her.

Not very promising. 'What does that mean?'

'Yes, I'd love to talk like we used to. God knows I need

someone to talk to. But you're with someone else now, or possibly two people.'

It was Lucy's turn to look confused. 'No, I'm not. There is no one else. I was so upset at losing you I've not wanted another relationship.'

He looked confused. 'But what about Harry?'

Harry? Of course! That's why he was on edge. Em's casual mention of Harry this morning had given him totally the wrong idea. How could Lucy have been so stupid not to realise that's what he would assume?

'Harry's a business partner, nothing else. And in any case, I'm not bisexual.'

He looked even more bemused now.

'Harry is a Harriet.' Surely that had reassured him. Why did he still look pissed off?

'And what about Charlotte's boyfriend? You were looking very pally with him in the kitchen earlier.'

'What are you talking about?'

'I'm not blind, Lucy. He'd got his arms around you while you were messing with the coffee machine.'

'Claudio was helping me load the beans, nothing else. I don't steal friend's partners.'

'Unlike me?'

Oh shit. Why did you say that? 'Sorry. I wasn't having a go at you. Can we start again?'

'This conversation or us?'

Was she imagining it, or did he sound like he wanted her to say us?

'Both?' she said tentatively.

'Oh, Luce.' He pulled her into a hug, buried his head in her shoulder and wept.

61

'I'm exhausted,' Em said to Jack as they stood in the doorway of the marquee. The last guest had left, and Nancy was supervising the tidy-up.

'You two go now,' Nancy said. 'I've got it all in hand.'

'Thank you for everything.' Em gave her a big hug.

'My pleasure, darling girl.'

'Was it a good day?' Jack asked Em as they walked up the path into the courtyard.

'My best day ever. Thank you.' She kissed him. 'What about out you?'

'Amazing. And now my beloved father has gone, it's even better. I'm so glad you and I are a team.'

'Me too. Can we go to bed now? I'm absolutely exhausted.'

'We just have to wait two minutes,' he said, checking his phone.

'Is this how it's going to be now you've got a ring on my finger? You don't normally keep me waiting?'

He grinned at her. 'You'll see.'

Em heard the crunch of tyres on gravel. She turned to look

as a vintage silver Rolls Royce pulled into the courtyard with a white ribbon tied in a massive bow around the Spirit of Ecstasy on the bonnet.

'We're going for a short drive,' Jack said.

'Are we? Where?' What was he up to? She was too tired to think about anything other than walking over to their flat and crawling into bed.

The driver held the rear door open for them.

'It's a surprise,' Jack said. 'After you.'

'You know I'm not good with surprises.'

'I know, but I'm pretty sure you'll like this one.'

She'd have to trust him. She got into the lush soft leather interior while Jack fetched his overnight bag from the house and handed it to the driver, who put it in the boot.

Jack climbed in beside her, and the car pulled out of the drive, heading to the village.

She snuggled into his arms. 'Have you booked us a night away somewhere boujie?'

'In a way. I think it's rather swanky, anyway.'

The car got to the outskirts of Dashford and turned up the hill towards the cliff-top road.

'This is the way to our house.' Em looked at Jack quizzically.

'No fooling you.' He laughed.

What had he been up to? With no heating, there was no way Octopus Cottage was habitable enough to spend the night there, but a few minutes later, that's where the driver pulled up. A string of brightly glowing bulbs led from the gate to the front door, and the lights were on in the hall. It all looked very inviting.

'Wait there a minute,' Jack said as they got out of the car.

He took the overnight bag from the driver, opened the front door and put it inside.

'Right, Mrs Carver, your turn now.' He scooped Em up in

his arms and carried her over the threshold.

'It's warm!' Em said as he set her down in the hallway. 'What witchcraft is this? It's never been warm in here.'

'The replacement part for the boiler finally turned up, so the plumber fixed the heating and the hot water yesterday.'

'And you didn't think to mention it?'

'You were too busy worrying about the party.'

There were fairy lights up the stairs.

'You're going to have to walk upstairs. I'm not sure I can manage to carry you all the way up to bed.'

Em grinned at him. 'You poor old thing.'

She walked up the stairs with Jack following her. She stopped outside their bedroom door.

'You can go in,' he said.

Fresh rose petals were strewn across the bed. Something caught her eye over by the window. A rolltop bath, positioned so whoever was relaxing in the water could look out over the bay.

Em gasped. 'I thought we couldn't afford that?'

'The plumber wasn't completely sure he could do it, so I might have fiddled with the spreadsheet to make you think it was beyond our budget. Pleased?'

'Delighted. Does that mean we can move in now?'

'I don't see why not. But before we worry about that, we need to christen our new bed,' he said, scooping her up again and dropping her on the duvet.

'I love you, Professor Carver.'

'I love you too, Mrs Carver.'

62

'Hey, sleepyhead,' Mark whispered in Lucy's ear.

'What time is it?' she asked, snuggling up closer to him.

'Time we got up.'

'Do we have to?' She could happily stay here in his arms all morning, making up for lost time.

'Unfortunately, yes. We're supposed to be having a tour of the new Carver mansion this morning. And I've got a plane to catch.'

'Aren't you staying here for Christmas?'

He must've heard the disappointment in her voice. 'I'm sorry. I need to be back in Nerja ready to hand over the business as soon as the festivities are done.'

'You've sold it then?'

'Yep. All gone through - well, nearly. I have to sign some papers, then give the new owner the keys.'

'Happy?'

'Yes. I need to move on.' He was looking at Lucy intently now.

'What are you going to do next?' Lucy asked, hoping she featured in his future plans.

'I was going to put in an offer for a property near where I am now, but that was when I thought I'd be staying in Spain with Hannah. Are we officially back together?' he asked.

'We most certainly are,' she said, pulling him into a kiss.

'You don't know how good that feels.'

'I think I do. I missed you so much.'

'I better look at moving back here, then.'

'Not necessarily.'

Mark looked puzzled.

'The whole point of partnering up with Harry is so she can run the Birmingham office while I go travelling. I'll still coordinate all the creative activities remotely, and Harry will handle the client-facing work. She'll be brilliant at it.'

'Can you trust her?'

'I've known her for years. We've worked on projects together in the past. I don't know why I didn't think of it before.'

'I'm glad you did think of it.'

'We've got my new business coach, Petra, to thank for that idea. I've never considered partnering with anyone else before. When she suggested it, it occurred to me that I knew the ideal person.'

'So where are you going to go?'

'I haven't worked that out yet. I'm going to plan it all out over Christmas.'

'Can I come with you?'

'I was hoping you'd say that. I prefer it when we're in the same country at the same time.' She grinned.

'As long as you're not going to Nerja.'

'Funnily enough, it wasn't on my list of potential places to visit. Somewhere else in Spain might be nice, though?'

'Or France?'

'Or Italy? Or Greece? The world is our oyster. Or at least the bits of it with a decent internet connection.'

***

Jack and Em were in the living room at Octopus Cottage decorating the large Christmas tree that Jack had put up yesterday morning with help from Mark.

'You do the star. I can't reach.' Em handed Jack the large silver glitter star that looked more like a comet. He expertly twisted it around the top of the tree.

'There. All done. We're ready for our guests now.'

He looked out of the window. 'Is that Mark and Lucy down there?'

Em looked down at the beach. A couple were walking hand in hand across the sands towards the shipwreck.

'Yes, it is.' She watched them kiss. 'Looks like they're back together.'

'I hope they're as happy as we are.'

'Hmm,' said Em distractedly

'You are happy, aren't you?'

'Yes, of course I am. I was just wondering how to tell you something.'

'Is everything OK?' Jack sounded concerned.

'More than OK.' She smiled. 'I think I might be pregnant.'

MORE FROM SUZANNE LISSAMAN

Dear Reader,

Thank you so much for reading *Be More Lucy*. I hope you enjoyed it. If you did, please leave a review on Goodreads or Amazon, even if it's just a few words. Reviews help other rom-com fans to discover my books, which means I can write more of them.

Talking of more books, if you'd like to find out what happened next to Em, Jack, Lucy, Mark and their friends, the third book in The Dashford series will be out in late spring 2024. And if you haven't read the first book yet, *Be More Octopus* is available in paperback and ebook format, too.

To get notified when book 3 is published and get a freebie or two that I'm working on as well, sign up for my newsletter via my website: www.suzannelissaman.com

With love and laughter,
Suzanne x

Printed in Great Britain
by Amazon

29077115R00169